April Raintree

April Raintree

Beatrice Mosionier

Foreword by Senator Murray Sinclair

HIGHWATER
PRESS

Canada Council for the Arts

We acknowledge the support of the Canada Council for the Arts, which last year invested $153 million to bring the arts to Canadians throughout the country.

Nous remercions le Conseil des arts du Canada de son soutien. L'an dernier, le Conseil a investi 153 millions de dollars pour mettre de l'art dans la vie des Canadiennes et des Canadiens de tout le pays.

HighWater Press acknowledges the financial support of the Province of Manitoba through the Department of Sport, Culture & Heritage and the Manitoba Book Publishing Tax Credit, and the Government of Canada through the Canada Book Fund (CBF), for our publishing activities.

HighWater Press is an imprint of Portage & Main Press.
Printed and bound in Canada by Friesens
Cover and book design by Relish New Brand Experience

April Raintree is a revised school edition of *In Search of April Raintree*, first published in 1983.

This book is also available in electronic format. See www.highwaterpress.com

LIBRARY AND ARCHIVES CANADA CATALOGUING IN PUBLICATION

Mosionier, Beatrice, 1949-
[In search of April Raintree]
    April Raintree / Beatrice Mosionier.

A revised version of the novel In search of April Raintree written for students in grades 9-12. This version originally published by Pemmican Publications, 1984.

ISBN 978-1-55379-660-2 (paperback)

    I. Title. II. Title: In search of April Raintree.

PS8555.U47515 2016   JC813'.54   C2016-900514-3

20 19 18 17   2 3 4 5 6

A note on the text: For this reissued publication of *April Raintree*, revisions have been made to spelling, punctuation, formatting, and style.

HIGHWATER PRESS

100–318 McDermot Avenue
Winnipeg, MB R3A 0A2
Toll Free: 1-800-667-9673
www.highwaterpress.com

In memory of Mom and Dad,
my sisters, Vivian and Kathy,
and my brother, Eddie.

Foreword

E veryone has a need to belong – to someone, to some place, to some thing. *April Raintree* is about that need. It's about the need to know where you come from, where you're going, why you're here, and who you are ... the most basic questions of life.

It's a fictionalized story about a real set of events, when governments removed Indigenous children from their parents and families and communities – the sources of the answers to all those questions – for the sole purpose of making them believe in another set of answers.

And it's about how one young heroic girl fights against all odds to find those answers for herself. The telling of this story is a wakeup call to the need for Indigenous children to feel value and validity in their sense of identity. It's about what happens to those who can't. There is a sadness buried between the lines, and yet it is a story of resiliency, of healing, and of triumph. Every child should read this.

– SENATOR MURRAY SINCLAIR, FORMER CHAIR OF THE
TRUTH AND RECONCILIATION COMMISSION OF CANADA

Preface

WRITING THE STORY OF THE RAINTREE FAMILY was an act of love for my family. Surprising for me, because, if I thought about it at all, I thought the bond with my parents and siblings was long gone. My sister Vivian committed suicide when she was in her early 20s. As a fourteen-year-old, there was nothing I could do for her but to accept it. To protect myself from possible future betrayals, I needed to stop caring about anybody else.

Sixteen years later, in October 1980, I was living on a farm in Vita, Manitoba, when I got a call. My brother-in-law told me that my sister Kathy had died – that she had committed suicide.

Having compassion is what I like best about myself, but I'm not always compassionate. At times in my younger years, I thought that if a person commits suicide, it's a betrayal, it's the final act of selfishness, it's a coward's way out. In my softer moments, I would wonder what kind of unbearable pain makes a person give up on life.

After I heard of Kathy's suicide, questions flooded my mind. Why did my sisters commit suicide? Why did we have to grow up in foster homes? Why did my parents become alcoholics? Why did we have to face so much racism? Why was I raped? If I wanted to try to find answers to these questions, I decided I would have to write a book.

With no connections to my Aboriginal community, I had a lot of research to do and much to absorb. Somehow, I tapped into memories that did not come from my life, but brought a true understanding of what we had been through as a people. Somewhere, during the writing, I realized I had been ashamed of being part-Indian. I also realized that it's possible to use the tragedies in our lives to achieve positive actions. And the ending to my first novel became the beginning of my life with my reclaimed identity. I am Métis!

When *In Search of April Raintree* was first published in 1983, I was able to reconnect to my parents. I am so grateful that they generously gave me permission to talk about their lives. Mom said, "If it will help others, that will be good."

I owe much gratitude to those who read *In Search of April Raintree* and encouraged me to revise it so that *April Raintree* could be used for high-school study. I especially appreciate the willingness of those readers who opened their hearts and their minds to gain a better understanding of April and Cheryl.

Thank you to those who work in publishing at Pemmican Publications Inc., Portage & Main Press, and its imprint, HighWater Press, with an extra thank you to Catherine Gerbasi and Annalee Greenberg. You've gone that extra mile, not just for me, but for so many.

To Murray C. Sinclair, thank you very much for your advice over thirty years ago and for your ongoing support.

And of course, my love and affection go to all my families.

I

MEMORIES. SOME MEMORIES ARE ELUSIVE, fleeting, like butterflies that touch down and are free until caught. Others are haunting. You would rather forget them, but they will not be forgotten. And some are always there. No matter where you are, they are there, too. I always felt most of my memories were better left untouched, but now I think it's best to go back in my life before I go forward. Last month, April 18th, I celebrated my twenty-fourth birthday. That's still young, but I feel so old.

My father, Henry Raintree, was of mixed blood, a little of this, a little of that, and a whole lot of Indian. My sister, Cheryl, who was eighteen months younger than me, had inherited his looks: black hair, dark brown eyes that turned black when angry, and brown skin. There was no doubt they were both of Indian ancestry. My mother, Alice, on the other hand, was part Irish and part Ojibway. My name is April Raintree, and like her, I have pale skin, not that it made any difference when we were living as a family.

We lived in Norway House, a small northern Manitoba town, before my father contracted tuberculosis. Then we moved to Winnipeg. I used to hear him talk about TB and how it had caused him to lose everything he had worked for. Both my mom and dad always took this medicine, and I always thought it was because of TB. Although we moved from one rundown house to another, I remember only one, on Jarvis Avenue. And, of course, we were always on welfare. I knew that from the way my dad used to talk. Sometimes he would put himself down, and sometimes he counted the days till he could walk down to the place where they gave out cheques and food stamps.

It seemed to me that after the welfare cheque days came the medicine days. That was when my parents would take a lot of medicine, and it always changed them. Mom, who was usually quiet and calm, would talk and laugh in a loud, obnoxious way, and Dad, who already talked and laughed a lot, and loudly, just got clumsier. The times they took the medicine the most were the times when many other grownups would come over and drink it with them. To avoid these people, I would take Cheryl into our tiny bedroom, close the door, and put my box of old rusted toys in front of the door. Along with the aunties and uncles out there, there were strange men, and they would start yelling, and sometimes they would fight, right in our small house. I would lay on my cot, listening to them knocking things over and bumping into walls. Sometimes they would crash into our door, and I would become scared stiff, even though I knew Mom and Dad were out there with them. It always took a long time before I could get to sleep.

There were days when they came with their own children. I didn't much like these children either, for they were sullen and cranky and wouldn't talk or play with us, or else they were aggressive bullies who only wanted to fight us. Usually, their faces were dirty, their noses were runny, and I was sure they had done "it" in their pants, because they smelled terrible. If they had to stay the night, I would put our blankets on the floor for them, stubbornly refusing to share our cot with them. Once Mom had let a little girl sleep with us, and during the night she had wet the bed. It had been a long time before the smell went away.

My mother didn't always drink that medicine, not as much as my father did. That's when she would clean the house, bake, do the laundry and the sewing. If she was really happy, she would sing us songs, and at night she would rock Cheryl to sleep. But that was one kind of happiness that didn't come often enough for me. To prolong that mood in her, I would help her with everything, chattering away in desperation, lest my own silences would push her back into her normal remoteness. My first cause for vanity was that out of all the houses of the people we knew, my mother kept the cleanest house. She would tell her friends that it was because she was raised in a residential school and then worked as a housekeeper for the priest in her hometown.

Cheryl and I usually woke up before our parents, so I would tend to Cheryl's needs. I would feed her whatever was available, then wash and dress her in clean clothes. Weather permitting, we would then go off to the park, which was a long walk, especially on hot summer days. Our daily routine was dictated by our hunger pangs and by daylight. Darkness brought out the bogeymen, and Dad told us what they did to little children. I liked all of Dad's stories, even the scary ones, because I knew that Cheryl and I were always safe in the house.

It was very rare when Mom would go downtown to the department stores where they had ride-on stairs. Mom didn't like going shopping. I guess it was because sometimes people were rude to her. When that happened, Mom would get a hurt look in her eyes and act apologetic. One day, I didn't notice any of that, because that day I saw my first black person. I was sure he was a bogeyman and wondered how come he wandered around so easily, as if nothing was wrong. I watched him, and he stopped at the watch counter. Since Mom and Cheryl were nearby and there were a lot of other people close enough, I went over to him. My voice was very shaky as I asked him, "Mr. Bogeyman, what do you do with the children you catch?"

"What's that?" his voice seemed to rumble from deep within him, and when he turned to look at me, I thought he had the kindest eyes I'd ever seen. Maybe, though, they changed at night. Right now, they twinkled with humour. No, he couldn't be bad.

"Nothing," I said and walked back to my mother's side.

When winter came, we didn't go to the park anymore. There was plenty to do with the snow around our house. Sometimes Mom would come out and help us build our snowmen and our houses.

One December, we all went downtown to watch the Santa Claus parade. That was such a thrilling, magical day for me. After that, we went to visit an aunt and uncle where Cheryl and I feasted on the most delicious cake ever, stuffed ourselves with fruit, and each drank about three cups of hot chocolate. Then we walked home. Dad threw snowballs at Mom for a bit before he carried our sleepy-eyed Cheryl in his arms. I was enchanted by the coloured Christmas lights and decorations in the store windows. Set against the sparkling imitation snow, the windows looked like doorways to wonderful white fantasies. I think that was the best day ever, mostly because Mom and Dad laughed for real.

Not long after that, many people came to our house to drink the medicine, and in the beginning, they all sounded cheerful and happy. Mom and Dad let us stay up for a while, and we sang Christmas songs. But after we had gone to bed, they started their yelling, and even the women were angrily shouting. One woman was loudly wailing, and it sounded like she'd gotten smacked a few times.

In the middle of the night when everything had been quiet for a while, I got up to go to the toilet. There were people sprawled all over the place, sleeping and snoring. I carefully stepped over one who was sleeping across the doorway. He grumbled and moved, and I quickly jumped away from him, thinking he might try to reach out for me. Once in the kitchen, I saw my dad sleeping on the bare floor, still in his clothes. I wondered why, so I went to their bedroom. When I switched the light on, I saw my mother in bed, and she was kissing a strange man. I guess she realized that someone was in the room, and she sat up. She squinted from the sudden light, and she looked both dizzy and scared, but when she saw that it was only me, she hissed at me, "Get out of here!"

I forgot about having to go to the toilet and went back to my bed. I tried to figure everything out, but I couldn't.

A few days later, I was sitting on my dad's lap, and Mom was doing the laundry. A woman came to visit, but then it became an argument. She was shouting terrible names, and she began to push my mother around. Meanwhile Dad just watched them and laughed, and even egged them on. To me this was all so confusing. I just knew that Mom shouldn't have kissed someone else; my dad shouldn't have slept on the floor; and right now, Dad ought to be trying to protect Mom, not finding the whole thing amusing. I squirmed off Dad's lap, walked over to that woman, and kicked her as hard as I could, yelling for her to leave Mom alone. I heard Dad laughing even louder. But it worked, because the strange woman left.

That winter, I noticed that my mom was getting fatter and fatter. When winter was finished, my mom got so sick from being fat she had to go away to the hospital. One of our aunties came to stay with us. She and Dad would sit around joking and drinking their medicine. I used to wonder how come they all drank this medicine, yet no one ever got better. Another thing, they couldn't all be sick like Mom and Dad, could they? So one evening while Dad and Auntie Eva were busy playing cards, I picked up his glass and took a quick swallow before he could stop me. It burned my mouth and my throat and made me cough and choke. I spit it out as fast as I could. It was purely awful, and I was even more puzzled as to why they all seemed to enjoy taking it. I felt so sorry for them, and I was real glad I wasn't sick.

When my mother came back, she wasn't as fat as when she left. The snow was all gone, too. We celebrated my sixth birthday, and one of my presents was a book. I took it with me everywhere. There was talk of my going to school in the fall. I didn't know what reading and printing were like, but I was very curious about it. I looked forward to school. I promised Cheryl I would teach her reading and printing as soon as I knew how. But for the time being, I would pretend to read to Cheryl, and as I turned the pages of my book like Mom did, I would make up stories to match the pictures in the book.

A few weeks later, we came home from a day's ramblings to find a real live baby in Mom's arms. Mom was rocking it and singing a soft melody to it. I asked, "Where did it come from?"

"The hospital. She was very sick. She's your new little sister, Anna."

"Will she have to take that medicine? It tastes awful," I said, pitying the baby for being sick.

"No, she drinks milk. The nurse came this morning and helped me prepare some," Mom answered. Then she turned to me and asked, "And how do you know that our medicine tastes awful?"

I looked her in the eye and assessed that she wasn't angry with me. She even seemed humoured by my slip of the tongue. "Aw, Mom, I just wanted to see what it tasted like."

"Well, it's for grownups only," she said. I knew from the way she talked that she hadn't taken any medicine so far. I hoped that from now on, she wouldn't have to take it anymore. I studied the baby for a while. It was so tiny and wrinkled. I decided I'd much rather play with Cheryl anytime.

That summer, Cheryl and I spent whole days at the park. I would make us sandwiches of bread and lard so we wouldn't have to walk back home in the middle of the day. That's when it seemed the hottest. We played on the swings and slides and in the sandbox, as long as they weren't being used by the other children. We would build sandcastles and install caterpillars and ladybugs in them. If the other children were there, we would stay apart from them and watch the man mow the park lawns, enjoying the smell of the fresh-cut grass and the sound from the motor of the lawnmower. Sometimes the droning noise lulled Cheryl to sleep, and I would sit by her, to wait for her to wake up.

Two different groups of children went to the park. One group was the brown-skinned children who looked like Cheryl in most ways. Some of them even came over to our house with their parents. But they were dirty-looking, and they dressed in real raggedy clothes. I didn't care to play with them at all. The other group was fair-skinned, and I used to envy them, especially the girls with blond hair and blue eyes. They seemed so clean and fresh and reminded me of flowers. Once I was up close to one as she was busily putting me down. I could smell the crisp newness of her cotton dress, and it made me think of one of those quaint little houses in my book where the front door could open on top like a window, and the home was surrounded by hedges and flowers and neatly kept lawns.

Some of them were freckled, but they didn't seem to mind. To me, I imagined they were very rich and lived in big, beautiful houses. I wondered what their lives were like, and I wished we could play with them. But they didn't care to play with Cheryl and me. They just called us names and bullied us.

We were ignored completely only when both groups were at the park. Then they were busy yelling names at each other. I always thought that the fair-skinned group had the upper hand in name-calling. Of course, I didn't know what "Jew" or the other names meant. Cheryl was too young to realize anything, and she was usually happy-go-lucky.

Our free, idle days with our family came to an abrupt end one summer afternoon. We came home, and there were some cars in front of our house. One had flashing red lights on it, and I knew it was a police car. When we entered the house, Mom was sitting at the table, openly weeping right in front of all the strangers. There were empty medicine bottles on the small counter and the table. I couldn't figure out why the four people were there. A nice-smelling woman knelt down to talk to me.

"My name is Mrs. Grey. I bet you're April, aren't you? And this little girl must be Cheryl." She put her hand on Cheryl's head in a friendly gesture, but I didn't trust her.

I nodded that we were April and Cheryl, but I kept my eyes on my mother. Finally, I asked, "Why is Mom crying? Did you hurt her?"

"No, dear, your mother is ill, and she won't be able to take care of you anymore. Would you like to go for a car ride?" the woman asked.

My eyes lit up with interest. We'd been in a taxi a few times, and it had been a lot of fun. But then I thought of Baby Anna. I looked around for her. "Where's Anna?"

"Anna's sick," the woman answered. "She's gone to the hospital. Don't worry, we'll take you for a ride to a nice clean place. You and Cheryl, okay?"

That was not okay. I wanted to stay here. "We can stay with Daddy. He will take care of us. You can go away now," I said. It was all settled.

But Mrs. Grey said in a gentle voice, "I'm afraid not, honey. We have to take you and Cheryl with us. Maybe if your mommy and daddy get well enough, you can come to live with them again."

The man who was with Mrs. Grey had gone to our bedroom to get all our things. When he came back, I became more uneasy. I looked from the woman to the man, then over to one policeman who was writing in a notepad, then to the other one who was looking around. I finally looked back at my mom for reassurance. She didn't look at me, but I said in a very definite manner, "No, we'd better stay here."

I was hoping Dad would walk in, and he would make them all go away. He would make everything right.

The man with our belongings leaned over and whispered to my mother. She forced herself to stop sobbing, slowly got up, and came over to us. I could see that she was struggling to maintain control.

"April, I want you and Cheryl to go with these people. It will only be for a little while. Right now, Daddy and me, well, we can't take care of you. You'll be all right. You be good girls for me. I'm sorry..."

She couldn't say anymore, because she started crying again. She hugged us, and that's when I started crying, too. I kind of knew that she was really saying goodbye to us. But I was determined that we were not going to be taken away. I clung to my mom as tight as I could. They wouldn't be able to pull me away from her, and then they would leave. I expected Mom to do the same. But she didn't. She pushed me away. Into their grasping hands. I couldn't believe it. Frantically, I screamed, "Mommy, please don't make us go. Please, Mommy. We want to stay with you. Please don't make us go."

I tried hard to put everything into my voice, sure that they would all come to their senses and leave us be. There were a lot of grownup things I didn't understand that day. My mother should have fought with her life to keep us with her. Instead, she had simply handed us over. It didn't make any sense to me.

The car door slammed shut on us.

"Please don't make us go," I said in a subdued, quiet voice, more to myself. I gripped Cheryl's hand, and we set off into the unknown. We were both crying and ignored the soothing voices from the strangers in front.

How could Mom do this to us? What was going to happen to us? Well, at least I still had Cheryl. I thought this to myself over and over again. Cheryl kept crying, although I'm not sure she really knew why. She loved car rides, but if I was crying, I'm sure she felt she ought to be crying, too.

We were taken to an orphanage. When we got there, Cheryl and I were hungry and exhausted. Inside the large building, all the walls were painted a dismal green. The sounds we made echoed down the long, high-ceilinged corridors. Then this person came out of a room to greet us. She was dressed in black from head to foot, except for some stiff white cardboard around her neck and face. She had chains dangling around her waist, and she said her name was Mother Superior, and she had been expecting us. My eyes widened in fear. It was even worse than I had imagined. We were being handed over to the bogeyman for sure!

When Mrs. Grey and the man said goodbye and turned to leave, I wanted to go with them, but I was too scared to ask. Mother Superior took us into another room at the far end of the corridor. Here, another woman, dressed the same way, undressed us and bathed us. She looked through our hair; for bugs, she told us. I thought that was pretty silly, because I knew that bugs lived in trees and grass, not in people's hair. Of course, I didn't say anything, not even when she started cutting off my long hair.

I was thinking that this was like the hen my mother had gotten once. She plucked it clean, and later, we ate it. I sat there, wondering if that was now to be our fate, wondering how I could put a stop to this. Then the woman told me she was finished, and I was relieved to find that I still had some hair left. I watched her cut Cheryl's hair and reasoned that if she was taking the trouble to cut straight, then we had nothing to fear. Between yawns, Cheryl complained that she was hungry, so afterward, we were taken to a large kitchen and fed some dry, tasteless food. When we finished eating, we were taken to the infirmary and put to bed.

We were finally left alone to ourselves, and it really did feel like we were completely abandoned in that pitch-black space. Cheryl groped her way to my bed and crawled in with me. She spoke for the first time since we got here: "Apple, them was bogeywomen?"

I smiled in the darkness for two reasons. I hadn't thought to call them that, and she had been thinking the same thing I had. "No, I don't think so. They didn't eat us," I said to reassure her.

For a minute, she was silent. "They didn't like us?"

"I don't know."

After more silence, she asked, "Apple, will we go home in the morning time?"

"I don't think so, Cheryl."

"But I want to."

"So do I," I said. By now, Cheryl had laid her head down, and I could hear the breathing she used for sleeping. I lay there for a while, thinking, wondering.

That was the last night we'd share the same bed or be really close, for a long time. The next day, Cheryl was placed with a group of children, four years old and under.

I found out from the other children that the women were called "nuns" and that they were strict, at least the ones who tended to my group. I'd seen the ones who looked after the younger children smile and laugh. The others, like Mother Superior, always seemed so unruffled, always dignified and emotionless. And the ones who took turns looking after us gave us constant orders that made my head spin.

Eventually, I figured out what the different nuns wanted and avoided many scoldings. My parents had never strapped us, and I never had to think about whether I was bad or good. I feared getting the strap. I feared even a harsh word. If I was quietly playing with some toy and somebody else wanted it, I simply handed it over because if we squabbled, we'd get heck. I longed to go over to Cheryl and talk and play with her, but I never dared cross that invisible boundary.

Most of my misery, however, was caused by the separation from my parents. I was positive that they would come for Cheryl and me. I constantly watched the doorways and looked out front-room windows, always watching, always waiting, in expectation of their appearance. Sure enough, one day I saw Dad out there, looking up at the building. Excited, I waved to him and wondered why he didn't come to the door, why he just stood there, looking sad. I turned from the window, saw that the attending nun was busy scolding a boy, so I left the room and went to look for Cheryl. I found her down the hall in another room. I looked in to see where the nun was and saw that her back was turned to Cheryl and the door. I tiptoed in, took hold of Cheryl's hand, whispering for her to stay quiet. I led Cheryl down to the front doors, but we couldn't open them. They were locked. I didn't know of any other doors except for the ones which led to the play yard at the back, but it was all fenced in. I left Cheryl there and raced back to the nearest empty room, facing the front. I tried to call to Dad, but he couldn't hear me through the thick windows. He couldn't even see me. He was looking down at the ground, and he was turning away.

"Oh no, Daddy, don't go away! Please don't leave us here! Please!" I pounded the window with my fists, trying desperately to get his attention, but he kept walking further and further away. When I couldn't see him anymore, I just sank to the floor in defeat, warm tears blurring my vision. I sat there and sobbed, for we had been so close to going home again.

"What are you doing in here?" the nun from my room yelled, making me jump. "Don't you know what a fright you gave me, disappearing like that? You get back into the playroom. And quit that snivelling." Then she asked why Cheryl was at the front, and what did I intend on doing. I wouldn't tell her anything, so she gave me the strap and some warnings. That strap didn't hurt nearly as much as watching helplessly as my dad walked away.

A few days later, I woke up feeling ill. My head hurt, my body ached, and I felt dizzy. When I sat at the breakfast table and saw the already unappetizing porridge, I knew that I wouldn't be able to eat it. I tried to explain to the nun at our table, but she merely looked down at me and said in a crisp voice, "You will eat your breakfast."

I made the attempt, but every swallow I forced down pushed its way back up. Tears came to my eyes, and I finally begged, "Could I please be excused?"

The nun responded in exasperation, "You will stay right there until you are finished. Do you understand?"

To my horror, I threw up just then. Instead of getting heck, though, I was taken to the infirmary room. I was bathed and put to bed, and by then I was feverish. When I slept, I dreamt I was somewhere near home, but I couldn't find our house. I was very hot, and I walked and walked, but our house was no longer where it should have been. I woke up and called for Mom and Dad.

The next time I went to sleep, I dreamt my parents were on the other side of a large bottomless hole, and I had to edge my way slowly and carefully around the hole to get over to them. But when I got there, they were back over where I started from. At last, I dreamt that I was finally running towards them, and there was nothing around that could stop me. They even had Cheryl with them. I felt such relief, such happiness! Just as I was about to jump into their outstretched arms, I glanced up at their faces again. The faces had changed. They weren't my parents. They were the two social workers who had taken us away in the first place.

Meanwhile, my temperature was rising, and the nurse decided I'd better be taken to the hospital. My dreams continued in the hospital. I was always on the verge of reuniting with my parents, but that was always thwarted by something beyond my control. I guess I was also delirious, because I began seeing this huge, white, doughy thing, kind of like a dumpling, and it would come at me, closer and closer. It would stop just in front of me, go farther away, and come in closer and closer again. I felt that if it ever touched me it would engulf me, and that would be the end of me. Sometimes, its huge bulk would whiz around, back and forth, in front of me. I was always scared it would bang into me, but I couldn't duck it or anything. It didn't matter if my eyes were open or closed. I remained in the hospital for about a week before the fever broke and the dreams became less intense.

2

I WAS GLAD TO GET BACK TO THE ORPHANAGE because I was
looking forward to seeing Cheryl. I had a new social worker
named Mrs. Semple. She told me she would find a home for
Cheryl and me together. Maybe she said she would try, but I
didn't understand that. When I found Cheryl was no longer
at the orphanage, I thought she had already gone to our new
home. I wondered how come I wasn't sent there, too. But the
day soon arrived when Mrs. Semple came for me. I was really
excited, but I pretended nonchalance. I figured if they knew
how much I wanted to move with Cheryl, they might take me
to another place or else leave me at the orphanage. So Mrs.
Semple was now taking me to the Dion family.

When we arrived, I jumped out of the car, looking for
Cheryl and wondering why she wasn't outside waiting for me.
The front door was opened to us by a pleasant-looking lady.

I walked in, looked around, and asked, "Where's Cheryl?"

Mrs. Semple realized then that I had misunderstood her,
and she tried her best to explain to me, but I wouldn't listen.

She assured me, "Don't worry about Cheryl. She'll be well taken care of in her new home."

"But I can take care of Cheryl," I said indignantly. "I want my sister."

"April, you'll be going to school now. So don't make a fuss." Mrs. Semple had a hint of impatience in her voice.

"Why don't you come into the kitchen, April? I've got some milk and cookies waiting for you," Mrs. Dion, my new foster mother, said. For some reason she reminded me of my mother. Obediently, I followed her and sat at the table. The two women went back into the living room, leaving me alone. My eyes were stinging as I took a bite of an oatmeal cookie. The tears spilled over and rolled down my cheeks. This was all too confusing for me. Why was all this happening?

The Dions lived on the outskirts of a small French-Catholic town, not far from the Red River, south of Winnipeg. It was September 9, 1955, when I moved there, and the three Dion children were into their fourth day at school. Usually, they came home for lunch, but on this day, it had been raining heavily, and they had been allowed to take their lunches to school. It was mid-morning when I arrived, and I spent most of that day moping around the house, fretting over Cheryl.

In the afternoon, Mrs. Dion turned the television set on for me. I'd never seen one before, and I sat in front of it transfixed. I was still sitting there when the Dion children came home. The oldest was Guy, who was twelve. Then there was Nicole, whose room I would be sharing. She was ten, and the youngest was seven-year-old Pierre. They were all friendly and polite, and only Pierre asked about my hair, which was still ridiculously short. Of course, I was very shy, and I couldn't look them in the eye. They reminded me of the rich white kids in the park, so I was amazed at their friendliness.

I had come on Friday. So the next day, I got up at eight with everybody else, had breakfast, then waited for Nicole to finish her Saturday chores. Meanwhile, Guy swept out the garage, washed the car, and collected all the garbage. When they were finished, we all went to the vegetable garden to do some weeding. Pierre and I carried the boxes of weeds over to a pile that was to be burned. We stopped for lunch, which Mrs. Dion brought outside for us. When we finished, some other kids came over, and we all played dodgeball. By the end of that day, I had forgotten how lonely I was.

The next day, when we got up, Mrs. Dion gave me a pretty dress from Nicole's closet and told me there were more clothes that were too small for Nicole. I was very happy. I thought now I was rich, too, just like those other white kids.

We went to Mass that morning. I didn't like it. I was fidgety from having to stay still for so long. But after Mass, we had a big Sunday dinner. When the dishes were done, we all piled into the car to go on one of Mr. Dion's excursions to find plants to bring back to his gardens. On these trips, Mr. Dion would tell us about the trees and the plants and the wildlife that lived in the forests. Of course, I didn't learn much on that first trip. I was excited about the adventure and explored things by myself.

Monday was my first day of school. Mrs. Dion came with me that day, while the others rode on their bikes. I was scared and excited at the same time. When I was introduced to the rest of the class, I was so shy, I couldn't look at any of the other children. All I knew was that there must have been at least a hundred kids in that classroom. By the end of that first week, a few of the girls decided that I was to be their friend and nobody else's. At recess times, I skipped rope with them or played hopscotch. Although I found my new friends bossy, even haughty, I was grateful to be one of them.

I learned that I had been baptized a Roman Catholic when I was a baby. Therefore, I had to study catechism to prepare for my First Communion in the springtime. We had catechism classes every day at school. Every evening, I was obliged to learn my prayers in French, so when they were said at church, I would be able to say them, too. I memorized all the Acts, and there were a lot of them: the Act of Love, the Act of Charity, the Act of Faith, the Act of Penance. I was allowed to learn the prayer for the confession in English, because later I would be telling the priest my sins in English. I also learned the answers to all the questions in my manual, and there were a lot of things in it that puzzled me. Was it possible that my parents had committed a lot of mortal sins because they had never gone to Mass on Sundays? That meant they were going to hell. I didn't think that I wanted to go to heaven so much, after all. Another thing was that the church was infallible, never to be questioned, but I couldn't help it – nor could I ask anyone else my questions about it, for fear they would know that I, April Raintree, had sinned.

By October, all the vegetables and crabapples had been canned, and Mr. Dion had made his last trips to get transplants for the gardens. I had settled in at school very nicely. And I now felt this home could be as safe and secure as the tiny one on Jarvis Avenue. Sometimes, when it was windy, cold, and grey outside, I even enjoyed the cozy feeling of being with this family. At the same time, I longed to be with my own.

Back then, there were a lot of good shows on television. It made me wish for adventure, and also for pets just like the ones on TV. First, there was Tornado, Zorro's black stallion. Then there was Rin Tin Tin, a big German shepherd dog. And, of course, Lassie. I wanted them all. When I grew up, I would have German shepherds and collies, black stallions and white stallions, and palominos too! I spent many church-time hours thinking what it was going to be like.

By November, my hair had grown long enough that the children in school who had teased me about it stopped. Mrs. Dion told me I could grow it long if I wanted. But even better than that, she told me that I would be going to visit Cheryl and my parents at the Children's Aid office. I circled the date on the calendar, then waited with impatience and excitement. When the day finally came, and Mrs. Semple came to pick me up, I suddenly remembered those horrible dreams. I was very quiet on the trip to Winnipeg. What if something happened? What if Mom and Dad got too sick and couldn't come? What if Cheryl couldn't come?

"Why the glum face, April? Aren't you glad you'll be seeing your parents and sister again?" Mrs. Semple asked me.

"Oh yes!" I almost shouted, fearful that Mrs. Semple would turn the car around, and it would end up being *me* who didn't make it.

I was the first one there, and I was taken to one of the small sitting rooms down the hall. Mrs. Semple showed me some books and toys with which I could occupy myself while I waited. Then she left, shutting the door behind her. I chose to sit on the edge of the chair, and I stared real hard at the closed door, wishing with all my might that the next time it opened, there would be Dad, Mom, and Cheryl. I could see movements going back and forth through the thickly frosted windows. What if they all went to the wrong room? Maybe I should wait in the front waiting room. Better yet, maybe I should wait downstairs at the front entrance. I settled for opening the door a crack so I could see. When I saw figures approaching, I shut the door quickly and went back to the chair. The door opened, and in walked Cheryl, followed by her worker, Miss Turner. When Cheryl saw me, her face lit up and she screamed, "Apple! Apple!"

I was just as happy to see her, and for a moment, I forgot my fears that Mom and Dad might not make it.

"Hi, Cheryl. I got a present for you. Mrs. Dion gave it to me to give to you." I presented the gift to her, and she tore off all the wrapping and held up a black-and-white teddy bear.

"Has he got a name, Apple?"

I nodded and said, "Andy Pandy. Do you like that name?"

"Uh-huh. I like Andy Pandy. I don't got a present for you, Apple. But you could have this." Cheryl put her hand in her pocket and pulled it out, her chubby little fist clutching something. She opened up her hand and offered me a brass button, which had obviously come off her coat.

Miss Turner and I both laughed. Then I said, "It's not my birthday, Cheryl. Don't you remember having a cake for your birthday?"

"I had lots of cakes," Cheryl answered, moving the arms of Andy Pandy.

"Why don't you girls take off your coats? I'll be back as soon as your mother and father come," Miss Turner said.

I helped Cheryl take her coat off, then took my own off. While I asked Cheryl questions, I kept my eyes on the door.

"What's your new home like? Mrs. Semple told me you live with the MacAdams. Are they nice?"

"Oh, yes. We have lots of good things to eat. There's lots of other boys and girls there. And I got my own bed. At night, Mrs. MacAdams reads us stories. But no one reads good stories like you, Apple. Cindy always reads the same story. You used to read me lots of different stories, remember?"

"I remember. I'm going to school now, and I'm learning to read and print for real. Pretty soon, I'm going to have my First Communion. Right now I have to learn a lot of prayers in French."

"What's French?"

"French is...well, it's not English. We talk in English. And the Dions talk in English, too, but they probably think in French. Do you go to Mass on Sundays, Cheryl?"

"Yes. I don't like going to Mass, Apple. We got to behave and not play. Mrs. MacAdams said so. Cindy was bad in church, so Mrs. MacAdams made her sit in a corner, and she couldn't have dessert. But I sneaked her some cake to eat when she was sitting there."

I was laughing when the door opened again and this time Mom and Dad entered. I was into my mother's arms, while Dad picked Cheryl up and twirled her around the room. Then I noticed the tears in Mom's eyes.

"Oh, did I hurt you, Mom?" I remembered that she was sick. "No, April. I'm just so happy to see you again."

"See the snack we brought you?" Dad said, after he had hugged me. We looked in the bag, and there were some doughnuts, milk, and candies.

"See what Apple got me?" Cheryl said, holding up her teddy bear. "His name is Andy Pandy. He's going to be my friend now. Right, Apple?" I nodded.

"So you're five years old. Happy birthday, Cheryl. My baby girl is growing up fast. And we brought you a present, too," Dad said to her. He nudged Mom who opened her purse and brought out a tiny leather purse with beadwork on it. Cheryl was delighted. Then she asked, "Could we come home now?"

We all became suddenly silent, and I looked at each one of them, hopefully. But Mom said very softly, "I'm sorry, my babies, but we can't take you back yet. Soon maybe."

To change the subject, Dad said to me, "So, April you're in grade 1 now, eh? How do you like your school?"

I realized he wasn't all that interested, but I told him anyways. I didn't tell him how much I liked the Dions and liked living there, because I felt that would hurt their feelings. Besides, going back home with them was my first choice. We had our snack and talked some more. Cheryl talked the most, because she liked to talk. Too soon, though, Cheryl's worker returned to say it was time to leave. As I was getting my coat on, I felt total despair. I didn't want to leave Mom and Dad and Cheryl again. I kissed and hugged my mom, then my dad.

I pleaded with him, again, "Please take us home with you. Please, Daddy?"

"April, we just can't do that. We want to, but we can't."

"Why not, Daddy?"

"Look, you're making your mother cry, and you're going to make Cheryl cry. If it was up to us, you would never have left home. But this isn't up to us, and you can't come home with us. I'm sorry."

I felt defeated. My shoulders slumped inside my heavy coat. I walked out of the room, my head down. I didn't want anyone to see that my eyes were wet. Then I remembered I hadn't even said goodbye to Cheryl. I ran back and kissed and hugged her and shot one last pleading glance at our parents. I knew it was of no use.

I had to wait a bit for Mrs. Semple. By then, the rest of my family had left. As we were going down the road, I saw my parents up ahead. Dad had his arm around Mom's shoulders. I wondered if they still lived in the house on Jarvis. They looked so much like they loved each other. It gave me a good feeling to see them like that. At least they were together; they had each other. As we passed them, I waved to them, excited that I was seeing them again in such a short time. They both smiled and waved back to me.

As we drove farther and farther away from them, and I could no longer see them from the rear window, I became sad again. I just wanted to cry, but I couldn't, not in front of Mrs. Semple. I figured that if I did cry, she wouldn't let me see them again. I answered "yes" or "no" whenever she asked me something, because I knew my voice would give me away. When we got to the Dions, Mrs. Semple explained to Mrs. Dion that I would be moody for a while because of the family visit, but not to coddle me, or I would carry on like this after every family visit. I didn't much like Mrs. Semple for saying that. How would she feel? I went off to my bedroom and was glad that Nicole wasn't there. I felt the same as when I first came there.

A little later, Mrs. Dion came into my room and asked me in a gentle voice, "April, do you want to come out for supper? It'll be ready in a few minutes."

"I'm not hungry," I said listlessly.

"I know how you must feel. But if you eat something you'll feel much better. How about if I brought a plate for you?

Nicole can do her homework in the kitchen tonight." Mrs. Dion patted me on the arm and left.

I ate all the food on my plate that night, knowing it would make Mrs. Dion happy. When I finished, I took my plate and glass into the kitchen. The Dions were all sitting at the table having their meal. They all looked at me. I felt shy and timid again. I wondered what had been said about me. I was an outsider and felt, more than ever, that I didn't belong to this family. They were being nice to me, that's all. I had my own real family. I wondered again how long it would be before I could go home.

"Are you feeling any better, April?" Mrs. Dion later came in to ask me.

"Yes," I replied. I had been half lying and sitting, so I sat up properly on the edge of the bed. Mrs. Dion sat next to me. I asked, "Mrs. Dion, why can't I be with my mom and dad?"

"You poor angel. It must be so hard on you." Mrs. Dion put her arm around my shoulders.

"I want to be with my mom and dad. I want to be with Cheryl." I tried hard not to cry, but I felt so sorry for myself that the sobs and tears broke loose. Mrs. Dion hugged me to her and rocked me back and forth.

She tried to explain, "Honey, sometimes we can't have everything we want. Believe me, living here with us is what's best for you right now. I know it's hard to understand that. You just have to trust in God's wisdom."

"Mom and Dad say they're sick. They say that when they're better, then we can go home to them. But they used to take a lot of medicine before, and it never made them any better. So, maybe they never will get better. Maybe they never will take us home with them, will they?"

"Honey, that medicine that your mom and dad take does make them feel better, but not for long and not in the right way. Someday you'll understand that. For now, just keep loving them and praying for them. And try to be happy with us. We all care for you very much, April."

"I know. It's just that...I belong to my mom and dad."

"That's true, April." Mrs. Dion gave me a big hug and then stood up. "Come and join us for the Rosary now. Tonight, we'll say it for your family."

I did feel a whole lot better, but I wondered about the mysterious medicine.

My first Christmas with the Dions was celebrated much differently than when I was with my family. We went to bed right after supper, but, of course, we couldn't sleep for a long time. Then when we did finally get to sleep, Mrs. Dion came to wake us up so we could go to the Midnight Mass.

As we walked to church, it was snowing, but it wasn't cold. The snow shone like a million sparkling diamonds. Our footsteps made crunching sounds, and I wished they were leading us back to the house so I could crawl back into my warm, cozy bed.

The Mass seemed endless that night, but relief was provided by the choir singing Christmas hymns. After it was over, we went back home and gathered in the living room to open all the presents. That's when I became wide-eyed awake, seeing all those presents. I got a set of books, puzzles, games, and a doll, all brand new! I couldn't decide which present to play with first. In the kitchen, Mrs. Dion had set out the best dishes and all the baking she had been doing was displayed. By the time we had eaten, it was almost four in the morning.

It wasn't long after Christmas that I received my very first letter from Cheryl. I was amazed that she could print, and she wasn't even in school or anything. There were spelling mistakes and some of the letters were reversed but I could make out exactly what she meant.

January 5, 1956

Dear Apple,

How ar you? Mrs. Madams tole me to ast that. I got lots a presnts. A dol and sum books of my very own and sum puzles an gams to play with Cindy an Jeff an Fern an some craons an a colring book. Wen they is at scool I colr an lok at my books. I am lerning to reed an print an count an Mrs. Madams says I is fast lerner. I wish I was going to scool. Jeff is bad boy. I is good. I is good girl like Dady tole me. I mis you, Apple. I mis Momy and Dady.

luv,

Cheryl Raintree

p.s. I had to ast how to spel sum werds.

I had never written a letter, but I sure learned how to write one that day! Nicole helped me write it, and I made sure my letter was a little bit longer than Cheryl's.

Our next family visit came in February. Up until then, I had begun to get the feel of being part of the Dion family. Like all our future visits with our parents, the pattern would be the same. From the day I was told about the coming visits, I would become excited, and the excitement would mount until the day of the visit. Then when I actually saw our parents and Cheryl, it was a constant high for those few hours. As soon as a social worker came to tell either Cheryl or me it was time to go, I turned instantly despondent, and I would stay that way for maybe a week or more. But for those few hours, I was with my real mom and dad, and I was with my real sister. I loved them, and they loved me. And there were no questions of ties or loyalties.

I loved the Dions, because they took care of me, and they were nice to me. They were deserving of my love, because I had nothing else to give. But Mom and Dad were different. It didn't matter that they were sick and couldn't give us anything. I thought then that I would always love them, no matter what. Cheryl and I did ask them when would we go back with them – we always asked them that. And they would promise us that as soon as they got better, we would all be together again. So, I had hope, and I knew it wouldn't be long before we once again had our own home.

The next big event for me was my birthday. Mrs. Dion gave a small birthday party, and some of the girls in my class came to it. I got a present and a card from Cheryl. After that came my First Communion. I felt more grownup, because from then on I was able to receive Communion. I bragged about this to my parents at our summer visit, but they didn't seem at all interested. Then I remembered they had never gone to Mass and realized they probably knew they would go to hell. I wanted to tell them that if they went to confession and then went to Mass every Sunday, they too could go to heaven, but I felt awkward about the whole thing, so I didn't say any more on religion.

Cheryl had been going to kindergarten, and she could read and print while most of her classmates were still learning their ABCs. She was still very funny, and she always made Mom, Dad and me laugh. Most of the time, she had no intention of being comical. I sure did miss them after the visits. It was after that family visit when I received another letter from Cheryl.

August 20, 1956

Dear Apple,

How ar you? Mrs. Madams got our scool things. I is so ecited to go to scool for reel. I wil be in Gr 1. Apple on Sunday I was bad. I did not meen to be. I wanted to see the litle peeple who lives in the radio. I kood see the lites on. The radio fel on the flor. The lites wont werk now an thos peeple is ded. I am skared. Mr. Madams is mad. He ast who brok it. I was to skared. I didnt say nothin. Dont tell Momy and Dady. Pleese Apple. I am so skarcd.

Cheryl

I felt so sorry for Cheryl. I used to feel scared like that at the orphanage. I knew what it felt like. I also knew that there weren't any people who lived in radios. I'd seen Mr. Dion fix their radio. Poor Cheryl. She was scared she'd killed some people, and she was scared she'd get heck. Mrs. Dion had told us that telling the truth was always easier and better than telling lies. I wrote to Cheryl and told her to go to Mr. MacAdams and explain exactly how she broke the radio. I told her to write me and tell me what happened afterward. Her response came on August 30th.

Dear Apple,

How ar you? Mr. Madams sed you was good to tel me what to do. He even laft after I tole him. He sed to me the peeples voice cum frum waves in the air or sumthin. I dont no. Now I is ecited agin bout going to scool. 1 week to wate. I try to be good. I promis.

luv,
Cheryl

I felt warm and happy that I had been able to help Cheryl. I was glad that Mr. MacAdams was the kind who could laugh at something like that. Not that I knew of any other kind, because Mr. Dion was just as understanding, and my dad, well, I really couldn't remember when we had broken anything in the house. Of course, we never had much to break. One of the good things about having nothing, I guess.

I don't remember the exact day when I began to call my foster parents "Maman" and "Papa." I just copied their children, and nobody made any comments about it. I was still shy, and if anyone had made note, I would have stopped. It did make me feel more comfortable in their home.

At the beginning of the winter when I was in grade 2, my classroom was overcrowded. I was among six students who were placed in the grade 3 class. With Nicole's help and patience, I was able to adapt very quickly to the higher grade. When I passed with a good average, all the Dions were very proud of me, and they made a little celebration. For an eight-year-old, I had a very large head for a while.

That summer and the following summer, we all went to a Catholic camp at Albert Beach on Lake Winnipeg. I loved those times at camp. I felt a twinge of guilt when I thought that if I were with my mom and dad, we probably couldn't go to summer camp. At home, all the neighbourhood kids would gather to play baseball or touch football. When there weren't many kids around, we'd play badminton. If it were raining, we'd find something to do indoors, like playing marbles or reading comics. There was always lots to do.

In winter, we'd go tobogganing down the slopes of the Red River. Sometimes, a man from a farm on the outskirts would come with a team of horses and hayrack and give the kids of the town a hayride. At the end, Mrs. Dion or some other mother would give us all cookies and hot chocolate. At Christmastime, we would go around carolling, even those of us who couldn't sing. And for me, there were my regular family visits. They always made me happy and sad at the same time.

Mrs. Dion had always been a happy, cheerful person, and as long as I had been there, she had never been sick in bed. I must have been the last to sense the change in her. Mostly, I was told that Maman was very tired, and Nicole urged me to help with the chores a little more. She didn't say why, and I resented that at first. I thought she was being bossy. When Maman took to her bed, I offered to do as much as I could, fully repentant. At the end of November, Papa coaxed her to see a doctor. She was supposed to be going to the hospital for a week to have some tests done, but her stay was prolonged to another week, then another.

That year, Christmas was a sad celebration. Maman came home and stayed for New Year's. Everyone was very sad but made a pretense of being happy. When I saw Maman, I wanted to cry. She looked so different. She used to joke about being too fat. She wasn't really – just pleasantly plump – but now she was skinny, and to me she looked grey. Any movement, even breathing, seemed to be such a strain for her. Yet, she led us all in forced cheerfulness.

I'd lay in bed at night, worrying about her. I'd say my prayers over and over, pleading with God to make her better. I must have overheard Papa and Grandmère Dion saying in French that Maman was dying, because my prayers to God changed to "Please don't let Maman die." I would think of Nicole, Guy, and Pierre. It would be so terrible for them not to have a real mother. Finally, I would cry myself to sleep.

One night, I sat up in bed and was wondering what had woken me. After a while, I put my robe on and went to the kitchen for a glass of milk. I was on my way back to my bedroom, when I heard a noise in the living room. Because of the bright moonlight, I could see everything clearly. There in his rocker was Papa, with his arms on the armrests and his back very straight. I knew he wasn't sleeping, that he was very, very sad. I went in without turning on any lights and sat on the stool beside him. I wanted to comfort him, but I didn't know what to say. I put my hand on his and said softly, "Maman says it's okay to cry sometimes. Maman says it makes you feel better."

I saw tears, glistening in the moonlight, run down his face. "Maman says we have to trust in God's wisdom."

I heard him restrain a sob and felt him patting me on my hand. I knew then I should leave him alone. I returned to my room and said another prayer for Papa.

In January, Mrs. Semple told me that I would be moving. At first, I thought I was finally going home. I was both happy and excited to be going home at last and very sad that I was going there only because Maman Dion was so sick and may be dying. But my happiness was short-lived, because Mrs. Semple began telling me about the farm which would be my new foster home. I was permitted a last visit with Maman in the hospital. She smiled when I walked into her hospital room, and after asking me about school and other things, she said, "April, I wanted to say good-bye to you. We're all very sorry to see you go, but the final decision was theirs. You understand that, don't you?"

I nodded slowly, trying hard to smile courageously. I couldn't talk because of the lump in my throat.

She continued, "I wanted to say some things to you before you go. Papa told me how you gave him comfort. We all love you very much, April. When life seems unbearable, remember there's always a reason. April, you're a very special person. Always remember that. Mrs. Semple says that the home you're going to is a fine home. I'm sure you'll be happy there."

"I love you, Maman." It was the first time I had ever said those words. To me, they were precious words to be used for very special people. When I saw how much she appreciated hearing those words, I was glad I had said them.

There were tears all around when I said goodbye to the rest of the Dion family. I had promised to write and always keep in touch with them. I left them with the hope of either coming back to live with them or returning to my own home.

3

I WAS TAKEN TO A SMALL FARMING COMMUNITY further
south of Winnipeg, on the outskirts of Aubigny, to the
DeRosier farm. It was a Friday afternoon when we arrived.
While Mrs. Semple talked with Mrs. DeRosier, I studied my
new foster mother with great disappointment. She was a tall
woman with lots of makeup and badly dyed hair. If she had
been a beauty once, the only thing left to her now was her vanity. Her voice was harsh and grating. The more I watched her,
the more positive I became that she was putting on an act for
Mrs. Semple's benefit. I wondered why Mrs. Semple couldn't
figure that out. If I had to stay here, I hoped Mrs. DeRosier
gave me a good home.

After my social worker's departure, Mrs. DeRosier turned
to me. I looked up at her with curiosity. She went to the kitchen
drawer, took out a strap, and laid it on the table near me. She
told me the routine I would have to follow but in such a way that
it made me think she had made this speech many times before.

"The school bus comes at eight. You will get up at six, go
to the henhouse, and bring back the eggs. While I prepare

breakfast, you will wash the eggs. After breakfast, you will do the dishes. After school, you'll have more chores to do, then you will help me prepare supper. After you do the supper dishes, you will go to your room and stay there. You'll also keep yourself and your room clean. I know you half-breeds; you love to wallow in filth. You step out of line once, only once, that strap will do the rest of the talking. You don't get any second chances. And if you don't believe that I'll use it, ask Raymond and Gilbert. And on that subject, you will only talk to them in front of us. I won't stand for any hanky-panky going on behind our backs. Is that clear? Also, you are not to use the phone. If you want letters mailed, I'll see to it. You do any complaining to your worker, watch out." She put the strap away and continued. "Now, I'll show you where your room is."

I was left alone in a small room at the back of the house. It was cold, smelled mouldy, and felt damp. There wasn't even a closet, just nails sticking out all over the walls. The Dions had given me a new set of suitcases, and I opened one up and started hanging a few things on the nails. I stopped and sat on the bed. The mattress was soft and warped. Maman Dion had told me that self-pity was not good for one's spirits, but right now, I felt justified in being sorry for myself. Mrs. DeRosier had said "you half-breeds." I wasn't a half-breed, just a foster child, that's all. To me, half-breed was almost the same as Indian. No, this wasn't going to be a home like the Dion's. Maybe if there were other children, they might be nice. Most people I'd met when I had stayed at the Dion's had been nice enough. With this thought, I finished hanging up my clothes, looking forward to the arrival of Raymond and Gilbert, who I thought must be at school.

I was waiting at the kitchen table in order to meet them.
Mrs. DeRosier was in the kitchen, too, but she only glared
at me as if to warn me to stay quiet. I saw the school bus
from the kitchen window and thought how nice it would be
to take a bus from now on. Four kids got off: two older boys
around thirteen or fourteen, and a girl and a younger boy. I
was hoping that they would like me. They all walked in, but
the two older boys walked by without looking at me, and I
heard them going up the stairs. The younger boy and the girl
eyed me contemptuously.

The boy said to Mrs. DeRosier, "Is that the half-breed girl
we're getting? She doesn't look like the last squaw we had."

The girl giggled at his comment.

"April, you may as well start earning your keep right now.
Here, I want you to peel these potatoes." Mrs. DeRosier got
out a large basket of potatoes and put them down in front of
me. The resemblance between these two children and Mrs.
DeRosier was more than physical. They made themselves sandwiches, making a mess in the process. When I finished peeling
the potatoes, Mrs. DeRosier told me to clean up their mess.

Mr. DeRosier came in at suppertime, and it became appar-
ent to me that Mrs. DeRosier towered over him not only in
size but also in forcefulness of personality. He and the two
boys, who had changed into work clothes, sat on one side, Mrs.
DeRosier was at the head, and Maggie and Ricky and I sat
on the other side. The only talking at the table was done by
the mother and her two children. I had finished my milk and
reached for the pitcher to pour another glass.

"You're not allowed more than one glass." Maggie protested. I froze, my hand still on the handle, waiting for Mrs.
DeRosier to agree with Maggie or to allow me another glass. I

wondered if I should give in to this girl, then realized I had no choice, because Mrs. DeRosier simply remained silent. Slowly, I withdrew my hand from the pitcher and looked over at the mother and daughter. Maggie had a smug look on her face. I wanted to take that pitcher of milk and dump it all over her head. At other meals, she would make a show of having two or more glasses of milk herself.

When Ricky finished eating, he left the table without excusing himself. The other two boys had also finished eating but remained seated until Mr. DeRosier got up to leave. Then they followed him outside. Mrs. DeRosier put the leftovers away and indicated I was to start on the dishes. While I washed and wiped them, Maggie sat at the table and watched. I wondered why this family was so different from the Dions, especially those three. So much malice, so much tension. It seemed to me that it was a lot easier being nice. After all, the DeRosiers were Catholics, too. How I wished that my own parents would rescue me, and right this minute would be a fine time. I finished wiping the last pot and put it away. I started for my bedroom, relieved to get away from Maggie's watchful eyes.

"You're not finished," Maggie said in a bossy tone. "You didn't even sweep the floor. I heard you half-breeds were dirty, but now I can see that it's true."

"You didn't do anything yet. Why don't you sweep the floor?" I retorted.

"Because it's not my job. My job is only to see that you do yours. So get the broom!" Maggie hissed at me.

I stood there for a minute, looking down at Maggie. She was still sitting, very composed, very sure of how far she could go. Helpless fury built up inside me, but I was alone here, unsure of what my rights were, or if I even had any. So I went to get the broom. After sweeping the floor, I went to my room. I had nothing to do but think. Was it only this morning I had felt loved and cherished? Now, I had been told I would have to earn my keep. I knew that Children's Aid paid for my keep. And I didn't like that word *half-breed* one bit! It took me a while to get over all these new things I didn't like so I could get ready for bed and say my prayers.

Maman Dion had taught me that praying could bring comfort. I had memorized the Lord's Prayer in French and English, but I had never really thought about the meaning of each sentence. Now, I said it slowly.

"Our Father, who art in heaven, hallowed be thy name. Thy kingdom come, thy will be done on earth as it is in heaven. Give us this day our daily bread, and forgive us our trespasses, as we forgive those who trespass against us. And lead us not into temptation, but deliver us from evil ... Amen."

I would have to forgive these people their trespasses, and no doubt there would be many. But, hold on there, God, I thought. I'm not going to have any trespasses for them to forgive. So how come I'm going to have to forgive theirs? I looked for the answers in the talks and the Bible readings at the Dion's. I remembered the saints and the martyrs. They had been tested. Maybe I was being tested. Maybe what I had to do while I was here was turn the other cheek. When I went to sleep, I was feeling very saintly.

Saturday morning, Mr. DeRosier rapped at my door, telling me I was supposed to go for the eggs. It had been windy all night, and I had not slept well in my chilly room. I sleepily got dressed and went to the kitchen. No one was there, but I saw a pail by the doorway, so I took it. It was still dark outside, and it took me a while to find the chicken house. There were deep drifts of snow, which had been whipped up by the wind overnight. Another thing I decided was that I didn't like winter anymore. Not as long as I had to live on this farm. I gathered the eggs, getting nasty pecks from the hens that were too stubborn or overly protective. As I floundered back to the house through the snowdrifts, my mouth watered at the thought of breakfast, but when I entered the house, no one seemed to be up. I was still cold and very hungry, but I didn't dare touch anything. I washed the eggs and found that a few had broken and many were cracked. I worried while I waited for Mrs. DeRosier.

A few hours later, she came down in her housecoat, and she looked a whole lot worse without her makeup. She started to put some coffee on to perk and noticed the eggs still drying in the trays.

"What on earth did you do with these eggs? They're all cracked. I can't sell them that way!" I jumped up when she screamed. She picked up a few of them and threw them down on the floor in front of where I was sitting. She went on ranting and raving, not wanting my explanations. Finally, she told me to clean up the mess, and she started breakfast.

When everyone had eaten, she and her two children got ready to go to town. She left me instructions to wash the floors and clean the bathroom after I finished the breakfast dishes. I thought to myself that I was just like Cinderella. When I finished my assigned chores, I washed out my own room, trying to rid it of the musty smell. I had a few hours to myself before they came back, but when they did, Maggie, with her boots on, walked all over the kitchen floor, and I had to wash it over again.

On Sunday morning, we all went to Mass. After the services, while Mr. DeRosier and the two older boys waited in the car,

Mrs. DeRosier chatted with some neighbours. I was by her side and she explained my presence, adding that I was a lovely little child and we all got along very well. She wallowed in their compliments on what a generous, goodhearted woman she was to take poor unfortunate children like myself into her home. I just stood there meekly, too timid to say differently.

I had looked forward to Monday because I would be going to school on a bus. It was already almost filled, and being too shy to walk farther, I took the first empty seat near the front. I could hear the DeRosier kids tell their friends that I was a half-breed and that they had to clean me up when I came to their house. They said I even had lice in my hair and told the others that they should keep away from me. They whispered and giggled, and once in a while, they would call me names. I sat all alone in that seat, all the way to school, staring straight ahead, my face burning with humiliation. Fortunately for me, no one on the school bus was in my classroom. By the end of the first day, I had made one friend, Jennifer. Unfortunately for me, I had to board that school bus again to go back to the farm. I had decided that I wasn't going to let them see that their taunts really hurt me.

The months went by very slowly. The kids on the bus tired of picking on me, mostly, I guess, because I wouldn't react. My tenth birthday passed without celebration. One evening in May, Mrs. DeRosier told me I wouldn't be going to school the next day because of a family visit. That was my first happy moment since I had arrived. She drove me in to Winnipeg, complaining all the way that these visits would disrupt the routine she had set for me.

I was waiting alone in the reception area when Cheryl came in, bubbling with enthusiasm.

"Hi, April, I got a present for you. Can we go to a visiting room now, Miss Turner?" she asked her worker.

After we were left alone in one of the small cubicle-sized rooms, Cheryl turned to me and handed me a gift-wrapped package. "Happy birthday, April. It's a book."

"You're not supposed to tell me what it is, Cheryl. Half the fun is trying to guess what it is while I unwrap it," I grinned at her and shook my head.

"A book about Louis Riel?" I said and crinkled my nose in distaste. I knew all about Riel. He was a rebel who had been hung for treason. Worse, he had been a crazy half-breed. I had learned about his folly in history. Also, I had read about the Indians and the various methods of torture they had put the missionaries through. No wonder they were known as savages. So, anything to do with Indians, I despised. And I was supposed to be part-Indian? No way. I remember how relieved I was that no one in my class knew of my heritage when we were going through that period in Canadian history.

"He's a Métis, like us," Cheryl said proudly. "Mrs. MacAdams says we should be proud of our heritage. You know what that means? It means we're part Indian and part white. I wish we were whole Indians."

I just about fell off my chair when I heard that. There were a few Indians or part-Indian kids in my class who couldn't hide what they were like I did. But here was my very own sister, with brilliant grades, saying such idiotic things. Well, I didn't want to argue with her, so I didn't voice my opinion.

She continued talking, which was usual for her. "Mrs. MacAdams is a Métis you know, but Mr. MacAdams isn't. He teaches somewhere. Not at my school. They got a lot of books on Indian tribes and how they used to live a long time ago."

Cheryl paused for a breath, then continued in a sombre tone. "Mrs. MacAdams gave them to me to read, because no one at school would talk to me or play with me. They call me names and things, or else they make like I'm not there at all. This one girl and her friends would follow me home and make fun of me, so I slapped her. And her mom called Mrs. MacAdams. And Mrs. MacAdams says that all the bad stuff was 'cause I'm different from them. She told me I would have to earn their respect. How come they don't have to go around earning respect? Anyway, I don't even know what respect is exactly. I just wanted to be friends with them."

I knew what Cheryl was talking about from my own experience on the school bus. Yet, I couldn't share that with her. I guess I was too vain. She had admitted to me that some people didn't like her, because she was different, but I couldn't return that kind of honesty. So, I told her about the DeRosiers, and how much I missed the Dions. Telling her how the DeRosiers were mean to me was easy, because they probably didn't like anyone, and it wasn't only me.

"Why don't you give those kids a whack?" Cheryl asked.

"Are you kidding? Mrs. DeRosier would kill me," I replied, as I leafed through the pages of my new book. "Besides, you can't go around whacking people you don't like."

"Well, that's what I do," Cheryl retorted offhandedly.

"And what if the kids are bigger and stronger than you?"

"Then I pretend not to hear them," Cheryl answered with a mischievous smile. We both laughed over that, and then we talked about the other kids at school who were nice.

I got to wondering what kind of present my mom and dad would be bringing. Our precious hours together slipped away, and Cheryl's good mood faded, too.

"Maybe they're not going to come," she said as she paced back and forth. She was puzzled and hurt, and she was fighting back tears.

Miss Turner came in to tell me that Mrs. DeRosier was there to pick me up. Cheryl begged for just a little more time. I sat back down, and Cheryl came to me and knelt before me. She looked up at me with her large, questioning eyes, now glistening.

"They're not coming?" she asked softly.

"Maybe they got mixed up on the days or something." I knelt down to face her on the same level. "Cheryl, no matter what, we'll always have each other." I hugged her close, knowing that what I said was of small comfort to her. She started to cry, and naturally, that made me want to cry. Miss Turner came and poked her head in, saying I really had to go. We started putting on our jackets. Cheryl looked so pitiful when I left her alone in the visiting room.

Mrs. DeRosier had been told that my parents had not come for the visit. That evening, at suppertime, she told her own children they were fortunate in having a parent like her, as my parents were too busy boozing it up to even come to visit me. I sat silently, not believing a word of what she said, and pretending the insult to my parents didn't even bother me. She was forever putting my parents down, so I was getting used to her remarks. But inside, I despised her more than I would ever despise my own parents, even if all the things she said about them were true. And I just knew they were not.

Later that night, I lay in bed, unable to go to sleep and unable to say my prayers. I couldn't forget that look on Cheryl's face when I had to leave her. I felt anger towards my mother and father, because they were responsible. They were responsible for me being in this foster home. While I was at it, I turned my anger on Our Holy Father in Heaven.

"Oh God, why did you let me be born? Why? Why was I ever born? Why do you let these bad things happen to Cheryl and me? You're supposed to be loving, protective, and just. But you're not, God! You're none of those things if you can let all these bad things happen. You're just a phony! And I hate you. You hear me? I hate you!"

That's how angry I was. I started crying, and by the time I finished, I was overcome with remorse for having thought those things. At last, I was able to say my prayers and ask God to help me be strong and good.

For the rest of that month, the DeRosier kids taunted me about having drunkards for parents. It was new ammunition for them to use against me, and it bothered me a lot. One Saturday morning, they started in on me again, and, finally, I made my feeble defense. "They're not drunkards! They're sick. That's all. Sick!"

"Sick? Boy, what a dummy you are. But then half-breeds are pretty stupid, aren't they?" Maggie said maliciously.

"Yeah. Your parents didn't know how to take care of you. They just know how to booze it up," Rick added. And then they started mimicking drunken people and talking to each other with slurred speech, laughing at intervals.

"No!" I screamed.

I ran out of the house, across the grain fields, running as hard and as fast as I could. They had acted and sounded just like my parents and their friends. I remembered. I could run all I wanted, but I couldn't run away from the truth. When I reached the edge of the woods, my sides were aching. I stopped and sat down, my back against a pine tree. I was panting and sobbing very hard. As I caught my breath, I could picture my parents.

"So, that's why you never got any better. Liars! That's what you are! All those promises of getting well. All those lies about taking medicine. Liars!

"You told us, 'Soon, April; soon, Cheryl. We'll take you back home as soon as we get better.' Well, you lied to us. You never intended to get better. You never cared about us. You made Cheryl cry, and you don't even care. And because of you, I'm stuck here. I hate you both for lying to us. And I hope I never see you again."

I got up and started walking back to the house, because I still had floors to wash. I stopped and thought, "No. Why should I? They can beat me if they want to. I don't care. I just don't care anymore. To hell with them! To hell with my parents! To hell with everyone, except Cheryl. Even the Dions didn't answer my letters. They lied, too. They didn't really care for me. But that's okay, because I don't care for any of them either!"

I turned back into the woods and made my way through the heavy underbrush. I don't know how far I walked before I came upon a small clearing that bordered the Red River. The sunlight filtered through the towering trees, warming even the shady spots. The area was alive with the sounds of birds, squirrels, and bugs. But I felt at peace, the tensions from the past months were lifted. I knew I felt this way because I was all cried out, and I had decided that for now I didn't care about anything. I didn't even feel guilty about using the words *to hell*.

I wasn't really thinking about anything when I noticed my arms and hands. They were tanned a deep, golden brown. A lot of pure white people tanned just like this. Poor Cheryl. She would never be able to disguise her brown skin as just a tan. People would always know that she was part Indian.

It seemed to me from what I'd read and heard that Métis and Indians were inclined to be alcoholics. I guess that was because they were a weak people. Oh, they were put down more than anyone else, but then, didn't they deserve it?

Anyway, I could pass for a pure white person. I could say I was part French and part Irish. If I had to, I could even change the spelling of my name. Raintree looked like one of those Indian names, but if I changed the spelling to Raintry, it could pass for Irish. And when I grew up, I wouldn't be poor; I'd be rich. Being a half-breed meant being poor and dirty. It meant being weak and having to drink. It meant being ugly and stupid. It meant living off white people. And giving your children to white people to look after. It meant that kids like me had to take what kids like the DeRosiers gave, and none of that was good. Well, I wasn't going to live like a half-breed. When I got free of this place, when I got free from being a foster child, then I would live just like a real white person.

Then a question came to mind: What about Cheryl? How was I going to pass for a white person when I had a Métis sister? Especially when she was so proud of what she was? I loved her. I could never cut myself off from her completely. And she wouldn't go along with what I planned. I would never even be able to tell her what I planned. I sat there thinking, but the problem wouldn't be resolved. Well, I had a long time to figure that one out. For sure, she would never turn out to be like the rest of the Métis people. She and maybe Mrs. MacAdams were special people. Cheryl was already a whole lot smarter than all the rest of the kids in her class, and that counted for a lot. I sighed, stood up, and stretched. Now I felt ready to face whatever the DeRosiers had in store for me. One day I would be free of them. One day...

For the first two weeks of the summer holidays, Maggie was going to Vancouver to visit her grandmother. I looked forward to the day when she would be leaving, because she, more than Ricky, made my life miserable. She had started coming into my room whenever she felt like it, saying it was her house, and she could go wherever she pleased. One night, she was looking at my suitcases thoughtfully, and then she said, "I'm going to borrow your suitcases for my trip."

I looked up at her surprised and said, "You can't just 'borrow' my suitcases. They're mine! Besides, what if I had to move while you're gone?"

"Move? My mother's not going to let you move from here. C'mon, Ape, I've got to start packing tonight," she said in what was supposed to be a sweet, coaxing voice. I knew very well that her mother would let her have her way, but I still felt stubborn.

"Look, you owe it to me. You live in my house and eat our food. You're just lucky I don't tell Mother about your selfishness." With that, she dumped all the things in my suitcases on the floor and took them with her.

When she came back from her trip, she kept my suitcases. I asked to have them back several times so I could put my clothes back in them. But she only ignored me. One day, I entered my bedroom, and my suitcases were there. They had been scratched up as if Maggie had deliberately tried to cut into them with a knife. Inside, there was dried red fingernail polish poured to form the words *Ape, the bitch*. I was angry, but there was nothing I could do about it. I couldn't even show them to my social worker, because it would be Maggie's word against mine. I thought that would be the end of it, but it wasn't.

That same night, during supper, Maggie said, "Mother, Ape let me use her suitcases, and I forgot to give them back right away. So you know what she did today? She went up to my room, threw my stuff around, and stole some of my money and my jewellery. I wasn't going to say anything about it, but it makes me mad that she can just come into my room and do that."

I couldn't believe what she'd said, and I looked over at her with complete astonishment. I practically growled at her, "You bloody liar!"

Mrs. DeRosier slammed her fork and knife onto the table, stood up, and came over to where I was sitting. She slapped me across the side of the head, took a vise-grip of my arm, and yanked me out of my chair to shake me. It seemed to me that all happened at the same time.

And she was screaming, "Don't you ever talk to my daughter in that tone of voice again! Who the hell do you think you are? We take you in because your parents don't want you, we give you food and shelter, and this is how you pay us back?"

Then she asked Maggie, "Is your room still in the same condition that April left it in?"

"Yes, it is," Maggie answered her, pathetically.

To me, she ordered, "March up there right now. We're going to see what you did. And then you're going to get the strapping of your life."

I'd never seen Maggie's room before, because the upstairs was off limits to me. Her room was beautiful. The fancy furniture all matched and was white with gold trimming. Her bed even had a canopy over it. The wallpaper was of pink and yellow roses. But right now, books, papers, and clothing littered the deep pile rug.

"You must be a sick girl, April, to do this kind of thing. What did Maggie ever do to you?" Mrs. DeRosier asked.

All the while, I was being shaken about like a rag doll. She marched me back down to my room and started to look through my things. In one of the pockets of my coat, she found some money and some earrings. Maggie was standing at the doorway with a deep look of satisfaction on her face. While Mrs. DeRosier went for the strap, Maggie said softly, "That's what you get for bugging me, April Raintree."

The beating I got that night was one of the worst, but I wouldn't cry. That seemed to infuriate Mrs. DeRosier all the more. I was sure that after that Mrs. DeRosier would have me moved. I thought the beating would have been worth it after all. I waited for things to start happening, but over the next few weeks, nothing more was said about the incident.

At the end of the summer, Cheryl and I had another visit. When we got to the Children's Aid office, we were told that our parents were not expected to come. I felt guilty about the resolution I had made a few months back. To make up for it, I told Cheryl how our family life had been when we were all together. That is, I told her the good things. I told her how Mom used to rock her to sleep and sing songs to us; how Dad always laughed and joked and played with us for hours, telling us lots of stories; how we would all go out to visit our aunts and uncles or that they would come over to our house; how Dad would bring out his fiddle and play while everyone danced jigs. I wondered if it was right to tell her only about the good things. Maybe I was lying by not telling her about the drinking and the fights. But then, Cheryl didn't need to know that just yet. I wanted Cheryl to be happy as long as possible.

At our next family visit in October, only Dad came. He explained that he had been up north and couldn't get back for our visits. Mom, he said, was sick. Cheryl easily accepted the explanations. She was, as usual, affectionate with him. But I knew the truth about them. I was aloof but polite. I had thought once of telling him about what a bad place the DeRosier farm was. But now I didn't bother. He wouldn't care. He'd pretend to care, but he wouldn't do anything about it. I didn't have much to say to him. As children, that would be the last time Cheryl and I would see him.

Winter and spring passed. Life with the DeRosiers was the same: miserable. I had become bitterly passive, and I now said fewer prayers. I was sure that God had heard me say I hated Him, but He had not heard me ask for His forgiveness. Three more visits were arranged, but our parents never showed up. Each time, Cheryl would end up crying. She was beginning to change. Before she had been outgoing, always talking and cheerful. At the last two visits, I tried my hardest to bring out her laughter but was rewarded only with sad smiles, and I suspected they were only to make me feel good.

By the end of June, I had passed grade 6 with a low B average, and that was because English, French and Math were easy for me. I felt torn in different directions and often changed my mind regarding my parents. Sometimes, I would think of the life I would have been leading if we were all together. So what if we were poor and lived in slums? Being together would be a million times better than living on this horrible farm. Other times, I would remind myself that my parents were weak alcoholics who had made their choice, and then I would loathe them. Or I would think of the Dions and all their religious teachings. What was the sense of praying to a God who didn't care about me either? Regarding Cheryl, it was still the question of how I was going to live as a white person with her around. I probably had seven more years of being stuck with the DeRosiers and if not them, then in some other foster home. Seven years of not having control of my own life.

Most of the kids in my class were excited about the summer holidays. Some were going away on trips. Me, I was just going to be alone and unloved, with nothing to look forward to. For seven more years...

I wondered how I was going to ride them out.

4

IN JULY, MRS. DEROSIER had her husband move an old musty-smelling dresser from one of the outbuildings to my room. It had a cracked, spotted mirror on it, and it looked like it was about to fall apart. But I was grateful to have something to put my things in and wondered why the small kindness. Later, Mrs. DeRosier went out and bought an old cot at an auction and had it put in my room. Since it was in worse condition than the one I already had, my curiosity was really aroused. I suspected that Maggie knew the reason, but I knew better than to ask her. She and Ricky had stopped calling my parents drunkards. I knew it was my lack of reaction that made them ignore me, for the most part. Now, they were constantly at each other, to their mother's mortification – and to my amusement.

I was weeding in the garden the morning the car drove into the farmyard. I glanced at it, not really caring who it was. I looked again, surprised to see Miss Turner get out. My face had a grin from ear to ear when I saw Cheryl getting out on the other side. I dropped my garden tool and ran over to them.

"Cheryl, what are you doing here? Are you here for a visit?" Mrs. DeRosier had her plastic smile showing, and she said to me in a pleasant tone, "I wanted this to be a surprise for you, April. Your sister has come to live with us. We all thought this would be a good idea, because your parents haven't been coming to your visits." She then took Miss Turner into the house for a cup of coffee.

I turned to Cheryl and asked her why she had moved from such a fantastic place like the MacAdam's.

"They asked me last month if I would like to move with you. I asked why you couldn't move there because it was awful here, but they said they didn't have the room. I told them that I liked them and all that, but I'd rather live with you. So here I am." Cheryl shrugged and grinned, as if she had pulled off a master plan.

From the day she arrived, I changed. I was more alert and openly defiant towards the DeRosiers. I mostly just wanted to protect Cheryl from them. We did all the chores together, and while we did them, we joked around a lot. While we did the outside work, Maggie would lay on a blanket, to tan herself, choosing a spot close to wherever we happened to be working.

Once, she ordered Cheryl to go in and get her a glass of lemonade. Cheryl said, "Get it yourself." We were weeding in the garden, and I was farther away from Maggie and behind Cheryl. I stood up and eyed Maggie with a silent threat. Maggie got up and went off to get her own drink.

"You lazy half-breeds," was her comment as she stalked off.

I bent down to resume my weeding.

Cheryl turned to me and said, "See? That's all there is to it. They got no guts."

Before Cheryl had come, the DeRosier's dog, Rebel, had always followed the foster boys around, down to the barns or out to the fields. Now, he stuck close to Cheryl's side. Whenever I took Cheryl down to my favourite spot by the river, the big yellow mongrel came with us. Cheryl told me the MacAdams had taken her to see this movie *Old Yeller,* and Rebel looked like Yeller. She'd tell me all about the television shows that she'd seen. Since I'd moved to the DeRosiers, I wasn't allowed into the living room, except to clean it.

Our privacy at the river was protected for us by nature. A few times before, the DeRosier kids had tried to follow me. Maggie found the underbrush too scratchy and too difficult, and she had given up. Ricky had come down with a bad case of poison ivy the first time. The second time, there had been too many mosquitoes for his liking.

When school started in September, the DeRosier kids got the other kids on the bus to pick on Cheryl and me. Cheryl was easy to goad, and she'd get into verbal exchanges of insults. It was impossible for me to convince her that was exactly what they wanted. At home, there was a constant testing of wills between the DeRosiers and Cheryl and me. I grew tired of feeling I always had to be on guard. I preferred the passive state I'd been in before Cheryl had come. I was worried that Cheryl would get into physical fights when I wasn't around. Fistfights were for people who couldn't keep their self-control. Furthermore, they were undignified. Cheryl hadn't made any friends in her own class, so she sat with Jennifer and me at lunchtime. We had different recess periods. I guess she managed to keep out of fights because I never heard of any.

When our report cards came out before Christmas, Cheryl had maintained her high grades, despite the extra chores she now had. My own average jumped considerably. Knowing by their mother's reaction that the DeRosier kids had done poorly, Cheryl and I gloated. It was one of the few things we could rib them about, and we took full advantage. We'd say things like, "Hey Maggie, you told us that half-breeds were stupid. Well, if we're stupid, you must lack brains altogether." Maybe we overdid it a little. It was the only time I referred to myself as being a half-breed – to spite them.

It was after Christmas that Cheryl got into trouble at school. She told me all about it at lunchtime. That morning, her teacher had been reading accounts of how the Indians had scalped, tortured, and massacred brave white explorers and missionaries. Cheryl's anger began to build. All of a sudden, she had loudly exclaimed, "This is all a bunch of lies!"

"I'm going to pretend I didn't hear that," the teacher had said calmly.

"Then I'll say it again. I'm not going to learn this garbage about the Indian people," Cheryl had said louder, feeling she couldn't back down.

Everyone else had looked at her as the teacher approached her desk. "They're not lies; this is history. These things happened whether you like it or not."

"If this is history, how come so many Indian tribes were wiped out? How come they haven't got their land anymore? How come their food supplies were wiped out? Lies! Lies! Lies! Your history books don't say how the white people destroyed the Indian way of life. That's all you white people can do is teach a bunch of lies to cover your own tracks!"

Jennifer interrupted Cheryl's story, "You said that? To the teacher?"

"Gee, Cheryl, tactful, you weren't." I teased.

Cheryl sighed impatiently, "You want to hear the rest of my story or discuss my tact?"

"Lack of tact," I corrected her.

She gave me an impatient look, and I said, "Okay, okay, go on."

Jennifer asked, "Yeah, what happened next?"

The teacher had marched her down to the principal's office. Cheryl had been scared, but she was also stubborn. She believed she was right, and she intended to stand up for her beliefs, no matter what they dished out.

Her teacher had explained Cheryl's disruptive behaviour and then left the principal's office.

"So what's this business of upsetting your history class? Learned men wrote these books, and you have the gall to say they're wrong?" the principal had boomed in his loudest voice.

"They are wrong. It was written by white men who had a lot to cover up. And I'm not going to learn a bunch of lies," Cheryl had said, more scared than ever.

The man then pulled a strap from his drawer and said, "Now, I don't want to have to use this, but I will. You'll go back to your classroom, apologize to your teacher and to the class, and there will be no more of this nonsense. All right?"

Cheryl had shaken her head defiantly. "No. I won't apologize to anyone, because I'm right."

Then she had put out her hand, knowing he would give her the strap. He did. Each time he hit her, her resolve had grown stronger and stronger. When he stopped to ask if she was going to come to her senses, she answered, "Giving me the strap isn't going to change the fact that your history books are full of lies."

Seeing he wasn't going to get anywhere, he put his strap away and phoned Mrs. DeRosier. She arrived in about half an hour and was angry. She told the principal she'd had nothing but trouble with Cheryl. He left her alone with Cheryl in his office. "You're going to do exactly as they wish or else I'll call your worker, have you moved, and then I'll make sure you never see April again. Now, are you going to co-operate?"

Cheryl nodded meekly. The fight had gone out of her.

Before Mrs. DeRosier left, she had turned and warned Cheryl, "I'm not through with you yet, Cheryl Raintree."

When Cheryl finished telling us this, the three of us thought it over. "That was a gutsy thing to do, kid," Jennifer stated, at last.

"Yeah, no tact, but a lot of spunk," I said, proud of her.

"I would never go through that, no matter how much I believed in something," Jennifer said.

"Goes double for me," I agreed.

"Aw, it was nothing. I would have backed off, but I got stubborn. Right now, I'm afraid of what's going to happen tonight," Cheryl said, getting up to leave for her classes.

I was worried by Mrs. DeRosier's parting threat. No doubt, Cheryl was in for a beating, and somehow I had to do something to prevent it. For the rest of the day, I was nervous. That night when we sat down to supper, Mrs. DeRosier said, "Cheryl, since you already got the strap at school, I'm not going to give you another strapping. Instead, you won't have supper tonight. Now, go to your room."

I let out a sigh of relief to find that was going to be Cheryl's only punishment. I told Mrs. DeRosier that I wasn't hungry, since Cheryl had to miss supper.

"Very well, go to your room, and stay there. I'll get you for the dishes," she said coldly.

After I finished doing the dishes, I returned to join Cheryl in our room. We were laughing about the fear we had felt over the heavy-duty punishment she was expecting, when Mrs. DeRosier came to our room to get her. Cheryl followed her to the kitchen. Cheryl was gone for quite a while, and I was worried. When she came back, I was shocked. Cheryl's long hair had been her pride and glory. Now, there was hardly any left, and it was cut in stubbles. As she told me what happened, my anger mounted.

After she had finished telling me about it, Cheryl added, "And she made me sweep all my own hair from the floor. But at least, I didn't cry, April. Not once."

Still, I wasn't going to let that woman get away with it without at least, saying something! Rage made me overcome my usual fear of Mrs. DeRosier. I stormed into the kitchen and saw Mrs. DeRosier there. She looked quite satisfied.

"You...you witch," I yelled, not choosing my words very carefully, "What did you do to my sister?"

Instead of answering me, Mrs. DeRosier turned and slapped me resoundingly. I had to give her credit, when she wanted to move quickly, she could. I ignored the sting from the slap and yelled, "You had no right to do that!"

"No two-bit little half-breed is going to yell at me like that," Mrs. DeRosier screamed back.

Out came the scissors, again. I actually pushed her hand away from my hair. I think we would have had a fight except that she used the threat of separating Cheryl and me for good. So, in the end, I, also, went back to our room minus my own crowning glory. I was still breathing hard when I walked in.

Cheryl looked at me and did a double-take. Her eyes, like saucers, remained on my hair. Her mouth opened and closed a few times but she remained speechless. She had heard the commotion in the kitchen, but Mrs. DeRosier's threat had kept her back. I looked in the mirror. My new hairdo looked worse than Cheryl's. There I was, the big, protective sister going out to avenge the humiliation of my little sister, and I came back, myself properly humbled. It all seemed ridiculously funny, and I started to laugh. Cheryl joined in. It was good to be able to laugh defeat in the face. After all, our hair would grow back.

The next morning, though, the DeRosier kids told the others that we had tried to dye our hair, and that's why our hair had been cut. We were jeered and laughed at. At lunchtime, I confided in Jennifer, and she went to the Home Economics room and got some scissors. In the washroom, she cut our hair so that we looked better. The aggravation over this incident gradually died down. The DeRosier kids were back to fighting with each other, although I sometimes felt they stopped long enough to plot against Cheryl and me.

Left to ourselves in our room, Cheryl and I did our homework and read a lot. Sometimes, she would read my geography book and daydream. But mostly, she'd read about animals and adventure stories. I was into Nancy Drew and other mystery books, and occasionally I would read some of Cheryl's animal books. So far, I had not read the book on Louis Riel. Whenever Cheryl wanted to talk about him, I would change the subject. I guess she got the hint, because she began staying away from such topics.

On Saturdays, Mrs. DeRosier would take her eggs in, and do her visiting and her shopping. Usually her kids would go with her. Mr. DeRosier, Raymond, and Gilbert went to work in the barns, or in the springtime, they would work the fields all day. Cheryl and I would have Saturdays to ourselves. Since I was good at doing the floors, I'd let Cheryl go rambling outside with Rebel. One Saturday morning, in late spring, Ricky and Maggie didn't go to town with their mother. Later that day, Cheryl and I would know why.

Cheryl was outside looking for Rebel. I was cleaning the kitchen. Ricky had already gotten hold of Rebel, and he had brought the dog close to the house for Maggie to watch. Then, making sure Cheryl didn't see him, he slipped out to the pasture where the bull was kept. When he saw Cheryl nearing the pasture, he climbed back through the fence as if he had just come through the pasture. He yelled to Cheryl that Rebel had been hurt and that the dog was on the other side of the pasture. He said he was going for help.

Thinking that Ricky had just come across the pasture, Cheryl climbed through the fence and started running. She didn't notice the bull raising its head to watch her. She didn't see it start moving towards her, either. Her mind was only on Rebel.

I saw all this through the kitchen window. Horrified, I flew out the door, saw Maggie giggling to herself, and ran towards the pasture. The bull was now charging across the field, straight at Cheryl. I called Rebel and raced towards Cheryl. I climbed through the fence and yelled to distract the bull.

Cheryl heard the pounding of the bull's hooves at the same time she heard me. She stopped to look around, and when she saw the bull coming directly at her, she froze in terror. I screamed for her to run, and at the last minute, she did move. The bull narrowly missed her. It slowed to stop and turned around. Cheryl heard Rebel barking, but she didn't know that he had streaked behind her and was now preoccupying the bull. I was running towards her, and when I reached her, I grabbed her hand, and we ran back to the safety of the fence. We turned to see how Rebel was doing. The dog was prancing around the bull, easily avoiding the short charges. Cheryl called him, and he came happily loping back to her.

Ricky and Maggie had stopped laughing, and they glared defiantly at me as I walked up to them. Without saying a thing, I hauled back and punched Maggie right in the face. Her nose started bleeding as she landed on the ground. Ricky jumped on me from behind, and his weight knocked me off balance. Cheryl, who was still shaking, walked over to him and kicked him hard. I motioned for Cheryl to leave things to me. Ricky and Maggie fought back and screamed bloody murder. I was silent as I ploughed into them. The fury in me wouldn't let their punches and their scratches hurt me. When my anger had subsided, I stepped back and looked at them with contempt. They were bloody and crying.

As I turned to ask Cheryl if she was all right, I noticed Mr. DeRosier and the two foster boys in the distance. The boys, who were standing just behind him, had big grins on their faces, the first time I had ever seen that. The expression on Mr. DeRosier's face was unreadable. He didn't say or do anything. He just turned and continued towards the garage.

At suppertime, Ricky and Maggie came down after everyone else was seated. Maggie wore a sleeveless dress to show off all the bruises and scratches she had received. Ricky had also dressed for the occasion. As expected, their mother noticed their appearances right away. "What happened now? Did you two get into a fight?"

Maggie turned the tears on, so Ricky explained. "April and Cheryl were teasing the bull this morning, and we tried to make them stop, so they beat us up."

Before Mrs. DeRosier could turn on us, Mr. DeRosier spoke up in a quiet voice. "Now try telling the truth for a change. The tractor broke down this morning. I came back for some parts. You didn't see me, did you, Maggie and Ricky? But I saw you, and what you tried to do. You're both darn lucky I didn't have time to get to you first."

"Are you calling my children liars?" Mrs. DeRosier asked him angrily.

"They're worse than liars! What they did this morning could have gotten Cheryl killed. What the hell's the matter with you? You three make me sick!" He slammed his fist on the table and silenced Mrs. DeRosier from saying any more. After a minute, he got up and stormed out of the house. Raymond and Gilbert looked lost. Even though they had barely begun to eat, they got up and left after him.

The rest of us finished our meal in silence. Mrs. DeRosier told Cheryl and me to go to our room when we finished the dishes. I knew she wasn't going to let this go by without doing something, but I kept this worry to myself.

On Monday, Mrs. DeRosier kept Maggie home from school. When we got off the bus that evening, Maggie was in her good clothes, and it looked as if they had gone somewhere. She looked gleeful and triumphant. She whispered to Ricky, and they went into the living room, laughing.

At the beginning of the summer holidays, about a month after the incident, I was in the house one morning when I noticed a car enter the driveway and saw that it was Miss Turner. Then it hit me. Miss Turner was here to take Cheryl away. Of course, that's what their secret had been. That's why we had never been punished. I panicked. I couldn't be separated from Cheryl again! I just couldn't! But what could I do to stop it? Nothing! Except...except run away with Cheryl! But where could we go? Cheryl was outside somewhere. I didn't stop to think what we would take. I just ran out the kitchen door and looked around the farmyard. I saw Cheryl coming towards the house. Ricky and Maggie were still upstairs, sleeping. I heard Mrs. DeRosier calling for Cheryl from the other side of the house. I ran towards Cheryl and urged her to duck behind a building.

"Cheryl, Miss Turner is here. I'm sure she's come to take you away." I was shaking. I was glad to see that Cheryl had her jacket on.

"April, I don't want to go away from you. They told me I'd never see you again."

"I know, Cheryl. We are going to run away. Right now."

I looked around the corner of the building. There was nobody in sight. We ran across the open grain field as fast as we could, trying to keep low. When we were into the safety of the woods, I said, "We're going to Winnipeg. I'm sure I know the way there. We'll just follow along the roads through the fields. When we get there, I'll try to find the Dions. I'm sure they'll help us. I know Mrs. Semple. She'll just believe whatever Mr. DeRosier tells her. Okay?"

Cheryl nodded, and we started on our journey. I had no idea how far it was or how long it would take. We followed alongside Highway 200, the same way we went to Winnipeg by car. We walked all that day, ducking low in the tall grasses in the ditch whenever we saw or heard a car. Sometimes, we walked through nearby woods. Once, we saw a car moving slowly, and when it came closer we saw that it was an RCMP car. I knew they were looking for us. We'd have to be more careful. It grew dark, and the darker it got, the harder it was for us to walk through the weeds. We waited until it was pitch black and returned to the road. Cheryl began complaining that she was hungry and tired, and wanted to stop and rest.

I urged her on, saying that we had a better chance to make it if we continued through the night. In the middle of the night, Cheryl insisted she just couldn't go on anymore. I knew how she felt, because I was dead tired myself. We left the road for a field. Cheryl fell asleep, her head resting on my lap. I sat for a while to guard her, but I soon lay back and fell asleep, too.

I was awakened by someone prodding at me. The sun was shining down on us, and when I remembered where we were, I felt exposed. I blinked and was dismayed to find a police officer standing over me. Cheryl was already sitting up, and she was still rubbing her eyes.

We were told to get into the car. I sat there, glumly. The Mountie talked to us, but we ignored him and didn't say anything. I was so disappointed, that I couldn't think of anything except that we wanted to stay together. I was surprised when we got to Winnipeg, after all. But we were taken straight to a police station. We were told to sit in the waiting area. After a while, the officer came back and gave us milk and cinnamon buns. I wondered why we had to wait there.

"We almost made it, didn't we?" Cheryl said. "If I hadn't gone to sleep, we would have made it."

"I went to sleep, too, Cheryl. Don't worry; we'll explain everything to them." I had read about the RCMP. I knew they were good guys and that they would listen to us. I began to wish that I had talked to the Mountie in the car, after all.

We never did get another chance to talk to the Mounties. Mrs. Semple came in first, and she gave us a disapproving look. "I never expected this of you, April. Mrs. DeRosier is worried sick. Don't you know how much she cares for you? You girls put a scare into all of us. You should be ashamed of yourselves. Do you know what could happen when you hitchhike? Why you, you could have been hurt."

"We didn't hitchhike. We walked," Cheryl said, sullenly.

"Don't try to tell me that you walked all that way. You girls have had a very bad influence on each other." Mrs. Semple turned to stare at Cheryl. "And you, young lady, I won't be surprised if you land in reform school."

"Why should *she* land in reform school?" I said, bitterly. "*I'm* the one who talked her into running away. I didn't want us to be separated again."

"And I suppose you're the one who attacked Maggie?" Mrs. Semple asked.

"I beat her up. And Ricky, too. They tried to kill Cheryl." After I said it, I realized it must have sounded ridiculous. Nothing was coming out right. I had wanted to explain everything in a logical, sensible way. Instead, here I was, sounding hysterical.

"You have too much imagination and not enough common sense," Mrs. Semple said. "Mrs. DeRosier brought her poor daughter in and showed us what happened. Now they have no reason to lie about who did what. It was a very vicious act, Cheryl. Furthermore, Mrs. DeRosier brought a report from school to back her claim that you are a troublemaker. April, it's touching that you want to cover up for your sister. But if we don't do something now, she'll end up in a reform school."

"I'm not covering up! I'm telling the truth!" I shook my head in disbelief. How come they couldn't see through

Mrs. DeRosier and Maggie? How could I convince them of our honesty? Then I remembered Mr. DeRosier and the boys. He had spoken up for us once. If he knew about this, surely he would speak up again.

"Did you talk to Mr. DeRosier and Raymond and Gilbert?" I asked excitedly.

Mrs. Semple eyed me suspiciously and said, "April, you're a beautiful girl. I advise you to keep your charms to yourself. Mrs. DeRosier told us that you've been flirting with them."

"And, of course, you believed her," I grumbled more to myself than to her. The witch would have had that covered, too. After that, I just didn't know what to say. Then Mrs. Semple gave us a little speech about what she called the "Native girl" syndrome.

"...and you girls are headed in that direction. It starts out with the fighting, the running away, the lies. Next come the accusations that everyone in the world is against you. There are the sullen uncooperative silences, the feeling sorry for yourselves. And when you go on your own, you get pregnant right away or you can't find or keep jobs. So you'll start with alcohol and drugs. From there, you get into shoplifting and prostitution and in and out of jails. You'll live with men who abuse you. And on it goes. You'll end up like your parents, living off society. In both your cases, it would be a pity, because Miss Turner and I knew you both when you were little. And you both were remarkable, well-behaved youngsters. Now, you're going the same route as many other Native girls. If you don't smarten up, you'll end up in the same place: skid row."

I thought if those other Native girls had the same kind of people surrounding them as we did, I wouldn't blame them one bit. Much of the speech didn't make sense to me anyway. I'd never heard the terms *shoplifting* and *prostitution,* and I didn't even know what drugs were. I'd been into drugstores and they sold all sorts of useful things. So far, I hadn't had a crush on a boy … well, not a major crush. And what the heck was skid row? All I knew for sure was that somewhere in that speech, she had insulted our parents, and I could see that it rankled Cheryl. I held her hand.

I thought of once more trying to reason with Mrs. Semple, but then Miss Turner walked in. Mrs. Semple went over to her, and they talked for a few minutes. Then they came to us and told us we were going to the Children's Aid office.

There, we sat alone in one room, while they discussed our futures in another. I was still angry and felt like a criminal. We hadn't done anything wrong. Well, maybe I shouldn't have laid such a beating on those two brats. But it was Cheryl who was getting all the blame. Between the two of us, she was the more innocent. It was unjust.

"Cheryl?" I said quietly.

"What?"

"I'm sorry."

"You're not the one who should be sorry. All of them are the ones who are doing wrong. They're the ones who ought to be sorry," Cheryl said, vehemently. After a few minutes, she said, "I guess I'm going that syndrome route, huh?"

"Of course not. Why do you say that?"

Cheryl smiled. "I just kind of accused everyone of being against us, didn't I?" We both laughed.

It was a while before Mrs. Semple and Miss Turner came back into the room. Mrs. Semple said to me, "April, we've decided it's in your best interest for you to return to the DeRosiers. You never got into any trouble until Cheryl came to live with you."

"No, don't send her back there! They're mean people. Mrs. DeRosier said we'd never see each other again," Cheryl shouted.

"Cheryl, we've arranged for you to go to the Steindalls'. If you give them a chance, you'll be happy there. And don't you worry. There'll be visits between you and April," Miss Turner said.

"But you can't send April back to the DeRosiers. They'll do something to her. I just know it. Why can't she come with me?"

"Because you're not good for each other. Now, I don't want any more nonsense, Cheryl. April, if you can talk any sense into your sister, you'd better try," Miss Turner said to me.

"I want to talk to Cheryl alone," I said. The two women looked at each other, shrugged, and left the room.

I knelt before Cheryl who was still seated, and said, "Cheryl, we can't fight them. I know I'll be okay with the DeRosiers. I don't want you to worry about me, okay? And I don't want to have to worry about you. I want you to be good at this new place. I want you to keep your grades up. This won't last forever. When we're old enough, we'll be free. We'll live together. We're going to make it. Do you understand me? *We are going to make it!* We are not going to become what they expect of us."

I sat back on my heels and looked her in the eyes. She nodded and smiled through her tears. "Okay, April, I'll try."

5

ON THE RIDE BACK TO THE DEROSIER FARM, I went over what I had said to Cheryl. Those were big words, said on the spur of the moment. I had this idea that anyone who went to reform school was doomed for life. I didn't want Cheryl to end up in one. I could let the DeRosiers suck out my dignity for now, and I could pretend they had me where they wanted me. But my future would belong to me. I had said to Cheryl that one day we would live together, and I had meant it. But that was a long way off. Maybe things would change, and I wouldn't have to live up to that statement. Or maybe if I became so rich and important, people wouldn't care that I had a proud Métis for a sister.

As we approached Aubigny, my thoughts returned to my present predicament. Just what was in store for me? It was easy to think to myself that I didn't care, but living it was different.

I'd often thought to myself that Mrs. DeRosier, Maggie, and Ricky were crazy. That night, when I did the dishes and they all sat behind me, silently staring at me, I was sure of it. Earlier that day, when I had returned with Mrs. Semple,

Mrs. DeRosier had made a big fuss over me. It had made me sick, and I hadn't been able to hide my hostility towards her. And throughout that whole summer, they wouldn't talk to me except to give me curt orders. Ricky and Maggie made no comments about Cheryl, and I thought this plan of theirs to give me the silent treatment must be hardest on Maggie, because she was such a verbal person.

The only companion I had was Rebel, who had now adopted me as his new friend. When I could sneak off, I'd go down to my spot at the riverbank, taking Rebel with me.

By the end of the summer, I didn't have anything good to tell him. "You know, Rebel, I think you're going to be my only friend around here for a long, long time. When I first came here, I ignored you, because you were *their* dog. Now I think of you as Cheryl's dog. You saved her life, you know. You must miss her as much as I do. But now, I don't have to worry about protecting her from them anymore. Doesn't help me from being jumpy, though. If it's not the hot, stuffy air in my room keeping me from sleep, it's staying awake, listening for sounds. I'm so scared they'll do something during the nights. They're crazy, Rebel. I don't trust them one bit. I wish you could sleep in my room."

Whenever I had one of those talks with him, Rebel would give a low whine and wag his tail to indicate he was still listening. "You want to hear the latest? That witch gave me my school clothes. You should see them, Rebel. All real old-fashioned stuff. And she told me that from now on I won't be able to use the sewing stuff. I'm going to look simply horrible. I don't know what I'm going to do. I'm glad they built that new high school. That means Ricky and Maggie won't be in my school. And I hope Ricky doesn't fail, or he could end up being in my class next year. This year, I'm going to ask Jennifer if she can mail my letters for me and if I can have letters sent to her place. I'm positive now that the witch has been throwing all my letters away. Cheryl said she wrote to me and I wrote to her but neither of us got any letters at all. I sure hate it here, Rebel. Except for you.

"Oh yeah, and you want to know what else that old hag came up with? Now, if I want my clothes washed, I'll have to do all the laundry and ironing. But if she thinks that's going to keep me from doing good in school, she's wrong. You know, Rebel, you and me, we talk the same language. We both whine." I smiled and scratched him behind the ears. Cheryl had said he liked that. Then I got up to walk back.

I started grade 8 as the laughingstock of the school, and from the first day on the bus, I was often called, "Gramma Squaw." It was more painful than I'd expected, and each time, I'd have to swallow hard. But when Jennifer teased me, I started crying. She immediately became contrite and sympathetic, and that got me crying even more.

"April, don't cry," she said. "I'm sorry. I didn't mean it. Hey listen, I'll bring you some of my stuff, and you could keep it in your locker, okay?"

I was wiping my eyes when our Home Economics teacher walked in to see what was taking us so long. "What's going on? What's the matter, April?"

Jennifer explained, "Mrs. DeRosier's making her wear these kinds of clothes, and she won't let April use the sewing things at home to make them look better."

"Would it help if I transferred you from the cooking class to the sewing class right now?" the teacher asked me.

Her kindness made me want to cry all over again, but I kept my self-control and simply nodded.

Between the chores I was assigned and all my homework, there wasn't much time to alter my clothing. Whenever I could, though, the first sewing I did was to shorten my skirts, as they hung down almost to my ankles. I'd still have to wear the black, ugly shoes to school, but once I got to school, I would change into a pair that Jennifer had brought from home. I asked her if she could see to my letters, and she checked with her mother. They agreed to be my go-between. I wrote first to the Dions. It would have been to Cheryl, but I didn't know her address. In November, my letter to the Dions was returned, marked *Moved*.

Before Christmas, I had a visit with Cheryl. She was full of enthusiasm about her new foster home. Mostly, it was because the Steindalls had horses. "Mr. Steindall gives lessons most nights, and when he's not busy, he teaches me to ride. We went on a sleigh ride last week. Oh, April, it's so much fun. It's easy being good there. The kids at school are okay. Some of the girls who like horses went out of their way to make friends with me. But that's only 'cause they figure I'll invite them over for horseback riding. Mr. Steindall gave me my own horse to ride. His name is Fastbuck. I have to help clean the stalls and feed them, but I like doing all that."

She went on telling me all the good things that were now happening to her. I hardly said anything. What could I say? That I was lonely and miserable, and my foster mother dressed me funny? I envied Cheryl. I envied her having her own horse to ride. I envied that she could feel so much excitement. I knew I should have been happy for her; it was what I wanted. But in comparing our lives, I only came up with envy. Before we parted, I got her address and gave her Jennifer's.

In early February, I received a letter through the new courier system. I had sent Cheryl a letter in January. I saved it until I was alone. I walked through the snow, with Rebel following behind, until I reached a fallen tree by the river bank. Then I read it aloud for Rebel's benefit.

Dear April,

How are you? Mrs. Steindall says we will have our next visit in April or May. I can't wait. We had to do speeches in front of the class. I made mine on buffalo hunting. I'm sending you a copy of my speech just so you know I'm doing good in school. Pardon me, doing *well* in school.

Have a Happy Valentine's Day, April. If nothing else, think of me. I've also enclosed a homemade card. Do you like it? I'm going to ask Mrs. Steindall if you could come to see me for the summer holidays. Then I could teach you what I know so far about riding. Would you like that?

I told them all about the DeRosiers, but I don't think they believed me. That is the one thing I don't like about them. They think because we're foster kids, we probably lie. Anyway, I feel sorry that you have to go through what you're going through. I wish there were something I could do to help. At least, you've got a friend like Jennifer.

And Rebel too. Does he miss me? I sure miss him. They have an Irish setter here, and it's a nice-looking dog, but it's got no brains. She's high-strung and follows me all over the place and is always chasing after the horses. I guess, after Rebel, it would take a mighty big dog to fill his paws. Get it?

I had thought of all these funny things I could tell you so you'd laugh when you read this letter but once I got down to

writing, all the funny stuff slipped my mind. Sorry about that.
I guess I'll close off for now and I'll see you in the springtime.
Write back soon.

Love,
Cheryl

Buffalo hunting? That was almost as bad as getting a book
on Riel. I looked at the card. Cheryl had drawn a picture of
a horse, a girl, and a red setter. I showed it to Rebel and said,
"Look at that. How lucky can one get? Me, jealous? Of course,
I'm not jealous, Rebel. I prefer the word *envious*. Anyways,
what are you so smug about? That dog there, that Irish setter,
she's with her and you're not."

Rebel made all the appropriate movements, as if he understood every word I said. So, I read Cheryl's speech to him.

The Métis hunters, equipped with buffalo guns, used one meth-
od known as "running the buffalo." This was perhaps the most
dangerous way but definitely the most exciting. Men on horseback would ride through the stampeding herd, shooting prime
animals. Once a shot was fired, the hunter had to pour some
more powder from his buffalo horn into the muzzle of the gun,
spit in one of the lead balls that he carried in his mouth, and
hit the gun butt on his saddle to shake down the powder and
ball. All this was done as he raced his horse among the stampeding buffalo. If a horse stepped into a gopher hole or if the
rider became dismounted for any other reasons, his time as a
buffalo hunter was probably reduced to mere seconds. Perhaps
a bull would turn on him or a stray shot could bring him down.
Or he may have loaded his rifle too fast or not properly and
it could explode and blow his hand off. The hunt required

steady nerves, much skill, and expertise in horsemanship and marksmanship....

There was more, but Rebel had gone off to chase a squirrel. "Hey, Rebel, I'm telling Cheryl you didn't appreciate her speech."

Then I wondered how she ever had the courage to stand up in front of her class and give such a speech. I never would have done it. I read the rest of it to myself.

Grade 9 became the very worst school year I'd ever have. A lot of the kids in my class had started pairing off and going steady. As long as I lived with the DeRosiers, I knew that I would have to give up any ideas about special friendships with boys, and the easiest thing to do was simply not to think about it. But then a new family moved into Aubigny. They had a boy who was in grade 11, the same class Maggie was in. I had a secret crush on him, but Maggie talked about him every night at the supper table. Mrs. DeRosier even went so far as to invite his family over for a Sunday dinner. The boy was named Peter. I guess he liked me, because after that Sunday dinner, he began talking to me at school. Being seen with him brought me more friends. I loved school.

Maggie had not been openly hostile towards me until the other kids' attitudes changed. I knew she felt that way because of Peter's friendship with me and not with her. It had even made me smug and more sure of myself. As soon as the whispering about me started, I knew that she and Ricky were behind it. Whatever they were saying spread throughout the school quickly. Kids were looking at me and snickering. I'd pass by a group of boys, and they'd whistle. I started getting notes on my desk that said things like, "If you want a really good time, meet me at such and such a place." Some of the notes had obscenities in them, and the comments I got from the boys were also obscene.

First Peter stopped talking to me, and then Jennifer began avoiding me. This confused me even more. Jennifer was the kind of girl who would stick by a friend no matter what. I finally asked her, "What is going on, Jenny?"

Jennifer had looked around quickly, because other kids were watching us and were obviously talking about me. "April, I have to go," she apologized and left.

She slipped me a note that said she'd still post my letters for me but that was all. I became so angry and hurt, my first impulse was to tell her to just forget it. But she was my only connection with Cheryl, and I had to accept things the way they were. Again I was a loner, and now I didn't have a single friend at school.

I was glad I still had Jennifer as a go-between on letters, because in January, I got another fat envelope from Cheryl. I was rather disappointed when I opened the envelope and found most of it was a speech on the Métis.

That evening, at the chicken house, I read the letter out loud to Rebel. I knew he didn't understand what was written, but it was a little more comforting to be able to share this one joy in my life with the last friend I had around here.

January 26, 1963

Dear April,

How are you? I just know you're waiting for my next speech with anticipation, right? Well, here it is. Actually, it's not really a speech. I'm just caught up in this stuff. I was going to deliver this speech, but now I think my fellow classmates might not be able to hack another speech on Métis people. I've decided I will keep it among my papers on the history of the Métis. I think it's important that we know our own history. It's a rather short history compared to other nationalities, but it's interesting, as I've already stated. I wouldn't have minded one bit living in those days. Mrs. MacAdams used to have so many good books on the subject of Natives. I've been babysitting lately and next time we go to Winnipeg, I'm going to spend all I've got on books. I wish I could afford to buy every book there is. Sally says I'm going to need glasses. I doubt it. I'd hate to have to wear glasses. Wouldn't you? It's un-Indian.

Oh, I made the volleyball team. We'll be going around to different places and playing other schools. It's too bad you couldn't try out for after-school sports. I know you'd be good. Come spring, I won't join any outdoor stuff because I'd rather practise riding. I've been trying to do trick-riding but all I've got to show for my efforts are bruises.

Write back to me, April, and tell me what you think of my project. I'm going to work on something about Riel. I need a few more books though. Well, I'll sign off for now. Got a load of homework to do.

Love,
Cheryl

Then I dutifully read through her essay. Again, she wrote about the Métis with a touch of pride.

The two armed parties met at Seven Oaks. Grant sent an emissary to Semple, demanding his surrender. An argument ensued, and a settler fired. The sound of gunfire brought a nearby group of fifty more Métis to the scene. The battle-experienced Métis fired their round of shots and then fell to the ground to reload. The settlers, thinking they had shot the men down, began to cheer. The Métis, with their guns reloaded, charged the settlers. Terrified, most of the settlers turned and ran. The horsemen took over, as if running buffalo. They overtook the settlers and shot them. Within fifteen minutes, twenty settlers and two of Grant's men were dead.

Cheryl went into further detail describing why The Battle of Seven Oaks had happened. I hated dates and company names. And why did all this matter so much to Cheryl? She said that she planned to keep it among her papers. It almost sounded like she was going to be a history professor or something. Did it help her accept the colour of her skin? Was that why we thought so differently? That and her superior intelligence? One had to be super-intelligent to find this kind of thing exciting. Skin colouring didn't matter in my school. Everyone treated me like a full-blooded Indian. I'd never forget being called "Gramma Squaw." I hated those DeRosier kids so much. I sure wished I knew what they had been up to this time.

A few months later, I found out. The guidance counsellor, Mrs. Wartzman, was waiting for me in the hall one day at lunchtime. She said she wanted to see me in her office. The counsellor came right out and said what was on her mind. "April, I've heard some disturbing things, and I feel I should talk this over with you. I know that you're a foster girl, and perhaps that's the reason. You feel a need to be loved. Well, what I'm really trying to say is that you shouldn't be letting Raymond and Gilbert fondle you. They're only using you, you know."

I sat in the chair with my mouth open. I felt a wave of humiliation wash over me. A tidal wave, I might add. I was sure my face was red. I thought later that Mrs. Wartzman probably assumed I was embarrassed because she knew all about my "indiscretions."

"Perhaps it's not my place to be talking to you. It's such a sensitive issue. I know that you're doing well in your grades, and I want to warn you that a pregnancy would disrupt your life. Let's see if we can't get your life on the right track again. And if Mrs. DeRosier has taken this up with your social worker, I can say that we had this little talk. Okay?" Mrs. Wartzman finished it with a smile.

I walked out of her office in a daze. It was a warm spring day, so I went outside to eat my lunch. I really wanted to avoid the lunchroom and have some privacy to myself, but there were kids outside. When they saw me, some of them snickered. I wanted to die, crawl away into some hole, and never be seen again. Instead, I sat and nibbled my sandwich. If it had been Peter I was accused of fooling with, I would have been embarrassed. But Raymond and Gilbert? Both? At the same time? Not only were they ugly and pimply, but they passed their grades only because of their age and their size. I didn't have anything against them, but I'd have to be plumb out of my head to even look at them in "that" way. Well, it was no wonder Jennifer and Peter stayed away from me. But then, how could Jennifer believe that of me? And had Raymond and Gilbert gotten that same kind of speech? Probably not. Only girls got pregnant.

For the rest of that week I walked around thinking about it. On Saturday, I found myself at the riverbank, talking to my old friend, Rebel.

"I know I shouldn't feel so sorry for myself. I know that other kids go through much worse than me. But knowing that doesn't make it easier. At least Gilbert and Raymond are getting out of this rathole. I wonder who Maggie and Ricky are going to accuse me of doing things with next? I'll bet Mrs. DeRosier knew all about their rumours, too. Rebel, I have to get out of this place. I just have to. Do you know how hard it is to walk around that school with those rumours hanging over my head?"

Rebel came over, put his paw on me, and licked my face. I just continued grumbling. "And if they don't get some other boys, I'll probably have to take the bales off the fields all by myself, on top of all the other work I have. How could Jennifer believe all those things about me? How could she? I thought she was such a good friend. Maybe she doesn't believe them. Maybe she's just scared to be seen with me. Boy! I'm going to get even with those DeRosiers. I don't know how, but somehow, some way, I'm going to get them. And when I get through with them, they're never going to get another foster kid. Never!"

6

I HAD NO IDEA how I was going to get even with the DeRosiers for those horrible rumours. It just made me feel a little better to think I could. I would entertain different ideas, but I discarded them all. Talking to my social worker was futile, because she'd already proven to me that she could be fooled too easily by the DeRosiers. And the same thing went for the teachers at school.

It was when I went into grade 10 that an opportunity presented itself to do something about the DeRosiers, though I didn't recognize it as such. Since I never saw Jennifer over the summer months, Cheryl and I hadn't written to each other. Then, in September, Jennifer came to me with a letter from Cheryl. I expected her to walk away, but she stayed, and after an awkward pause, she said, "April, about last year...I guess I should have told you what was going on when I first heard about it. But there are these sayings, you know, about being judged by the company you keep. Well, I didn't want to get the same hassles you were getting. I'm chicken. I couldn't take that kind of thing."

I looked at her and said, "Did you believe any of it?"

"No. I knew you. I knew you wouldn't do anything like what they said. I'd like for us to be friends again."

"I'd like that, too," I said, gratefully.

"One more thing, April. I'm sorry I didn't stand by you," she added.

I smiled. "It's okay, Jenny. I understand. You've done a lot for me already."

In October, Mrs. Gauthier, our English teacher, told us that the *Southern Journal* was holding a competition for Christmas stories, and we'd have two weeks in which to submit entries. At lunchtime, Jennifer and I talked about the competition. English was my strongest subject, and compositions were easy for me. It was mostly just a matter of choosing a topic that would attract attention.

"Why don't you write about your life with the DeRosiers?" Jennifer asked with a grin.

I thought it was a great idea. But then I said, "It has to be a Christmas story, and they have a way of destroying Christmas for me."

For a week I pondered over how I could work my life at the DeRosiers into a Christmas story. Finally, the idea came to me, and I worked on my story at lunchtimes. The title was "What I Want for Christmas," and I ended the story with the sentence, "What I want for Christmas is for someone to listen to me and to believe in me." I handed it in to Mrs. Gauthier.

The next day, Mrs. Gauthier asked me to stay at lunch. I waited and was surprised when Mrs. Wartzman came into the room with my story in her hand.

Mrs. Wartzman said to me, "This is an incredible story, April. Is this really what's been going on?"

I nodded, unable to speak, because that perpetual lump in my throat was back. I was sure they were going to throw my story in the garbage after giving me a good scolding. Maybe they would even show it to Mrs. DeRosier.

Mrs. Gauthier's next words gave me hope. "I believe the story. I've heard the rumours about April, and she's never done anything to indicate that they were true. She's a very good student. One of the best."

"Oh, I'm sure she is. I've checked with Cheryl's former grade 5 teacher, and she confirmed what you wrote, April. I can't believe that workers would place children in this kind of home."

"Why didn't you ever tell your social worker or one of us?" Mrs. Gauthier asked.

"We tried. We tried to tell our workers, but they would only believe what Mrs. DeRosier told them. And when you said those things to me last year..." I looked at Mrs. Wartzman.

"I owe you an apology, April. I am so sorry I jumped to conclusions," Mrs. Wartzman said.

It was decided that my story would not be entered in the competition, and they urged me to write another one in its place. From what I understood, Mrs. Wartzman was going to call my social worker herself. That was good enough for me.

I waited impatiently. In November 1963, something happened in the United States that made me forget my impatience temporarily. The president of the United States, John F. Kennedy, was shot. I was just coming back from lunch when I heard the news. The whole class was subdued, and I was shocked. Cheryl and I had talked about him a few times. She admired him for many reasons. In the weeks that followed, I saved clippings from the newspaper about his funeral and his family. I wasn't allowed to watch television, so I missed an awful lot, including the death of Kennedy's killer, Lee Harvey Oswald. I planned to give my clippings to Cheryl. We were supposed to have a visit, but for some reason it was put off.

I returned to my impatient waiting. Had the wheels of motion begun, or was nothing going to come of my story, after all? Christmas passed, and then it was 1964. The only consolation I had until then was that two grownups were aware of my predicament. Then, in January I got a letter from Cheryl.

January 16, 1964

Dear April,

How are you? I got your letter and obviously you didn't know you missed a visit with me. I waited at the Children's Aid office all afternoon December 23rd. Then Miss Turner came and told me that Mrs. DeRosier called to say she wasn't able to make it to town because she'd gotten stuck. Is that true? Anyway, I'm glad you've gotten through to your teachers. Have you heard anything further? We are getting a new social worker, did you know that? I sure hope she's going to be better than what we've got now. Wasn't it terrible about President Kennedy being assassinated? I wanted to see you so much to talk about it. I cried all that night and the next few days. I read a lot on history and politics. All the Kennedys were so interesting and young and vital. I used to collect items on them. I'm sure that Robert Kennedy will get in as President, though. I hope he keeps the same speechwriters. Kennedy's speeches were just marvellous.

Anyway, I've enclosed my historical piece on Riel at the Red River Insurrection. You ought to see this rubbish we have to take in history. I don't know if you took the same textbook. It makes me wish those white men had never come here. But then we would not have been born. At least, the Indians would have been left in peace. Nothing those tribes ever did to each other matches what the whites have done to them. Whoa, there, Cheryl. You probably don't agree with me, do you, April? But history should be an unbiased representation of the facts. (Unfortunately, I'm not unbiased but fortunately, I don't plan on writing a history book.) And if they show one side, they ought to show the other side equally. Anyway, that's why I'm writing the Métis side of things. I don't really know what I'm going to do with it, but it makes me feel good.

Well, I hope you like my essay. I'll sign off for now. Let me know what happens. Sure is taking a long time.

Love,
Cheryl

As I read her letter, I was infuriated to learn of Mrs. DeRosier's usual deceit. Stuck, was she? Well, she'd be stuck once the social worker got through with her. Any new social worker had to be better than what we had now. Then my feelings changed to regret when I read about her reactions to President Kennedy's death. That had been so unnecessary, so senseless. Suddenly, a thought hit me. Had Mrs. DeRosier learned of my essay? And was she going to stop me from seeing Cheryl? I felt a chill. She *did* know. As usual, it was going to be me who got stuck...stuck here until when? It just wasn't fair.

To preoccupy my mind, I read Cheryl's essay on Riel and the Red River Insurrection. But reading her essay didn't help. Knowing the other side, the Métis side, didn't make me feel any better. It just reinforced my belief that if I could assimilate myself into white society, I wouldn't have to live this way for the rest of my life.

That afternoon, I didn't pay much attention to classwork. My mind was on my present problem. I firmly believed Mrs. DeRosier knew about my essay. I felt I had been betrayed. What could I do about it? I could think of only one thing. Come summer, I'd take off. But then I had wanted to finish school so much. I had wanted to be able to get a good job. I wanted to be rich. Oh, to heck with being rich. I'd run away anyway, maybe to some other city so they wouldn't find me. I'd lie about my age if I had to, and I'd get a job. For the moment, being free was more important than anything else in the world.

That night, I lay in bed still thinking about my soon-to-be future. Another problem came up. I had no money at all to even start out. I'd have to get some. But how? Steal it? I'd been accused of stealing already, so why not? That would be justice of a sort. Oh, sure, April, and when you run out of money in the city, you can just sell your body. What else do Native girls do? By now, I knew what skid row meant. I bet all those girls who ended up on skid row just wanted freedom and peace in the first place. Just like me. I'd had good intentions about my life. But here I was, forced to go out into the world, unprepared and alone, with only a grade 10 education and no money. No matter; I'd still run away. I felt such pity for myself as I thought about what I'd end up being, about having to give up my plans, about facing a hard life ahead. But staying here would be harder. I felt I had no choice.

My running away plans were discarded when rescue did come at the beginning of spring break. It came in the form of Mr. Wendell, my new social worker. When I saw him enter the house and introduce himself, I was downright disappointed. He was short, thin, balding, had glasses, and worse, he had a meek, mild demeanor. To put it bluntly, he was no match for Mrs. DeRosier. I studied him as he exchanged preliminaries with her. Suddenly, he said, "I'd like to see where the boys slept."

"The boys?" Mrs. DeRosier asked. She was obviously flustered by his unexpected question. I could tell, and I was glad she was off balance. But the thought that she was going to get more boys must have hit her the same time it hit me. Her face lit up, and my face grew long.

"Oh, yes, Raymond and Gilbert. How are they doing now that they're on their own? I hope they're not getting into any trouble. They were such good boys when they were with us. And such hard workers. You couldn't get any better workers. I believe that hard work is good for the soul, don't you?"

"You lying, phony hypocrite," I said to her in my mind.

Mrs. DeRosier led the way into the living room towards the stairs, saying, "They used to share my son's room. We moved their bunks into the storage closet for now."

Upstairs, Mr. Wendell had a look in the storage closet and nodded without saying anything. He asked where my room was. Mrs. DeRosier took him down the hall to Maggie's room. I followed them everywhere, and when she could, Mrs. DeRosier scowled at me as if trying to tell me to get back downstairs.

"I can only see one bed, Mrs. DeRosier. I understand you have a daughter. Isn't this her room?" Mr. Wendell said.

"The girls share it. The other bed was so old I've ordered a new one. It should have been here by now." She smiled at him.

This was probably my only chance to prove what a liar Mrs. DeRosier was. I said, "My bedroom's really downstairs, at the back."

Mrs. DeRosier said quickly, "Well, the girls have been having trouble, so I moved April there, but only temporarily." She glared at me when Mr. Wendell turned to start back down.

"I've been in that room since I first came here. And so was Cheryl." I was beyond caring about the later consequences.

"How about if you show me where your room is, April?" Mr. Wendell said to me when we were back in the kitchen. Mrs. DeRosier said nothing as Mr. Wendell looked at my belongings. "Well, Mrs. DeRosier, I think that under the circumstances, I can only recommend that April be moved as soon as we find a new foster home for her." He was about to say more, but Mrs. DeRosier cut him off.

"And I think you can take her, and get out of my house right now," she bellowed.

"Mrs. Semple has had a very heavy caseload. Otherwise I'm sure you wouldn't have been able to fool her for so long," Mr. Wendell said to her calmly.

He told me to get my things ready. When we started for the car, Rebel came to me. I stopped to pet him one last time. "Poor old Reb. I wish I could take you with me. Thank you for being my friend here. Bye, Rebel." Rebel wagged his tail, and as we drove off, I saw him lay down by the roadside, probably to wait for me to come back.

7

ONCE WE ARRIVED at the Children's Aid Office, arrangements were quickly made for me to attend St. Bernadette's Academy once their spring break ended. I waited the rest of that morning in the waiting area, not quite sure I wasn't dreaming all this. I would actually be going to an academy. Rich girls went to academies. When Mr. Wendell returned, he brought back news that increased my excitement. I was going to the Steindalls to be with Cheryl until the spring break was over. All of this excitement was inside me. Outwardly I might have smiled slightly, but I was now used to keeping my feelings to myself.

When we arrived at the Steindall's place in Birds Hill, Cheryl was waiting for me on the veranda. When she saw our car pull into the driveway, she bounded off the steps and came running up to greet me. She was practically jumping up and down. I greeted her in a cool, reserved manner and that put an injured look on her face. At the time, only Cheryl and Mrs. Steindall were home. Their own daughter was away in the city for the holidays, visiting an older sister. After Mr. Wendell made sure I was settled in, he left. I had a snack while Cheryl chattered away. Mrs. Steindall seemed nice enough, but she didn't attempt to join in Cheryl's questions. Cheryl seemed used to her being quiet, because she wasn't at all self-conscious about what she said.

Afterward, she took me out to the barn to show me Fastbuck. As I admired the horse, she asked, "You know what I used to think about doing all the time?"

"What?"

"I used to think of riding him to the DeRosiers to rescue you from them. But then I probably would have gotten lost, and I couldn't figure out how to feed and water the horse. Anyway, Mr. Steindall only gave me Fastbuck to ride, not for keeps. If I'd taken him, I'd have been a horse thief." While I smiled, Cheryl seemed to ponder for a minute before she spoke again. "April, how come you didn't seem very glad to see me?"

"I was Cheryl. Honest. It's just that I'm used to keeping the way I feel inside of me. I've been doing that for such a long time now. It just seems it's safer not to show your feelings in front of other people. Like, if the Steindalls were mean people, or even Mr. Wendell, and they saw that we liked being together, they might try and keep us apart. Remember, DeRosier did that."

"Yeah, I guess you're right."

After that, Cheryl and I talked every minute that we could, catching up on things we didn't say in letters. I must have made up for all the laughing I didn't do while I was living at the DeRosiers. But too soon, I had to leave for school.

I finished my grade 10 at St. Bernadette's Academy. When I'd been living at the Dion's, I had known nuns, and they were okay people. I was able to relax at the convent. I followed a daily routine, and all the girls had chores assigned to them. It was wonderful not to have to be the only one to work. I made friends with a lot of the boarders. The only thing was that they spoke of their friends and families back home, and I had no one to speak of except Cheryl. It wasn't until June that I came up with an outright lie, an excuse for being with the Children's Aid. I told my friends that my parents died in a plane crash. I didn't plan on that lie. It just came out on the spur of the moment, when I was being asked about my family. They were so sympathetic towards me that I knew I would never be able to take those words back. I credited my ability to make friends easily to the fact that none of them knew I was part Indian.

The Steindalls agreed to take me for the summer holidays. Mr. Steindall and Cheryl taught me how to ride. Sometimes, we would all go out riding, even Mrs. Steindall, who looked out of place in her jeans and cowboy boots. When I became a good-enough rider, Cheryl and I were allowed to go camping overnight by a small creek about four miles away. The first time, Mr. Steindall rode over in the evening and helped us set up the tent.

One night, when we were sitting in front of our small fire, Cheryl told me the things she had dreamt of when we lived together at the DeRosiers. "Remember how I used to look at your geography book?"

"Yeah, and daydream."

"Well, I used to think that when Mom and Dad got better and took us back, we could move to the B.C. Rockies and live like olden-day Indians. We'd live near a lake, and we'd build our own log cabin with a big fireplace. And we wouldn't have electricity probably. We'd have lots and lots of books. We'd have dogs and horses, and we'd make friends with the wild animals. We'd go fishing and hunting, grow our own garden, and chop our wood for winter. And we wouldn't meet people who were always trying to put us down. We'd be so happy. Do you think that would ever be possible, April?"

"It's a beautiful dream, Cheryl." She was watching me, and I didn't want her to know then that I had my own plans. I wanted to be with people, not isolated in the wilderness.

"But do you think it's possible that it could happen?"

"Maybe. Maybe our parents might start coming to see us again. But it all depends on them." I realized that moment that I had stopped thinking of our parents as Mom and Dad, and that now it was hard for me to refer to them as Mom and Dad.

"I wanted to ask our social workers about them, but I was too scared. I don't know why. I still think about us living out there together. When I'm feeling down, that picks me up. Mom and Dad would become real healthy again. I always think of Dad as a strong man. If he had been pure Indian, he would have been a chief or a warrior in the olden days. I'd sure like to know what kind of Indians we are. And I remember Mom was so beautiful. To me, she was like an Indian princess. And since this was only a daydream, Rebel would be with us, of course." Cheryl's eyes sparkled. I could tell that this fantasy had meant a lot to her. It had probably helped her get over her loneliness. She looked so wistful that I knew this was not the time to tell her the truth about our parents. I felt it was more important to let her hang on to her impossible dreams. If only Cheryl would forget about them, forget that she was Métis. She was so smart that she could have made it in the white world. White people has a great respect for high intelligence.

When I first came for the summer, I had talked about how great it was to be at the academy. But by the end of it, Cheryl started talking about going there, too, so I changed my tune. I then told her, "You wouldn't want to leave this place and Fastbuck to go to a convent, would you? I'm sure you wouldn't like it there. There are hours and hours of praying in the chapel, and then there's also the hours of study periods. There's hardly any sports activity. You'd be bored to death." I didn't want Cheryl at the academy because of the lie I had told about my parents and because I was white, as far as the other girls were concerned. I wanted to keep it that way as long as I could.

"Sounds to me as if you don't want me there," Cheryl said, tilting her head to one side.

"You know it's not that. You have it so good here. And I could probably come and visit you for holidays. Besides, I'll be finished school in two years, and you still have four years to go. What would you do if you didn't like it? When I graduate, you'd be alone. If you left there, they might put you in another home like the DeRosiers'." Cheryl shrugged and accepted my reasoning. I was greatly relieved.

Going to St. Bernadette's was good for me. I had many friends, and it was easy to study and do well in my school work. On weekends, I was invited to go to other girls' homes, with Mr. Wendell's okay. I never told Cheryl about those weekends, knowing she'd probably feel slighted. Long weekends I always went to the Steindalls.

I'd often wish that I had been placed as a boarder at this school long before. There were no hassles about not having a family. There was no one who made fun of my parents. Of course, that was due to the lie I had told. I might not have known a family life as I had at the Dion's, but I would not have known the cruelty of the DeRosiers, either.

I spent Christmas with the Steindalls. Perhaps Cheryl had put her family fantasy aside, because while I was there, she had something new to tell me.

"You know, April, I think that since we're going to make it, we ought to help other kids like us make it, too. You know what I've been thinking? I'm going to go on to university and become a social worker. And I'm going to be one of the better social workers, just like Mr. Wendell. What about you? What are you going to be when you grow up?"

"I am almost grown up. And I haven't got a clue what I'm going to be. I used to think of being a lawyer, but I'm too shy. All I know for sure is what I don't want to be. I don't want to be in anything medical, I don't want to be a teacher or a social worker. I just don't know."

"Well, geez, April, you better start thinking about it, because you've only got a year and a half to go."

True, I did have only a year and a half to go before I would graduate. But even so, I'd only be seventeen. What I wanted to do was start working and make money.

At the end of my grade 11 school year, Mr. Wendell gave me the option of returning to the Steindalls for the summer or going to Winnipeg and finding myself a summer job. He said my room and board would be provided. Not another foster home but room and board! I opted for the city. To ease the guilt I felt for not choosing Cheryl's company, I told myself that I had to start making my life, for me, and that both of us should have friends of our own, not always relying on each other. I wrote Cheryl a hurried letter to tell her all this.

I moved to Spence Street, just off Portage Avenue, near the heart of the city. It didn't take me long to find a job as a waitress, and I made new friends among the other boarders. Some of them were Native people from northern communities and were there to go to the University of Winnipeg. Others were former foster children who were working at steady jobs, on the verge of going into the world on their own, but who still required the security of the Children's Aid to fall back on. I would work from eight in the morning to four-thirty. After supper, I would go with the other girls down to a coffee shop where a lot of other kids hung out. On Fridays and Saturdays, we would all go to the Hungry Eye, a discotheque on Portage Avenue, near Carlton.

I found these people fascinating. Compared to them, I was all tensed up inside, but they were so free and easy that it wasn't long before many of them became my friends. I liked the way they dressed, and I liked the way they danced. They were good and bad at the same time. Good in that the Native people were good-looking and seemed self-confident, contrary to those few I'd seen in school. Good in that the different peoples mixed easily. Good in their open acceptance of others. Bad in that they went shoplifting, drank liquor even though they were underage, and had easy sexual relationships with each other. At first when they talked about this, I thought they meant kissing. By the end of that summer, I knew it was more. When the discotheque closed, all-night parties followed, but I always went back to my place. I felt at home with these new friends, but a lot of times, I imagined I was better than they were. The girls made me think of Mrs. Semple's speech on the "syndrome." So, I enjoyed the good things they offered but stayed away from the bad.

I worked hard all that summer and put all my earnings in a savings account. I hadn't written to Cheryl; I had kept putting it off, and then I figured there would be more time once

I was in school. When I returned to St. Bernadette's to complete my grade 12, I felt a bit more worldly. It was less than a week before I received a letter from Cheryl.

September 7, 1965

Dear April,

How are you? In case you've forgotten, it's me, Cheryl, your sister. How come you never came to see me once this past summer and you never even wrote to me? Your last letter made me very sad. It's like you don't want to have anything to do with me anymore. Your pretense about not caring seems to be turning into reality. I was looking forward to our spending the summer holidays together again. Instead, all I get is a short letter. I know we each have to have our own friends and make our own lives. But it was you who said all we've got is each other. We're family, not just friends. Are you coming for Christmas? I hope so.

I finally got another essay done on Riel. I didn't have much time in school with sports and other things going on. I did have a lot of rainy days when I was alone this past summer. I'll probably grow up to be a nag, huh? You're so lucky to be in grade 12. They really should have let me skip a grade, too, don't you think? Well, I'm going to sign off now. This was just going to be a short note to let you know how much you hurt my feelings. Hope you like Riel at Batoche.

Your loving sister,
Cheryl

I felt guilty all over again after I had read the letter. She was right. I should have written to her and given her my address in the city. I should have made a special effort to go and see her. I tried to imagine myself in her place. Yes, she must have felt abandoned by me, more than she showed in her letter. I had to write her a long letter to make up for it. I even sent her lavish compliments on her essay. It *was* quite extraordinary for someone her age, but it had no big effect on me. Riel and Dumont: they were men of the past. Why dwell on it? What concerned me was my future. And this essay proved my point once again. White superiority had conquered in the end.

By Christmas, I had decided what I was going to do. Some of the girls had talked about becoming secretaries. That sounded good enough for me. I would take a quick secretarial course after I graduated. Over the Christmas holidays, I told Cheryl my plans. She was disappointed. She was sure I could do something better, something professional. She figured I would be wasting my life away. I told her she was beginning to sound like one of those ambitious white mothers she scorned so much. We teased each other back and forth, but I knew she was serious. She really did want me to attend university. And, of course, she was still set on becoming a social worker.

After my graduation, I got my old job as a waitress for the summer months. It was arranged that I would attend the Red River Community College in September. I lived once again on Spence Street, expecting everything to be the same as the previous summer. It wasn't. The Hungry Eye had closed down. I ran into a few of the old crowd. They told me that some of the others had gone to other cities and a few were doing time in jail. Another discotheque had opened on Graham Avenue. I went along with them to check it out. One of the girls I had met last summer now had a baby at home and was living on welfare. That bothered me a lot, and somehow the magic of that kind of nightlife was gone for me.

By September, I had over eight hundred dollars in the bank from my two summers of working. I thought I was quite wealthy. My first boyfriend wasn't really a boyfriend. He spent most of his time pining away over his old girlfriend, and I spent my time telling him that maybe in the future, they would get back together again. We went to school socials, concerts, and movies, but I always insisted that we go Dutch. What I liked most about Ted was that he was safe to be with. We made no demands on each other. When I completed my course, I knew I would never see Ted again, except by accident.

Children's Aid assured me they would support me until I found a job. About three weeks later, I became employed as a legal secretary at the law firm of Harbison and Associates. I was thrilled when I found out I'd be making more than four times the amount I had as a waitress.

When I had my last talk with Mr. Wendell on what I called my Independence Day, I showed no outward reactions. He gave me the accumulation of my family allowances along with reassurances that if I needed assistance of any kind, I could always come to him. Then I heard myself asking about my parents and what the chances were of finding them. He went off and returned with a list of names and addresses. I didn't know why I had asked, as I had no plans to look for them. I thanked him and said goodbye. I'd probably see him again, but I would no longer be a foster child. I was free. Free! FREE!

8

I FOUND FREEDOM RATHER BORING, once I'd settled into my new routine. I'd found an apartment on Cumberland Avenue, which was within walking distance of where I worked. Then I furnished it with used furniture. Working was easy – that is, after the first couple of weeks when I got over my nervousness. I worked for Mr. Lord, a young lawyer who did real-estate work. I was nervous about making mistakes when I typed up all the legal forms; a mistake could be costly. I was nervous about answering the phone; I could get names, numbers, or messages wrong. I was nervous each time I handed in letters I had typed for his signature; I could have made mistakes with my shorthand or my typing. Mr. Lord was generous with his compliments, though, and that soon put me at ease. The other girls in the office were pleasant. Several were around my age, and when I got to know them better, we would go to movies or go shopping together.

Evenings and weekends I spent on the search for my parents. I'd take the list and a map of the city and go to the addresses on the list. Sometimes the addresses would lead to a parking lot or a new building. The house where we had lived on Jarvis had been torn down and replaced by a government building. I would feel a vague kind of relief when this happened, because I didn't like the people I met who said they once knew Henry and Alice Raintree "a long time ago." I found out they both had relatives in the North. I couldn't go looking for them in the northern towns because of my job, and because there was too slim a chance that I would find them, anyway.

At one address on Charles Street, I was practically dragged into the house by a rather large, squat woman. When I told her who I was and that I was looking for Henry and Alice Raintree, a grin spread on her face from ear to ear. All happy and smiling, she took me by the arm and led me into the house. She hadn't seen my parents for the last couple of years but maybe Jacques had. I figured Jacques to be her husband. I didn't want to stay there, but I could think of no polite way of leaving. Besides, she assured me that Jacques would be home in a short while. Meanwhile, she offered me some tea, then a beer, but I refused both. She'd been cooking, and she resumed her position at the old stove. I sat at the kitchen table, looking around.

What a horrible place, I thought. The linoleum was coming apart at the seams, and here and there, pieces were missing. I could see why it hadn't been washed. The cupboards had been painted white, maybe twenty years ago. The plaster was also coming off the walls and the ceiling was warped and water-stained. And flies! They were everywhere and reminded me of the book *Lord of the Flies*. One fly landed on the rim of an uncovered lard can, which sat on the table with some bread. It rubbed its legs together, as if with glee. How could anyone eat that food and not be sick? Suddenly it was very important to me that those flies not touch me, and I waved them away. Of course, the windows couldn't be closed, but hadn't they ever heard of screens? I wondered what they did in wintertime when the smell of the place must be rank. They were probably immune to all the germs in the house, but me, I feared going home, getting sick, and missing work.

I stared over at the old woman, her back was to me, and now probably unaware of my presence. From our initial encounter, I thought she would have been the talkative type, but no. Silently, she occupied herself with peeling and dicing vegetables. I thought she probably used the flies for meat, and then I told myself I should slap myself silly for thinking like that.

I couldn't help it, though. I looked down at her feet, stockingless and stuck into a pair of men's backless slippers. Her legs were lumpy with varicose veins or some disease. Her heels were dried and scaly. Ugly! Her, this house, this kind of existence. I finally cleared my throat, mostly to remind her that I was still sitting behind her.

"I really have to go now. I'm supposed to meet someone. I could come back another time," I lied. I really would have to slap myself or something.

"Oh, I'm sorry, I was sure Jacques would have been back by now," she said, turning to me. "Are you sure you really have to go? You could stay for supper."

"Well, thank you, but I really have to go." I turned to leave, knowing I would not return.

Later, as I sat in the bathtub, washing off all those germs I'd probably picked up, I thought about the scene I had witnessed. If I had been brought up in those slums, I would have been brought up with flies and mice and rats and lice and germs. I would have been brought up by alcoholic parents, and what would I be like now? Would I have any ambitions? Or would I come to live just for today, glad when each day would end? I would not go back to that house on Charles Street. I would not go out of my way for a long, long time to try and find the parents who had abandoned Cheryl and me – all for a bottle of booze! When I finished my bath, I put all the papers Mr. Wendell had given me, along with new addresses I had been given recently, into a box and stuck the box in the back of the closet, out of sight and out of mind. If I did find my parents, there would be emotional pain for Cheryl and me. It would probably tear me apart once again. That part of my life was now finished for good. I had a plan to follow, and from now on I would stick to it, whether Cheryl agreed with it or not. It was the only way for me to survive.

Mr. Steindall usually came to get me for long weekends so I could spend them with Cheryl. Otherwise, I would stay home, watch television, read books or magazines, and if I wanted to go out and do something, I would go to the movies or to the stores. On paydays, I would go to both.

I'd buy magazines that featured beautiful homes and study how they were decorated. Then I would lay back and have daydreams about owning one of those homes, giving lavish parties, and having lots of important friends. I also studied fashion magazines, and I'd spend hours shopping for just the right thing. I had no idea how I was going to become rich. All I knew was that one day I would have a beautiful home, a big fancy car, and the most beautiful clothing ever. Yes, when fortune kissed me with wealth, I'd be well-prepared.

I had been working at Harbison's law firm for almost six months when another lawyer was added to the eleven already there. When I first saw Roger Maddison, I thought to myself,

"Now there is somebody I wouldn't mind spending the rest of my life with." It wasn't that I was a sucker for all good-looking men, just that his rugged looks were the kind one could look at forever. Since some of the other girls obviously shared the same opinion, I figured I'd be cool about my infatuation with him. But then I had to do some work for him, because he didn't have his own secretary. He was a perfectionist, and when I made my first small mistake, he tore into me. I was so angry that he would criticize me. Or maybe I was dismayed to find our feelings weren't mutual. I practically yelled right back at him. Needless to say, that infatuation ended quickly. From then on, we were sarcastic towards each other, making snide remarks, always trying to outdo the other. Even when he did get his own secretary and she began to do all of his work, we still glared at each other whenever it was appropriate. Or he would smile and greet everyone, excluding me. What I couldn't figure out was that he seemed to study me an awful lot. I'd be hard at work and then I'd feel someone watching me. I'd look up and there he was. But he'd give me a dirty look and turn away.

While I worked, Cheryl was finishing her grade 12. In June, she graduated at the top of her class and even won a scholarship to go to the University of Winnipeg. If she hadn't, Children's Aid would have paid for her education anyway. There were some advantages in being a ward of the CAS.

Cheryl moved in with me, even though she wouldn't be eighteen until October. Children's Aid agreed to pay all her expenses. The day Cheryl moved in with me, July 6, 1968, was more like a real Independence Day. The Steindalls brought Cheryl and her belongings to my place that Saturday morning, had lunch with us, and then left. Cheryl and I went shopping for a sofa that opened into a bed. Then we went to other stores. We dropped off shopping bags back at the apartment, then went out for supper. That evening, we sat around talking. We both couldn't get over how wonderful it felt being together with no one to control our destinies but us.

I went to work on Monday, and Cheryl went to the Winnipeg Friendship Centre. She volunteered her services for the rest of July and August, believing the experience would help in her future career as a social worker.

Cheryl began her first year of university in September. I began to meet her for lunch in the university cafeteria. She quickly accumulated a number of friends, both white and Native. To my biggest surprise, she started going out quite steadily with a white student, Garth Tyndall. I was amazed, because the way she had talked in the past, she didn't seem to like anything white. I wasn't surprised she could attract the opposite sex, because she was very beautiful and outgoing. She reminded me of the Native girls from the Hungry Eye, and I wondered how she got that way and I didn't. As always, she was stubborn when she made up her mind about anything. When she was home, she'd usually have her friends around. And when she was over at Garth's place in the evenings, I would be alone.

I gave a party for her eighteenth birthday. That night, I could see how close she and Garth had become. He seemed to care more about her than she did about him. I was very pleased. If anyone could change a woman's mind about some things, it was a man.

But my hopes were dashed when, a month later, they split up. At first Cheryl wouldn't tell me what happened. That night, they had gone out, supposedly to dinner and then a movie. But later in the evening, Garth called for her.

When she came in a few minutes later, I said, "I thought you two were going out tonight."

"No. Something more important came up. If he calls again, tell him I'm not in. I'm going to take a bath and go to bed." She seemed very depressed.

"Hey, Cheryl, did you two have a fight?"

"No, not a fight. More of an insight." With that she stalked off to the bathroom.

Garth called again, and I was tempted to ask him what had happened, but I felt I should hear it from Cheryl. The next day was Saturday, and Cheryl was still in a state of depression. I asked her again what had happened.

Reluctantly, she finally told me. "We were walking down Portage, and Garth saw some of his friends coming towards us. He told me to keep walking, and he'd catch up. I pretended that I was window shopping so I could listen to them. You know what he did? You know what that creep did? He left me there and went for a beer with them. He didn't want them to know about me. That hypocrite! He's ashamed of me."

I didn't say anything. I didn't say anything because I was guilty of that, too. I had never invited Cheryl to meet me for lunch because I didn't want anyone at work to see her, to know she was my sister. Even now, I knew this wouldn't change me. I would continue to walk the five blocks or so at lunchtime, so I could meet her where she was already accepted.

That night, Cheryl decided she was going to keep a journal. I smiled and told her she shouldn't start a journal with an unhappy opening. "Wait until something good happens to you, something special."

"Well, I haven't got a lifetime. I want to start this thing right now. I have a feeling there will be a lot more of this kind of thing."

I thought to myself that I would be added in there one day, in a negative light.

Not long after Cheryl's breakup with Garth, I met someone I thought was very special. I was waiting for Cheryl outside one of her classrooms, when another of Cheryl's professors approached me. We talked until Cheryl came out. His name was Jerry McCallister, and whenever he saw me alone after that, he'd stop to chat. One day, he asked me to go out with him. I guess he thought I shared some of the same ideals as Cheryl, because he talked about Native subjects, like housing and education. Having heard Cheryl often speak about such things enabled me to carry on a reasonable conversation with him. When he dropped me off at my apartment, he asked me to go out with him again, but he didn't try to kiss me. I had gone out with some of the students to plays and concerts but they had only one thing on their minds at the end of the evening. So Jerry's behaviour was refreshing. We'd go out together frequently after that, even during the week. He was always a perfect gentleman. The more I saw of him, the more I appreciated him.

Finally, one night when we stayed at my place for dinner and some conversation, he made his first advance. I held back. Good girls didn't do that kind of thing. Furthermore, and more important, if things got out of hand and we went all the way, there was the risk of getting pregnant. Maybe that was my worst fear, because when Jerry tried to get too close, I would always back off. Jerry's initial amusement and patience waned, and one night he was trying to coax me again. Finally, he said, "April, what are you scared of? Are you scared of getting involved with another human being? Or is it sex you're afraid of?"

"I'm not afraid of anything," I said. It was my trick way of saying, yeah, I'm afraid of something, but I don't want to tell you what.

"Well then? You know how much I like you. I like being with you. I admire you a great deal. You're beautiful. You're intelligent. I like everything about you, April."

He had not complimented me this way before, and I was slightly surprised that this was what he thought of me. I felt warm and comfortable. He pulled me closer to him as if what he had said was enough to have made me change my mind. But I said, "I don't know. I never...well, I never...well, how would I know if I never?" I hadn't wanted to reveal that I was a virgin. It made me feel so immature.

Jerry smiled and said, "April, if you feel the same way that I feel, then making love is the most natural thing in the world. And if it's respect you're worried about, I'll certainly not respect you any less. We're not teenagers anymore. We're man and woman. Adults, with adult feelings and adult needs." He pulled me close again, and I tensed up.

"I can't."

"Why not? There's nothing wrong with it. Now stop acting so childish." He took his arms from around me and sat up.

"No. I'm sorry, Jerry. I want to, but I just can't." I looked at him for some understanding.

He stood up, went to the closet, and got his coat out. As he put it on, he said, "I don't like playing games, April. Either you want me or you don't. When you make up your mind, I'll be at the university."

In the following weeks, I agonized over Jerry's absence. I had really liked the intimate suppers, long talks, and having a steady friend to go out with. I had planned to ask him to the law firm's Christmas social and show him off, especially to Roger Maddison. I didn't attend the law firm's social, after all. I went with Cheryl to spend Christmas with the Steindalls and returned alone because of work. I was so lonely during the holidays that my resolve broke down, and I decided to call him. I had never been out to his home, and I looked up his name in the phone book. As I dialed the number, I thought of being flippant about the whole thing. I'd say something like, "Hi, Jerry. I was wrong, and you were right, so I'm yours for the taking." No. That wasn't my style. I'd just play it by ear.

"Hello?" a small child's voice answered.

"Uh, hello. Is Jerry McCallister there, please?"

"No, Daddy's not home. Do you want to talk to my mommy?" And before I could say no, I heard the child calling to his mother.

"Hello," came the voice of a woman. I tried to picture what she looked like.

"Oh, hello, Mrs. McCallister? I'm a student at the university, and I was working on a project over the holidays, but I needed Mr. McCallister's advice on something. I'm sorry to be bothering him at home." My cheeks were burning red.

"Oh, that's all right. He should be back any minute now. Could I have him call you back? Oh, just a minute. I think he's at the door now. Hold on." She also left before I could stop her.

I thought of hanging up, but if I did then it might arouse his wife's suspicions.

"Hello," Jerry's voice came on.

"It's me, April. I guess I made a terrible mistake. I'm sorry." I hung up before he could say anything. I felt incredibly stupid. I had been going out with a married man! Not only that, he had a child, maybe more than one. And I was about to try out a bedroom scene with him? I shook my head and sat there for a long time.

He came to see me one evening, after the New Year. "April, I'd like to explain."

"There's nothing to explain. You're married! You wanted me to...to...well, you know. And all the time, you were married. And *you* don't like playing games?" I said sarcastically.

"My wife and I have been talking about getting a divorce. Then I met you, and I wanted to get to know you right away. I'm sorry I didn't wait until it was all proper and legal."

"And I'm sorry, too. But I don't go out with married men. That is when I know they're married. It's finished. Over. Just leave me alone!" I opened the door for him to go and then stood back waiting.

"But April, you know how I feel about you. We could have a promising future together," Jerry said, stalling.

"Goodbye, Jerry." I gave him the coldest, hardest look I could muster. He had no choice but to give up and leave. He looked dejected, and I felt sorry for him. For a second I almost said, "It's okay, we could still be friends, at least." But I didn't. I closed the door on my almost-first lover.

For the next few months, I didn't go out on dates. I just stayed in and moped. When Cheryl brought home another of her strays for supper, I didn't even mind. That's what I called the Métis and Indian girls she befriended from the Friendship Centre. Nancy was a dark-skinned Native girl with long, limp black hair. The story of her family life was similar to that of other Native girls Cheryl had met. Drinking always seemed to be behind it. Nancy had been raped by her drunken father. Cheryl remarked that people called that incest, but Nancy insisted it was rape. Everyone in Nancy's family drank, even the younger kids. Or the new rage: sniffing glue. Both Nancy and her mother had prostituted themselves, sometimes for money, sometimes for a cheap bottle of wine. Nancy was like a wilted flower. She had a defeatist look to her. What a life to have led! I suppose she had stayed at home because there was nowhere else to go. I was shocked when Cheryl told me Nancy was only seventeen. She looked at least twenty-five.

How Cheryl could stand to hear those kinds of stories all the time was beyond me. That she wanted to make a lifetime career out of it was impossible for me to understand. It was depressing, especially when I knew that Nancy and the other strays came from the same places that we came from.

I'd go with Cheryl and Nancy to nice restaurants and treat them to suppers. I began to notice what being Native was like in middle-class surroundings. Sometimes, service was deliberately slow. Sometimes, I'd overhear comments like, "Who let the Indians off the reservation?" Or we'd be walking home and guys would make comments to us, as if we were easy pick-ups. None of us would say anything. Not even Cheryl who could be sharp-tongued. Cheryl and I never talked about these incidents either. Instead of being angry with these ignorant people, I just felt embarrassed to be seen with Natives, Cheryl included. I began to go out with them less and less.

Anyway, Cheryl was starting to spend more evenings at the Friendship Centre, leaving me alone with my magazines and my daydreams. I was even reading books on proper etiquette, preparing myself for my promising future in white society. If Cheryl had known I was reading that kind of material, she would have laughed or criticized me. It wouldn't have mattered, because I began to think I would be dreaming such dreams right into my senility. Oh, well. Cheryl once had a fantasy, which comforted her, and now I had mine.

I gave a lot of thought to the kind of man I would eventually marry. If I were going to be successful and happy, he would have to be carefully scrutinized. I would not be able to afford to let my heart rule my head. Nor could I marry just for money, or I'd be rich but not happy. Actually, it was quite simple. I'd have to find somebody who was handsome, witty, and charming. He'd have to be making a good living. He'd be good and honest, with a strong character, but he would also have a fine sense of humour. He would be perfection personified. "Oh yeah? Dream on, April Raintree. If such a man existed, he'd already be married," I sighed. I'd probably end up falling in love with a farmer, and we'd be dirt poor, and I'd have to work for the rest of my life.

But that spring, Prince Charming did come into my life. I was typing a mortgage agreement when he walked into the office. He was there to see Mr. Lord, and the receptionist sent him to my desk. I let him stand there, without even looking at him, while I finished typing. Then I looked up into his merry, blue eyes. He was one of those smooth, handsome men, the kind I didn't like, the kind who was so polished, he just had to be conceited.

He smiled at me as he said, "Hello, I'm Bob Radcliff. I have an appointment with Mr. Lord."

I knew immediately that he was a big deal from Toronto. I told him that Mr. Lord had been delayed at another meeting that morning and asked him to return at one o'clock.

"Well, I suppose I could be persuaded to return by your having lunch with me."

I thought of flatly refusing, since it was obvious he was the conceited type. Instead, I surprised myself by asking, "How do you know I'm not married?"

"I looked for a wedding ring. There's none." He spread his fingers before me to show he was not wearing a ring, either.

I scrutinized his finger for telltale marks. At the same time, I figured he couldn't be so conceited after all, since he didn't wear any flashy rings. I realized some of the other secretaries had stopped to watch. I smiled self-consciously and said, "Well, I don't take lunch until twelve."

"I'll wait."

For almost the next hour, I felt him watching me from where he sat. My fingers fumbled over the keyboard, as I made a show of being efficient by finishing page after page, all filled with mistakes.

Over lunch, he told me more about himself than I already knew. I had been impressed that a man of his importance was not upset by having his appointment delayed. Furthermore, he had sat for forty-five minutes waiting for me, patiently. He had his own wholesale furniture business, which he ran with his mother. His father had died when he was in university, and he and his mother had taken over the business. He was in Winnipeg with plans for expansion. Since I knew his home was in Toronto, I had no intention of becoming further involved with him. Just this lunch, and that would be it. But then on our way back, he asked me out again for that evening. Okay, so he must be lonely. But after this one night, that would be it.

It wasn't. For the next few months, we spent nearly every evening together. He met Cheryl and showed no negative reaction. They got along quite well, considering Cheryl had resumed her "I-don't-like-white-men" stance. I found Bob gentle, good-natured, and very considerate. He was every-thing I thought a good husband should be. It was just too bad he had to go back to Toronto.

Bob delayed his return trip to be with me. By the end of the third month, he proposed. He asked me, April Raintree, to be his wife! He wanted to get married in a small civil ceremony in Winnipeg. My dreams were coming true, and I ecstatic-ally floated through those days. Everything seemed to happen overnight.

The only note of discord came when I told Cheryl that Bob had proposed to me. I expected her to be as excited and happy as I was. "What do you want to go and marry this dude for? You're asking for trouble. You don't know anything about him, really."

"I know all I need to know. You're just saying that because of Garth, aren't you?"

"Maybe I am. Even if Bob isn't prejudiced, maybe his friends are. And what will they think when they find out he's married a half-breed? If he had to choose, do you really believe he'd stick with you?"

"Cheryl..." I said in a warning, angry tone.

"Or what would you do if you had children that looked Indian. Could you both cope with that?" Cheryl paused but I made no answer, so she continued, "You'll probably go over there and pass yourself off as white, won't you? You're not going to tell anyone who and what you are."

"Well, I'm certainly not going to go around saying, 'Hi, I'm April Radcliff, and I'm a half-breed.' So just knock it off, Cheryl."

I stormed into the bathroom, cutting our discussion short. I was more disturbed than angry. Not so much by Cheryl's telling me I shouldn't marry Bob, but by her questions, which were like needles pricking into my bubble of happiness and satisfaction. We'd never talked about this before, and I was sure she had not suspected how I felt. But all this time, she knew. She knew I was ashamed of being a half-breed.

We were married on July 25, 1969, on a Friday afternoon with only Cheryl and a "not-anyone-special" male friend of Cheryl's to witness our exchange of vows. I wondered why he hadn't even invited his mother, but he had said that was the way he wanted it. I accepted it, I was so happy. From that moment, I wouldn't have to worry about changing the spelling of my name, because it was now legally April Radcliff.

Cheryl came with us to the airport on the Saturday afternoon that we were to fly to Toronto. I guess Bob knew I wanted some time alone with her, because he left to buy some last-minute items. At first, Cheryl and I let some of our precious minutes slip by, just looking at each other and not saying anything.

Cheryl spoke first. "April, in spite of what I said the other day, I do hope you'll be happy. I really do. I was just mouthing off, you know. I'm sorry."

"Don't be, Cheryl. I guess I got on the defensive, because some of the things you said were true. And I've never wanted to admit them. You didn't come right out and say it, but I am ashamed. I can't accept.... I can't accept being a Métis. That's the hardest thing I've ever said to you, Cheryl. And I'm glad you don't feel the same way I do. I'm so proud of what you're trying to do. But to me, being Métis means I'm one of the have-nots. And I want so much. I'm selfish. I know it, but that's the way I am. I want what white society can give me. Oh, Cheryl, I really believe that's the only way for me to find happiness. I'm different from you. I wish I weren't, but I am. I'm me. You have to do what you believe is right for you, and I have to go my way. Remember, though, I'll always be there if you need me."

Cheryl was smiling, but sadly. Finally, she said, "April, I have known how you felt for a long time. And I decided that I was going to do what I could to turn the Native image around so that one day you could be proud of being Métis." To lighten the mood, she added, "Of course, you may be old and grey when the day does come, but it will come. I guarantee it."

Bob came back, and it was time for us to board the plane – and for me to say goodbye to Cheryl. When we hugged each other, I felt good, like there was a new kind of honesty between us. I was moving into a new phase of my life with a man I loved and who loved me. And I had just had a good honest talk with the other most important person in my life.

But once we were airborne, I was still thinking of Cheryl. I missed her so much already. For a younger sister, she was a lot wiser than me in some ways. So she had known about my shame for a long time. And she had never said anything. She had just accepted me the way I was in silence. I wished I could do that whole part of my life over again. She was such a giving, unselfish person. What was it that made us so different, even though we were real sisters?

9

I WAS TOTALLY UNPREPARED when we arrived at Bob's home, now mine. When he had spoken of his business, I assumed it was a small operation. There had been the plans for expansion in Winnipeg, which I had worked on, but I had assumed there would be mortgages attached. Many of the documents and letters had gone to the typist, as Mr. Lord's workload had increased substantially. I had also made a special point of not taking note of the legal arrangements, as I had not wanted to be influenced in my relationship with Bob.

But from the moment I saw their house, excuse me, mansion, I knew I had underestimated the wealth I had married into. The English Tudor-style house was huge and was located on a sprawling estate. Bob took me on a tour. I was overwhelmed. The living room, with its oversized fireplace at one end, was twice the size of our apartment in Winnipeg and was to the right of the two-storey foyer with its open staircase. There was a recreation room to the rear, also with an enormous fireplace. The length of the room was flanked on the left side with French doors leading out to a swimming pool and terrace.

Bob said that when they entertained, sometimes these two large rooms were crowded. I simply could not imagine that. The long stately dining room also overlooked the terrace and the impeccably manicured gardens, which enclosed the terrace.

I felt Barbara Radcliff's disapproval of me from the very start. I couldn't blame her, though. She had missed out on her son's wedding, and that's when I realized why she hadn't been invited. He had, in effect, eloped. She was, however, very polite to me and extended a gracious welcome to their home. Somehow I had the feeling I had landed in another foster home. I was even subtly ordered to call her "Mother Radcliff," although, at times, later, I thought of her as Mother Superior, and religion had nothing to do with it.

We entertained a great deal, and, in turn, we were invited to social events and theatres and concerts and dinners and clubs. Because it was all new to me, it was thrilling. I had plenty of moments of being nervous and tongue-tied, committing social gaucheries, and I was forever wondering what the other women thought of me. In all fairness to Mother Radcliff, I must say she taught me all I hadn't learned from my books. She took me on shopping excursions and on weekly appointments to hair salons, always giving me advice in her detached way. Although we spent a good deal of time in each other's company, we never did become close. I felt small in her presence and never knew what to say. We never joked or laughed together. Her laughter seemed reserved only for those on her social level. I used to wonder what Bob's father had been like. He must have been a good-natured man, because Bob was so easygoing.

As for Bob, we got along very well. We had none of the problems that face most newlyweds, no hassles over finances, work, or even in-laws. I suppose, because of my childhood, it was easy enough for me to play second fiddle to a woman like Mother Radcliff, even to the point of allowing her to run our lives.

By November, it occurred to me that it would be nice if Cheryl could see how right I had been in my decision to marry Bob. I checked with Bob to see if it would be okay to invite her for the Christmas holidays. He thought it would be a great idea and urged me to phone her. I did and was surprised that she accepted, just like that. She told me then that Nancy had moved in with her. I thought once again that Cheryl didn't belong with a bunch of Native people. Then, the other thought struck me. Not once had nativeness been discussed in this household. Mother Radcliff had resented me simply because Bob had married me without her approval. What would she think once Cheryl came? And Christmas times were for gatherings. What would all the others think?

I should have thought twice about inviting Cheryl to visit. I wanted to show off to her so much that I had forgotten that, in turn, I would have to show her off to these people. I looked over at Bob who was smiling at me. Well, if it didn't matter to him, why should it matter to me? Still, I felt that perhaps Cheryl's predictions would come true. If Bob were ever forced to make a choice, what would it be? In his mother's hands, he was like putty. I was beginning to realize that my Prince Charming had a flaw.

Cheryl came on the Saturday before Christmas. Bob and I went to pick her up at the airport, and when we arrived home, I was dismayed to find that Mother Radcliff had some of her friends over for dinner. I watched her face for a reaction when Cheryl was introduced, but there wasn't any. It was the same when I had been introduced five months earlier, gracious but cool. I showed Cheryl around the "mansion" after dinner, and although she was complimentary, I could tell she wasn't all that impressed. I was put off. She was so religiously Métis!

Every minute we were alone, she would talk about the Friendship Centre and the program she and some other counsellors had started for teenage Native girls. She loved what she was doing, though, and that was great. It was when she criticized my lifestyle that I got on the offensive.

"What you aim to do is very commendable, Cheryl, but I can't see you changing a whole lot of people. You may turn a few lives around, but they're not the ones who are going to make an impression on the rest of the population. It's the ones who look filthy and look like they've just gotten out of bed with a hangover and who go to your neighbourhood department stores: they're the ones who make a lasting impression."

"Well, there are just as many white people out there who are in the same state," Cheryl shot back.

"It's not the same. I don't remember the white ones. I only remember the drunk Natives. It seems to me that the majority of Natives are gutter-creatures, and only a minority of whites are like that. I think that's the difference."

"I still think our project is worthwhile. Darn it, April, why do you have to be so prejudiced?" she exclaimed.

"I am not prejudiced, Cheryl. I'm simply trying to point out to you how I see things."

"Through white man's eyes."

"Maybe so, but that should be an advantage to you. How many white people would honestly tell you what they think? I don't want to discourage you completely. Helping some of the teenage girls avoid that 'Native-girl syndrome' thing is certainly worth the effort. Remember Mrs. Semple telling us about that? First, you do this, and then you do that, and next you do this, and next you do that, and she had our whole lives laid out for us. Well, we didn't do any of the things she claimed we would. But the thing is, you'll never change the image of the Native people. It would take some kind of miracle," I said, attempting to lighten our conversation.

That's how our private talks went, and I was grateful that Cheryl kept the Native subject private. As I expected, we had a full social calendar over the Christmas holidays, and I tried to coax Cheryl, unsuccessfully, to go shopping with me for the evening gowns I was sure she would need. She could not see the sense in spending money on clothing she would never wear again. So, I insisted she wear some of my dresses, since we were the same size. As a matter of fact, we could have been almost identical twins, except for our skin colouring. No wonder I had always found her so beautiful, my pretentious way of admitting my own beauty.

I had taken it for granted that Cheryl would be able to attend the dinners to which we had been invited, but Mother Radcliff took me aside – actually she summoned me to her study – and informed me that it would cause upsets to have an uninvited guest. She also stated that Cheryl would feel out of place, and although I agreed and understood, it was unthinkable that I would leave Cheryl alone. Mother Radcliff pointed out that we were giving a New Year's party so Cheryl would not be left out of *all* the festivities. I left her study, wondering how much of this I was going to tell Cheryl. At the same time, I was relieved that Cheryl's debut into my society was to be delayed. When I made my explanations to Cheryl, she made it easier by saying it was all right, because she hadn't really wanted to go to the big, fancy gatherings anyhow, and she was relieved to be able to avoid them.

On New Year's Eve, all the important people I had met over the past months, and many I had never met, gathered in our living room and adjoining family room. Bob had not exaggerated when he had said those rooms could get crowded. That party confirmed for me how wealthy and important we Radcliffs were. I guess I was the only one who was so greatly impressed, because when I took Cheryl around to introduce her to some of the people I had already met, I got a few surprises. After praising all these people to Cheryl, some came out with the most patronizing remarks.

"Oh, I've read about Indians. Beautiful people, they are. But you're not exactly Indians are you? What is the proper word for people like you?" one asked.

"Women," Cheryl replied instantly.

"No, no, I mean nationality?"

"Oh, I'm sorry. We're Canadians." Cheryl smiled sweetly.

Another woman, after being introduced to Cheryl, said, "Oh, we used to have a very good Indian maid. Such a nice, quiet girl and a hard worker, too." I suppose she meant it as a compliment, but I felt like crawling into a hole, I was so embarrassed for Cheryl.

Then two men came along, and one asked Cheryl what it was like being an Indian. Before she could reply, the other man voiced his opinion, and the two soon walked away, discussing their concepts of Native life, without having allowed Cheryl to say anything. Cheryl and I shrugged at each other, and I was wondering how she was taking it. The questioning stares didn't help, either. Some of them had tried hard to smooth things over, after realizing their initial blunders. But it was the fact that they felt they had to say something accommodating that was the most annoying.

About an hour later, my discomforting thoughts about what people must be thinking were interrupted when I noticed the entrance of an actress we had seen recently at a theatre production. As I watched Mother Radcliff greeting her, I remembered her name. Heather Langdon. She seemed to know Mother Radcliff quite well. I saw Heather look around the room in anticipation. I noticed the satisfied look on her face when Bob appeared and kissed her on the cheek. They looked like they knew each other quite well, and I felt a twinge of jealousy and worry. Mother Radcliff spotted me just then and indicated I was to come over.

When I reached them, Mother Radcliff said, "April, I would like you to meet Heather Langdon. We saw her play the other night, remember?"

"Yes, I do. I enjoyed your performance," I said as I shook her hand. Was that the right thing to say to an actress?

"April, go find your sister. I am sure she would like to be introduced to Heather," I was ordered. I obeyed.

I thought it was very nice of Mother Radcliff to give Cheryl the opportunity to meet a beautiful and talented actress. I found Cheryl and brought her back to be introduced. I noticed an exchange of looks between Mother Radcliff and Heather. I couldn't read any meaning into it, though. Heather seemed to make a point of socializing with me for the rest of that evening, and my initial worry and jealousy disappeared.

On Friday, Bob went to his office, so Cheryl and I had the whole day to ourselves. It started out being a good day. We talked about the people at the party, laughing and joking about their reactions. I found myself feebly trying to explain their positions. Cheryl didn't buy it.

"You really like this new lifestyle of yours? I mean, deep down, honestly? You like associating with these rich snobs?" she asked with sarcasm, the humour of a few moments ago suddenly gone.

I think the only thing that really aroused me in those days was when someone criticized me. So I answered, with equal sarcasm, "Cheryl, get off my case, will you? I don't ask you to live my kind of life. I know why you're doing this. You want me to take up your glorious cause. Well, I'm happy here. I love the parties, and I do like the kind of people I meet. I love this kind of life, and I have no intention of changing it. So, go home and live by what you believe in. But stop preaching at me. I admire your devotion and your confidence in Native people, but to me, they're a lost cause. I can't see what anyone can do for them, except the people themselves. If they want to live in their rundown shacks that are overridden with flies, and who knows what else, and that stink of filth and soiled clothing and mattresses, and if they want to drink their lives away while their children go hungry and unclothed, then there's not much that can be done for them except to give them handouts and more handouts. So don't ask me..."

"How the hell would you know how they live? You wouldn't go near them if your life depended on it! Who are you to sit around up here in your fancy surroundings and judge a people you don't even know?" Cheryl cut in, now openly angry.

"I know because I looked for our parents in those kinds of places. So, don't tell me that I don't know what I'm talking about. I went..." I'd been shouting, and I stopped abruptly as I realized I had just revealed the search I had meant to keep secret.

Cheryl and I looked at each other for a few silent seconds, and our tempers were forgotten. Then she asked in a quiet, accusing voice. "You went to look for Mom and Dad? How come you never told me, April?"

I sighed and wondered which way to go. "There was nothing to tell. I never found them. I came to a dead end. And, later, when I thought it over, I figured it was probably just as well. Finding them would most likely have opened old wounds for them and for us."

"What do you mean? It wasn't their fault. The Children's Aid had to take us because they were sick. You told me that. You told me Dad had tuberculosis, and Mom just had poor health all the time. Anyway, you should have told me. How did you know where to start? I thought of looking for them. That's one reason why I spend so much time down at the Friendship Centre, to listen for names."

"Cheryl, I still think it's best to leave it alone. Just pretend that we never had parents. Leave all that behind us." I thought that now was the time I should tell Cheryl what I already knew about our parents: that they were liars, weaklings, and drunkards; that all the time we were growing up, there was a more important reason for them to live, and that was their booze. But no, I couldn't do that to Cheryl. I couldn't tell her that alcohol was more important to our parents than their own daughters. I had given her cherished memories of them. I couldn't take them away now. They were too important for her. Those memories and her too-idealistic outlook for the future of Native people helped her and gave her something to live for.

I added, "Pretend that we're orphans."

"No! They're our parents, April! And we're not orphans!" Cheryl eyes blazed. "I want to see them again. Please, April?

I have a right to make that decision for myself. You have to tell me where to begin. How do I find them? You've got to tell me, April."

I silently argued with myself. The information I had was dated. Even the notations I had added were now dated. The chances of Cheryl finding our parents were so slim that I was sure she wouldn't find them. And because I felt that way, I relented.

"Okay, I guess you're right. Mr. Wendell is the one who gave me the old addresses and names. I guess they were places where our parents used to stay. A lot of the places have been torn down, and I've marked that down so you won't have to go there. But Cheryl, when I went to those places and saw the living conditions, well, I would hold my breath so I wouldn't smell the stink or breathe in the germs. I'd try not to touch anything, everything was so dirty. And if they offered me anything to eat or drink, I'd refuse, because I was sure their cupboards were infested with bugs. I'd back away from people so I wouldn't get their lice. I didn't feel sorry for them, Cheryl. All I felt was contempt. They were disgusting people. And maybe, just maybe, our parents are part of that. And if that's where we came from, I sure don't want to go back. That's why I'm happy with my life here. Happiness to those people was a bottle of beer in their hands. I vowed to myself then that no way was I ever going to end up like them or live in places like theirs. So, Cheryl, if you want to criticize me for my lifestyle, then go ahead, because if I can help it, I'm not ever going to change it."

"Oh, April, I didn't know why you felt the way you did. I didn't mean to criticize you. I just wanted to rouse you out of your passive state. I just wanted you to be aware of who we are, what we are, and what's been happening to us."

"If you're referring to all the negative aspects of Native life, I think it's because they allow it to happen to them. Life is what you make it. We made our lives good. It wasn't always easy, but we did make it. And they are responsible for their lives."

"I don't agree with you. We had a lot of luck in our lives. We've had opportunities that other Native people never had. Just knowing what being independent is like is an opportunity. But that's not the point right now. I still want to look for our parents. Okay?"

"I doubt that you'll find them after all this time, but okay." I sighed and went over to one of my dressers. As I looked through the dresser drawers, I said, "They usually move from town to town from what I understand. I really think it's going to be a waste of your time."

"Well, I've got to give it a try. Need some help looking? What do you need all these clothes for? I bet you don't wear half of them."

"Criticizing again, are we? Here it is. My shoebox. Now this is classy, isn't it?" I held up the old shoebox where I had hidden away my past.

Cheryl looked through the papers and asked, "How come you kept all this stuff if you weren't planning to ever look for them again?"

"I don't know. Some deep, profound motive, I guess. Maybe my last link with our parents. Who knows?"

We copied the names and addresses down, and Cheryl said confidently, "When I find them, I'll let you know. Wouldn't it be great to have a family reunion?"

I smiled. Realistically? Nothing could be worse.

This time, when Cheryl and I parted at the airport, I knew it was more realistic to acknowledge there would never be a complete honesty between us. And, then again, as long as my mouth kept running over, I just might spill out everything I had tried to protect her from. Cheryl, on the other hand, had nothing to hide. For one thing, she never worried about what people thought of her. What she thought about them was all that mattered to her. She was like a stalk in a field of grain that never bent to the mighty winds of authority. At the same time, that stalk could bend to the gentle breezes of compassion. That was Cheryl.

10

I WATCHED HER PLANE TAXI DOWN THE RUNWAY and gather speed, until its wheels no longer touched the ground. I watched until I could see it no more. Suddenly, I felt so empty. So alone. Funny I should have felt that way when Bob was right there beside me. On the drive back home, he was as preoccupied with his thoughts as I was with mine, so we didn't say much.

Sunday dinner that evening was eaten in silence, and not even Bob and his mother made any conversation. The atmosphere reinforced my feelings of loneliness. As usual, Bob and his mother retired to his office to plan the coming week's business strategy. I went upstairs to our room. I was restless and didn't know why. I turned the television set on, but there were no programs that interested me. I left it on just for the sound of voices. I looked at a book, then another. That was no good, either. It wasn't the first time I had felt this way, but it was the worst – this bored restlessness that usually came after big parties or large gatherings. And now Cheryl was gone. She was the one person with whom I felt completely relaxed and comfortable. Maybe if I had something of my own to do, something that involved...what? Useless, that's what I was. Bob had his business. Cheryl had her great cause. I had nothing.

I had everything I ever wanted, yet I had nothing. Bob's mother and I were involved in many charitable organizations, but none of them grabbed my heart or loyalty. Bob and I had our group of friends, but I felt I had access to them only as long as Bob was with me. Of course, I did find our own age group much more interesting than the older ladies with whom Mother Radcliff surrounded herself.

Cheryl and I wrote monthly letters to each other, but the chasm between us had widened, and there was less to say in our letters. I found that I was writing about Heather Langdon, who had joined our crowd. I told Cheryl that I wanted to be more like Heather, because she so enjoyed living. Then I scratched that part out and rewrote that Heather was a lot like Cheryl in that she lived by her own approval, not that of others. Just like Cheryl.

I guess Cheryl was having the same problem, because in her letters, she dwelled on her ongoing search for our parents. Where I had spent a month of weekends and quit, she wouldn't. I worried. Then in May, her letter said that she had finally given up. I was relieved. I didn't know what she would have done if she had found our parents. I hadn't even wanted to think about that possibility. Now that she had ended her search, I no longer worried about how shocked and disillusioned she would have been. My conclusion about alcoholism was that once an alcoholic, always an alcoholic. And if one's own children weren't enough reason for one to recover, then there could be no reason at all.

Her letters began to arrive less and less frequently. When she did write, it was about her education and her work at the

Friendship Centre. I found myself again in the position of envying her. She had a reason for being. She was her own person. I merely existed: comfortable and surrounded by socially prominent people. But I felt that I really didn't belong. That feeling grew worse as the months went by. I didn't belong, because I didn't care – not the way the others did. I was quite content to let Mother Radcliff and Bob run my social life. I performed all my duties as expected.

That September, I picked out a very expensive IBM Selectric typewriter for Cheryl's birthday. That was something she could appreciate. I even thought it might be nice to go back to Winnipeg to spend some time with Cheryl. I tried phoning but found that the service had been disconnected. I wrote Cheryl immediately, offering financial aid if she needed it. She wrote back to say that she was hardly ever home and didn't need a phone. As if to emphasize her point, she also told me that she had been invited to Brandon over the Christmas holidays. I felt as if she were abandoning me, because I read between the lines that she didn't want me in Winnipeg.

Christmas passed. New Year's 1971 came, and all the festivities were meaningless to me. I continued to feel blue. Actually, I don't know why they say blue when it's more like grey. The year of 1971 was to be a year of many changes for me. My feelings of inadequacy and boredom turned to resentment and jealousy. I came to hate how Heather and Bob could laugh together so easily as if they were sharing private jokes. Suspicions set in, and I began nagging Bob in private. Meaningful conversation between us had all but disappeared, not that we had all that much to begin with. I guess all he could see was my totally negative side, and he couldn't see any reason for it. I couldn't have explained it to him at the time anyhow, since I didn't quite know what was going on inside of me. Mother Radcliff even showed an open disgust for me, because on different occasions, I had rebelled and refused to perform my social duties. But that was okay, because I was just as disgusted with her and her snobbish friends and her card games and her charitable works, done only so she would be identified as a philanthropist. All these people lived for one or two things: money and power. They were hypocrites, all of them. Charming to each other when they were face to face, but get them into separate rooms and their tongues could cut like knives. They were such superficial people.

I became quite adept at this, seeing all the negative sides of everybody and criticizing them to high heaven to myself. It occurred to me that I had thoroughly criticized the Native people, and here I was now doing the same thing to white people. Maybe that's what being a half-breed was all about, being a critic-at-large.

I suppose things could have continued like that for a long time, but in August, I overheard a conversation between Mother Radcliff and Heather that roused me out of my passive state and got me fighting mad. A few days earlier, Bob and I had had a big fight. To make up for it, Bob had decided to take time off work and take me out for the day. We had planned to start out right after breakfast. I was amused at Mother Radcliff's obvious chagrin. But then Bob and I had another difference of opinion in our bedroom that morning, and he left in his car without me. I was so embarrassed that I stayed in my room, planning to wait until Bob returned. Our bedroom, on the second floor, had a covered balcony that overlooked a private garden. I had moved to the balcony when the maid had come to clean our room.

It was about noon when I heard a car drive up. I checked to see who it was and saw Heather walking up to the front door. I wondered why she was here. I knew she and Mother Radcliff didn't have that close a friendship that they would lunch together. I went back to the lounge to continue reading, curious about what was going on downstairs. I didn't have long to wait. They came out into the garden below, where we sometimes had our lunches. Their voices drifted up to me, and I could clearly hear everything they were saying.

"I would like to get straight to the point. Is this affair with Bob serious, or are you just toying around with him?" The voice was Mother Radcliff's.

An affair? With Bob? Serious? I couldn't believe I was hearing right. Not Heather. She was my friend. Bob was my husband.

"Of course it's serious. And there's nothing you can do about it this time. You knew how we felt about each other when you broke us up before. And don't deny it. I'm not as naive as I used to be. No, it won't be long before Bob asks April for a divorce." Heather sounded smug.

"As I told you on the phone, I have no intentions of breaking anything up. As a matter of fact, I fully approve. But it doesn't appear that a divorce will take place all that soon when he starts taking time off work to spend with her," Mother Radcliff responded.

I heard Heather scoff and say, "Well, he's taken a lot more time off for me, I'm sure. But I can't help wondering why, now that he's married, you approve of Bob and me? I know you purposely went out of your way to have me at that New Year's party. What do you have against April, anyway? Why don't you want her for a daughter-in-law? I just want to know, so I don't make the same mistake she's obviously made."

"Didn't you notice her sister? They're Indians, Heather. Well, not Indians but half-breeds, which is almost the same. And they're not half-sisters. They have the same father and the same mother. That's the trouble with mixed races. You never know how they're going to turn out. And I would simply dread being grandmother to a bunch of snivelling little half-breeds! The only reason I can think that Bob married her after knowing what she was, was simply to get back at me. This has been on my mind since the first time I saw her sister. I had hoped that a natural course would have followed and that Bob would see reason. I certainly don't know what he sees in her to have remained married to her all this time." Mother Radcliff sighed as if she had suffered so much. Then, she continued. "Well, I had my doubts as to how serious he was with you because of days like today."

Heather shrugged it off. "So, you knew all about it. Well, don't worry. Bob's a husband with a guilty conscience. He'll realize that April's not in our league, and the best thing for her is a divorce. I'll make sure."

"Yes, I suppose you're right. Of course, we'll give her a nice large settlement."

'You are so bloody right,' I almost shouted. Perhaps they said more about me. I don't know. With my face burning and my heart pounding like a war drum, I headed downstairs to confront them. They were both surprised and off balance when I stepped out on the terrace to face them.

I had always treated Heather with a certain amount of awe and respect, even after my suspicions had set in, because

I had hoped it was all my imagination. And I had also given Mother Radcliff her due respect. But in that moment, I eyed them contemptuously, and they realized I had overheard them.

"What are you doing here?" Mother Radcliff asked.

I was still breathing hard. Ignoring her question, I said, "You two make me sick!"

I looked at Heather. "You, you pretended friendship all this time. I trusted you! Oh sure, I suspected. I'm not blind. But I thought it was my imagination. I hoped it was my imagination. That Bob's mother would rather have a person like you, a hypocrite, an adultress, as her daughter-in-law, rather than risk a few grandchildren who would have Indian blood in them, well, that's beyond my comprehension."

"Now, there's no need..." Mother Radcliff started to cut in. I turned on her and cut her off. "And you! You make everyone who comes within your reach into puppets. But thank you very much for cutting my strings. And thank God I didn't become pregnant by your son. I wouldn't want the seed of your blood passed onto my children!" With that, I turned my back on them, leaving them sitting there open-mouthed.

A little later, when I was up in my room, I heard Heather's car start up, and she drove away. My heavy breathing returned to normal. My trembling rage subsided. I had to figure out what to do. Only one thing was certain. They were going to give me a large settlement. A very large settlement.

Well, I had seen through them, yet didn't even know it. All my criticisms were justified. My big fight with Bob had been about Heather. Turned out he was a liar, too. Just like my parents had been. Married me only to get back at his mother. Heather, deceiving me with friendship, while all the time she only wanted Bob. Mother Radcliff, making me call her Mother when she so detested what I was. And then there was Cheryl. She had told me how it would be, but I hadn't believed her. And although I had the same thoughts as Barbara Radcliff about children, it was unforgivable for her to tell them to Heather. I did have a fear of producing brown-skinned babies. How could I give my love to such children when I still felt self-conscious about Cheryl? Well, this wasn't the real issue. I had to plan a course of action. First thing I'd have to do would be to see a lawyer.

I called Ronald Feldman, whom I heard from past conversations was a good divorce lawyer. I phoned him, and he said he couldn't see me for two weeks but he suggested that if I were serious about filing for divorce on the grounds of adultery that I should cease living with Bob. I thought that meant I had to move out immediately.

Next, I phoned Bob at work. I wasn't surprised to find him there, nor that he was cold and distant with me. I demanded that he come home at once as an urgent matter had come up. While I waited for him, I looked through the newspapers and phoned to inquire about different apartments for rent. The thought of living in a huge, empty place was depressing. I didn't know anyone who would go out of their way to come and visit me. I also needed a job to keep me occupied. Still, I knew from past experience that evenings could be long and lonely. Maybe I would get so lonely I'd join the ranks of women who frequented singles bars.

I spotted a column under the heading of Shared Accommodation. That would be better than living alone. I phoned and was able to make some appointments for the following day. For now, I could stay in a hotel. I looked forward to a new life where I wouldn't be controlled by anyone else.

I felt as if the sun were coming out from behind the clouds, and it was a wonderful relief to know that there was still a sun. Aloud, I said, "Oh, I know you didn't mean to, Mother Radcliff, but you've made me a happy woman."

When Bob finally came home, I must have sparkled with excitement, because he said, "I thought something was wrong, the way you sounded on the phone. But you look like the cat that swallowed a mouse."

"Well, Bob, I understand you're about to ask me for a divorce. I'll save you the trouble of having to ask."

"Oh, not that crap about Heather again. Is that what this is all about?" he turned from puzzled to angry, instantly.

"Well, sweetheart, if you like, I could call a meeting of all those involved: 'We are gathered here today to establish whether there is or there is not an affair going on between my loving husband, Bob, and my good friend, Heather.' I was planning to be very bitter about all this, but I've changed my mind. I'm going to be sarcastic, instead." I smiled as I watched Bob sit down, his anger now dissipated.

The look on his face acknowledged the affair. "How did you find out? Did Heather tell you?"

"In a manner of speaking, yes. And your mother told me. And in a lot of different ways, you told me, too," I said. "I would appreciate it if you took me to a hotel for now. I'll look for a place to stay, and then I'll send for my things."

"Are you sure you want to do this? We could talk..."

"We can't talk. We never could, and we're not going to start now. Are you going to drive me to a hotel, or do I have to get a taxi?" I asked coldly.

"Don't you even want to make any explanations to Mother before you leave?"

"I'm sure your mother knows I'm leaving. I've packed a few things, and I'd like to go. Now."

In less than a week, I had found a place to my liking. It wasn't far from the subway on Woodbine Avenue, so I had easy access to the downtown area, where I planned to find a job. The rooms were in a large three-storey house, and the kitchen and dining room were shared by all the tenants, as were the laundry facilities. Most of the men and women who lived there were artistic, intelligent, and sociable. They created a homey atmosphere with their friendliness and willingness to be helpful to each other.

Once I was settled in, I turned my thoughts to getting myself a job. Money wasn't a problem, because Bob had given me more than I'd ever need, and that was just for one month. One of the other boarders, Sheila, suggested I do temporary work like she did. I signed up with her agency and was sent to different locations, filling in for absent secretaries.

Mr. Feldman, my lawyer, told me in December that the court hearing was to be held on January 26th. He assured me that everything was going extremely well. We were both pleased with the settlement Bob had offered. I remembered when I was starting Red River Community College, and I had eight hundred dollars in the bank. I had thought then that I was rich. And independent.

That same day, when the mail came, I found that the letter I had sent to Cheryl in November had been returned. On it was marked ·"Moved. No forwarding address." That was strange. Why hadn't she written to me to let me know? Or she could have called. I had given her my new phone number and address and had told her about my situation. She should have written or called. After all her thinly disguised refusals and excuses why she couldn't come or why I couldn't visit her, I began to feel like my own sister was giving me the cold shoulder. Did she think I was such a failure? On the other hand, I had always said she ought to go her own way, and I'd go mine. Maybe that's what was wrong.

Since Cheryl didn't write to me about any Christmas plans, I spent it with the other boarders who also lacked families to go home to. On Christmas Day, we all went to an old folks' home where Sheila's grandmother was living. That's when I got my first understanding of how Cheryl must have felt when she made somebody's day a little brighter.

One Saturday morning in early January, I received a phone call at eight o'clock. Thinking it was probably the agency looking for last minute secretarial help, I was tempted to let it ring. But I wasn't one who could ignore a ringing telephone. In a second, I was wide awake. It was a nurse calling from the Health Sciences Centre in Winnipeg, asking if I was related to a Cheryl Raintree. Then she said that Cheryl had been brought in during the night. I immediately asked how serious it was, and the nurse said she was still unconscious, so they couldn't be positive. Serious or not, I felt I had to at least be by her side. That afternoon I was on a flight back to Winnipeg.

II

A S SOON AS I ARRIVED AT THE WINNIPEG AIRPORT, I rented a car and drove straight to the hospital on William Avenue. There, a doctor informed me that Cheryl had been found in the early hours of the morning suffering from hypothermia and a possible concussion. They were holding her for observation. I thought immediately that she must have been assaulted, and I became resentful when the doctor asked me if Cheryl had a drinking problem.

"Why? Because she's part Indian?"

"No, Miss, but when she came in she was highly intoxicated. We thought she might have passed out in the cold."

"What about the concussion you mentioned?" I demanded.

"It does appear she may have been beaten," he admitted. Satisfied, I nodded and stalked off towards Cheryl's room.

Drinking problem! I was sure it was implied because she was part Indian. I entered the room, and Cheryl was at the far end. At first, I wasn't sure it was Cheryl. I mean, I knew it was Cheryl, but it didn't look like Cheryl. Her beautiful, strong face was now puffy and bruised, and her cheeks were hollow. She had lost so much weight. Under the fluorescent lights, her skin was yellowish. Her arms, resting on the white covers, were thin. She really had lost too much weight. And aged! I stared. It had been around two years since I had last seen her. Two years. It hadn't seemed that long. It looked to me as if Cheryl had been possessed. A cold chill ran down my back as I recalled the doctor's words, "...highly intoxicated." Oh, God, please don't let her be an alcoholic.

I pulled a chair closer to her bed and sat down. Maybe Cheryl had some kind of disease, and she hadn't wanted me to find out about it, and that was why she had refused to come to Toronto and had put off my coming to Winnipeg. People did that. They would find out they had a terminal illness, and they didn't want to tell anyone until the very end. Knowing Cheryl, that's the kind of thing she would do. She'd try to protect me from that kind of truth. Cheryl stirred and woke up briefly.

"Cheryl, it's me, April. Everything is all right. I love you, Cheryl."

She gave my hand a squeeze and dozed off again. I left when visiting hours were over and took a room in a hotel on Notre Dame, within easy walking distance of the hospital.

I returned the next day and found Cheryl fully awake. She didn't seem to want to talk about what had happened, so I didn't push her for answers. I sat there for the longest time, in silence. My mind was on what happened to her, and everything else that could have been said was blanked out. It was Cheryl who started talking.

"I'm sorry your marriage didn't work out, April."

"Well, I've been thinking that maybe it's for the best. Bob and I were never passionately in love or anything. And now I've gotten...well, used to the idea." I was almost going to tell her I would be getting a very generous settlement, but for some unknown reason I decided not to.

"Did you get a full-time job yet?" Cheryl asked.

"No, I decided to work for a temp agency. I'm not at all sure what I want to do once the divorce goes through. I'm changing my name back to Raintree. I was thinking of returning to Winnipeg for good, though."

Actually, the thought had just come to me. It looked like Cheryl could use any support I could give her by staying. If I missed Toronto, I could always go back once Cheryl got a job as a social worker. In June, she'd be finished university. It wouldn't be that long.

"Well, you're almost finished university, huh? And pretty soon, you're going to be a professional." I emphasized the word *professional* and smiled, but she didn't smile back.

"April, I quit university. I've got a lot more to tell you, but let's not get into it now, okay? I'm tired."

"Sure. Okay, we'll talk about it, maybe tomorrow, if you feel like it." I was shocked by what I had just learned, but I tried to cover it up. I left with a faked understanding smile on my face.

All the way back to the hotel, I thought about Cheryl quitting. Why had she quit? Had she failed or given up? All the letters she had sent me: they were all about her courses and her work at the Friendship Centre. Were they lies? No, she must have just quit recently.

When I got to my hotel room, I took a bath, then got into bed with the television set turned on. But all I could think about was Cheryl. I speculated on the different reasons why she may have quit and what other things she had or hadn't done, so that when she told me, I'd at least be partially prepared.

Maybe I could talk her into going back to university. As long as she didn't tell me she was dying of some incurable disease, then I could accept anything. I turned the television off and got back into bed. What if she were an alcoholic? How could I accept that? That was an incurable disease. And one was as good as dead if that was the case.

The next day, as Cheryl and I talked, we both avoided the issue. Towards evening, I figured it might help if we discussed my marriage failure first.

Afterward, Cheryl said to me, "Well, April, at least, you've experienced what you always longed for, and now you know that it's not for you."

"I know. I could almost treat the marriage as if it were one long holiday, especially since I didn't get all broken up about it. It's funny that I don't feel more pain. I really thought I loved Bob when I married him."

"Well, everything happened so fast, you never really had time to find out for sure. And maybe you convinced yourself that you loved him."

After she said this, Cheryl became thoughtful, and I wondered if she had been similarly involved with a man.

"Cheryl, have you ever been in love?"

She looked at me and smiled. She didn't say anything for a few minutes, and then she sighed and said, "I lived with a man. I thought, too, in the beginning that I loved him. I know that I wanted him. Before I actually met him, there was this great physical attraction between us. So, we moved in together. His name's Mark DeSoto. I was living with him right up until I landed here. He doesn't even know where I am."

"Do you want him to know where you are? Do you want me to tell him?" I asked.

"Oh, no. I should have left him a long time ago, but I didn't. I should have." She seemed to be talking more to herself. "Are you serious about staying in Winnipeg? You're not going to stay here just on my account, are you?"

"Well, I haven't any close ties in Toronto. And this is my hometown. If you wanted to come to Toronto, then I would go back. But no, I'm not staying here on your account. I would like to be with you for a while, though. Does that make sense?" I didn't know how to say I was staying because of her without telling her that.

Cheryl laughed and said she got the general idea. Since she was in a better mood, I figured it would be as good a time as any to bring up the past. "About those things you didn't want to discuss last night, you feel like talking about them now?"

"I was...I wanted to tell you that I've been living with a man who wasn't good for me."

"Oh."

"Well, what did you think I was going to tell you? That I was dying or something?"

"As a matter of fact, yes."

Cheryl started to laugh, and I sat there watching her closely, trying to determine whether she was being honest with me. When she realized I wasn't going to join in the laughing, she asked, "What's wrong?"

"It's the letters you've been sending me for the past two years. When did things begin to change? Why didn't you tell me the truth?" I tried to be tactful.

"Oh, the letters. Sorry about them. I just didn't want you to worry about me. You seemed happy enough out there."

"But why did you quit university? How come?"

"It wasn't going very well," Cheryl shrugged. "And the stuff I was doing at the Friendship Centre...well, I believed I was accomplishing something at first, but then a lot of girls we were trying to help just kept getting in trouble. In different ways it all boiled down to one thing: as a social worker I don't think I would have made the grade. So, I quit and got a job instead.

"That was two years ago. It's funny, you know. I was right about it not working out for you in Toronto, and you were right when you said that the Native people have to be willing to help themselves. It's like trying to swim against a strong current. It's impossible."

"I thought if anyone could do it, you could."

"You're disappointed that I've given up?"

"After all the griping I did against it, yeah. I suppose I am. There were so many days that I sat around the pool, listening to Mrs. Radcliff – Mother Radcliff is out now – and her friends discuss their charities, or we'd be at big, fancy dinners and I'd listen to all those people talk about what was important to them, and I was out of it completely. Like nothing was important to me. Except you, of course, but you had your life. And I used to envy you for having something so meaningful in your life. I mean, I couldn't do it, because I didn't believe it was possible – making a better way of life for Native people, giving them a better image. So what kind of job did you get?"

Cheryl made a face and said, "Oh, it doesn't matter, because I lost it. Mark and I used to party a lot, and I started drinking a bit. Anyway, the day I got fired, I had a big row with Mark, and then I went out and got all tanked up. So that's how I ended up here. I feel so stupid."

"Well, anyone who drinks goes overboard once in a while. I remember I got fuzzy once at a party, and then Bob's mother poured a pot of coffee into me and...I bet she thought I was getting to be an alcoholic. Just because she knew I had Indian blood. When I think of it now, a lot of things make sense in the way Mrs. Radcliff treated me."

Visiting hours ended then, so I had to say goodnight to Cheryl. On Tuesday morning, the doctor told Cheryl she would most likely be discharged on Wednesday. When she told me, I asked, "What are you planning to do when you get out?"

"You make it sound like I'm in jail or something. I don't know. I don't want to go back with Mark. I don't even want to go back there to get my things."

"Are you scared or something?"

"Oh, no, it's not that. He might want me to stay, and then there'd be a scene, maybe."

"I could go and get your things for you. Just tell me the address, and I could go tonight. Then you could come and stay at the hotel for now until you get a permanent place."

"Are you sure you wouldn't mind? It's in a rather rundown section of the city."

"If Mark is there, will he give me any problems?"

"No, just explain that I'm in the hospital, and you're going to look after me for a while. He looks tough, but he's okay. When he laid into me, he was drunk, and I pretty well asked for it. Besides, I'm sure he'll be out. Oh, April..." Cheryl's face had a guilty look on it.

"What?"

"You know all the things you left me? Well, I sold them. I'm sorry."

"That's okay, Cheryl. If you needed money, though, you should have asked me. I would have sent you some."

"No, I couldn't do that. You see, I was kind of supporting Mark. He's out of a job. Anyway, it would have just gone to him." Cheryl was looking down at her hands and nervously twisting her fingers together. "Two suitcases should do it. All I've got is clothing. Our room is right at the top of the stairs to the left. And there's two boxes under the bed with my papers and books in them. You can just take them."

That night, I had supper before looking for the address on Elgin Avenue. I had a lot to digest about Cheryl's past. I had thought mine was full of turmoil and dark secrets. By the time I got to the address, I was thinking of the future. With the money from Bob, I could buy a house in Winnipeg. Maybe we could even rent out some rooms, and that way, we'd have an income every month. On second thought, Cheryl would probably insist we take in only Native boarders. Besides, people make up creepy stories about two sisters renting out rooms. It wasn't very classy. Heck, with the money I had now, I could buy two houses and rent one out. No, then I'd be responsible for the taxes and repairs, and what if someone couldn't pay their rent? I'd end up letting people stay for free all the time.

I spotted a parking space not too far from the house. It was too bad I couldn't get a spot right in front of the house. I got out of the car, and a cold gust of wind struck me. I shivered. The temperature seemed to have fallen. I looked around. Cheryl hadn't been kidding when she said it was in a rundown section. It was dark and downright spooky. I got to the gate and wondered why on earth they would have a gate that closed when most of the fence was down, anyway. At the same time,

I was wondering if Mark would be home. And what was he like? I had to take my glove off to fiddle with the latch.

Suddenly, a male voice close to me said, "Can I help you with that, baby?"

I jumped. Where had he come from, so suddenly? I looked up at him, and he seemed to be leering at me. This couldn't be Mark. Maybe I should get back to the car.

Before I had a chance to move, an arm came from behind and grabbed me by the front of the neck. There were two men! I stepped back into the man as hard as I could, ramming my elbow into his side. He released his grip. The other man was now grinning.

"Oh, no, you're not going to get away from us."

He grabbed my arm, but I twisted loose and pushed against him. We were on a patch of ice, and he slipped, lost his balance and fell backward, all the while swearing. This all happened in a couple of seconds, and I was able to run back towards my car. I didn't know what their intentions were, but it was my intention not to find out. I opened the car door and was about to jump in when one of them reached for me and got hold of me. They were yelling to someone to bring the car up. Headlights were turned on, and I saw the two men clearly. I struggled desperately to free myself. The other man who had fallen reached our side, and when the car was beside us, he opened the door and shoved me in the back seat and got in beside me. The other one closed the door on the rented car and got in beside the driver.

Like a helpless animal, I was trapped and terrified. They meant to kill; I was sure of it. Otherwise, they would have disguised themselves or something. They whooped it up and congratulated each other on their catch. I figured if I was going to die, I was going to go down fighting. But then I thought I'd have a better chance if I watched for a police car. I watched for one at the same time as I kept an eye on the man beside me. They were crazy men, and now they were probably aroused from chasing me. Crazy men with crazy grins. The one beside me put his hand on me. I hit it away. He hit back much harder as if he had a right to do whatever he pleased.

"So, you're a real fighting squaw, huh? That's good 'cause I like my loving rough." He laughed at that.

The driver said, "Hey, we're only supposed to give her a scare. You're talking rape, man."

"Shut up, dummy. And slow down. We don't want to get stopped now. You're in this as much as us," growled the man beside me. So, he was the leader, I thought.

The other man in the front snickered and turned to eye me. I wondered how he knew I was part-Indian. Just because I had long black hair? I didn't pay too much attention to what the driver had said about just giving me a scare. I figured that this had started as a lark to scare women, and now the leader and his accomplice wanted to rape me. Maybe I could count on the driver to help somehow. And maybe they weren't out to do any killing. I just didn't know. I hadn't been in Winnipeg long enough to know whether there had been a rash of rapes and killings going on. Maybe that's what was going to happen to me. If they had knives it would be a whole lot worse. They could torture me to death, cut me to pieces, or beat me up and leave me to die in the cold somewhere, all bloody and broken.

Oh, God, I want to live. This isn't the way I want to die. This isn't my moment to die. I trembled with fear. More horrible thoughts rushed through my mind.

The night ahead could only be shameful, humiliating, and even if they didn't physically wound me, it would be torturous. I braced myself mentally and physically so I would be able to face up to anything they did. I knew I wouldn't be able to stop them from abusing me physically, so I'd try to be like a rag doll. But I'd close my emotions and mind off. Maybe it wouldn't affect me so much.

The leader was groping at me, and he grabbed me again, roughly. I gritted my teeth and sat rigidly, trying hard to ignore his hand, trying hard to be like a rag doll, trying hard to show no reaction. I smelled the liquor on his breath as he leaned toward me. Then his hand slid across me. I pushed his hand away and pressed against the side of the car. He was saying vulgar things to me, watching my face at the same time. I guess he wanted to reduce me to nothingness.

"Hey, you guys, we're going to have to teach her some manners. I'm trying to make her feel good, and she pulls away. The ungrateful squaw."

As they laughed, the leader grabbed a handful of my hair and pulled my head back. One minute he was laughing, the next he was saying in a low, frightening voice, "Listen, you little Indian, I know you want it, so quit pretending to fight it, okay? Or I'm really going to give it to you."

The man beside the driver was watching, and he asked, "Hey, man, could I have a turn with her?"

"Don't worry, you'll get your turn soon enough," the leader said ominously.

We were out in the countryside somewhere. I didn't know where, because I had lost all sense of direction. They had turned the interior lights on. The leader moved in on me, trying to take off my jacket. I pushed his hands away, and for a few minutes my anger overcame my fear.

"You filthy, rotten freaks!" I yelled. I threw myself at the leader, trying to scratch and bite him. "You keep your filthy, rotten hands off me!" I was panting from a mixture of anger and exertion.

I could hear them laughing like lunatics. The leader held me from him with ease, but I managed to scratch his face, drawing blood. This enraged him, and he swore. Then he followed his cursing with a hard punch to my midriff. That knocked the wind out of me and sent me flying back against the left side of the car again. My head hit the window. The leader then grabbed the front of my blouse and ripped it open, tearing the buttons off. Undaunted, I tore back into him, again.

"Why you little savage! You're asking for it." He gave me a backhand across the side of my head, which made my ears ring. He resumed trying to take my clothes off, and I tried my hardest to stop him. That's when he systematically started hammering into me. I could hear the driver making weak protests.

After his merciless onslaught, I was too weak to try to defend myself anymore.

"All right, you guys, mission accomplished. Hey, dummy, you gonna drive all night? Park this thing someplace. Maybe we'll let you join the party," he laughed, as he turned his attention back to me. "Yeah, you little savages like it rough, eh?" As he prepared to actually rape me, I shifted, trying to block him once more. Without saying a word, he slammed his fist into my ribs, which felt as if they'd already been broken.

Then he said very softly, "You do that again and I'm going to lay you wide open. You understand?"

Defeated, I lay there listlessly, my eyes half-closed because I didn't want to see his face, but at the same time, I didn't trust him enough to close my eyes completely.

Suddenly, I felt the pain of his thrust tear into my body and my eyes opened wide with terror. I struggled again to get away from him. Again, he grabbed my hair and yanked my head to the side. "You want me to lay you open?" He could see the terror in my eyes. I think that was what he enjoyed the most. "What's the matter, she giving you trouble?" the man in the front seat with the driver asked.

"Shut up! I can handle her."

He thrust into me again as if he were stabbing me with a deadly purpose. It was pure agony. Inside my head, I screamed long and loud, trying to block everything out.

"Hey, she likes this, boys. These squaws really dig this kind of action. They play hard to get, and all the time they love it. You love this, don't you, you little squaw?"

After what seemed an eternity, he withdrew, only to exchange places with the man beside the driver.

I don't think I could have fought anymore, even if my life had depended on it. Besides, I thought, the worst was over. But it wasn't. The rape by the second man inflicted a whole new pain but of the same intensity. My moans were muffled into the car seat. And all the while, he giggled wildly.

When he finally withdrew, he said to the driver, "It's your turn, dummy."

"Naw, I don't think so. I don't feel like it," the driver said, and I knew he was scared. The others knew it, too.

"You're going to, dummy, whether you like it or not. You're in this with us all the way. Now get back there, and do it," the leader ordered.

The driver came to the back. He pretended to, and then he told them he was finished.

"You sure?" the leader asked suspiciously.

"Yeah, I'm sure," the driver answered.

I lay there not daring to move, lest it drive them back into more activity. But now that they had finished, what would they do with me? Would they kill me or let me go?

To my great dismay, the leader exchanged places with the driver and came to the back again. I raked my mind desperately for thoughts on how to put a stop to all of this, but my mind was jumbled up. Then one idea came. I put it into action. I began to pretend to vomit. That had its desired effect.

The driver yelled, "She's going to puke all over the place. Get her out of here."

The leader and the driver both jumped out of the car, the leader to put on what clothing he had taken off and the driver to reach in the back and drag me out. Then he grabbed all my clothing and my purse and threw them out after me. I continued with the pretense of retching.

When the three of them had straightened their clothing, the third man who had been laughing through all this, yelled, "You dirty squaw!"

I heard the leader also begin laughing, as the car doors slammed. I didn't let up on my pretense. When the lights came on, I was able to make out the license number just before the car sped off.

12

I WAS FREE, AND I WAS ALIVE! As I put on my clothes, I kept looking in every direction, fearful they might return. I would run for safety into the fields, even in the deep snow in my bare feet if I had to. Tears ran down my face, but I didn't sob. I was finally dressed and started down the road in the opposite direction that they had taken, praying I wouldn't run into them again. As I walked, I repeated the license number. Out in the open with no obstruction to impede it, the wind shrieked with icy glee. But it didn't touch me. It must have been thirty below, but I didn't even feel the cold. I was numb and beyond feeling. I strained for any sounds of an approaching vehicle and often turned to look behind me. I had no idea where I was.

Finally, I saw a light in the distance. I felt fear and hope at the same time. When I neared the light, I saw that it was a farmyard light. Then I heard a dog barking. As I walked down the driveway, a large German shepherd came out to inspect me. It continued its thunderous barking all the way to the porch door. A porch light was turned on, and a man looked out cautiously. From the way he looked at me, I'm sure he at first thought I was some drunken squaw who had gotten into a fight and had been thrown out of a car. Begrudgingly, he asked me in only after I told him I had just been raped, and would he please call the police? His wife came into the kitchen where we were, and she offered me a cup of coffee. I asked if I could use their washroom and left while he called the police.

When I came out of the washroom, they asked me what had happened. The chill that hadn't touched me outside caught up with me in the warmth of their kitchen, and I began to tremble so violently that the woman went and got a blanket off their bed. Tears streamed down my face and my teeth were chattering, although I still didn't sob.

When the RCMP came, I expected that they would insinuate I had somehow provoked the rape. But the two officers were soft-spoken and kind. They wanted me to show them where the car had been parked, and on the drive there, I had the unreasonable fear that they, too, might turn on me. We soon came to the place where I had walked into the deeper snow to get my purse. When they finished examining the tire tracks and the area, they drove me to the hospital back in Winnipeg. I sat in the back seat, my teeth still clicking together from a coldness that just wouldn't leave me.

They took me to the Emergency at the Health Sciences Centre where Cheryl had been taken just a few days earlier. The doctor on duty examined me and took the swabs and samples that would be required for court purposes if they ever caught those rapists. Then I was sent for x-rays because of all the bruising.

The x-rays showed no fractures or broken bones, so the police took me to their headquarters to take my statement. They told me to recount everything exactly as I remembered it.

The whole thing took a long time, and it was taxing. While I quietly talked, tears rolled down my face. It seemed to me my voice droned on and on and on, but at last I was finished. They told me they would be talking to Cheryl in the morning to see if she had any ideas on possible motives, since I was initially picked up at her door. When they drove me back to the hotel, they informed me that they would later have me look at some pictures to see if I could make any identifications.

They also said they would have to take all my clothing for purposes of evidence. They waited outside in the hall while I changed into a nightgown and robe.

Once they had gone, I took a long bath. My whole body was aching. Although I stayed in the bath for a long, long time, I couldn't get rid of their smell. I tried to fathom why they would do such a thing, but I couldn't. It was beyond reason. Later on, in bed, every once in a while I'd give a shudder when the visions of the night became too clearly realistic. It was a long time before my tensions eased off. I stopped shivering, and I finally drifted off to sleep.

I was awakened by the sound of someone knocking on my door. It was Cheryl and two officers, although not the same ones as the night before. They had picked her up from the hospital and brought her to the hotel. Cheryl at first was going to throw her arms around me, but as she saw me brace for the pain, she stopped.

"Oh, April, I'm so sorry. It's all my fault you came here in the first place. I'm sorry."

"It's all right, Cheryl. I'm okay. Really."

I looked at the two officers. One of them said they would like me to go with them to look at a car. They said they'd wait for me in the lobby while I got ready.

After they left, Cheryl again said, "This is all my fault."

I was dead tired, and I snapped, "Oh, Cheryl, stop it. It's not your fault. It just happened." I felt awful for using such a tone of voice so I added in a lighter tone, "I need a hand getting dressed. I can barely move. You available?"

She nodded and helped me in silence.

Before I left, I asked her to wait for me, and we would go together to get her things and the rented car.

On our way to the Public Safety Building, one of the officers told me they had seized the car and arrested the owner. I would have to identify both the car and its owner. Some of my buttons had been found in the car, so my identification was merely routine. But a little while later, I identified the owner as one of the rapists from a lineup. He looked very scared, almost like a little boy. Even though he had taken part in the heinous crime against me, I couldn't help feeling sorry for him. All I really wanted to do was hate him. I remembered that he, Stephen Gurnan, had done nothing to try to stop what had happened. My feeling of sympathy disappeared.

When I returned to the hotel, Cheryl was waiting for me. "April, you look exhausted. Maybe you should try and get some sleep, and I'll go and get the car and that. Do you want something to eat?"

"Yes, I'm starved. And I need some coffee. Are you sure you want to go back alone?"

"Oh, sure. After this, I don't care if Mark does make a scene."

After we had eaten, and she made sure I was comfortable, Cheryl left. I got out of bed and ran some water into the tub. I got in and then ran the rest of the water as hot as I could stand it. I lathered myself with lots of soap. I had to get rid of that awful smell on me. I could smell it as if they were in the same room as me. Their dirty, stinking bodies. I could feel their hands all over me. I had to get rid of that feeling, too. I scrubbed wherever I wasn't sore or bruised, sometimes hitting a sore area that brought back new pain. But no matter how much I scrubbed and lathered, I still felt dirty and used. It was no use. I cried, my tears rolling down my cheeks into the water, because it was no use. I couldn't get myself clean. I would never be clean again, free from the nightmarish visions.

In bed, I realized just how much I had learned to hate. It wasn't a natural emotion for me. I had known deep resentments, but if I had been given choices, I would rather have been friends with people like the DeRosiers, Mother Radcliff, and Heather. But a real cold, deep hatred had crept into me, and I knew that I wouldn't want to let go of it, not for the rest of my life. I wanted two of those men, in particular, dead. By my hand. Yes, I wished with all my might that I could be the one to kill them and make their deaths prolonged and painful. And I knew exactly what I would do to them. Oh, how I wanted them dead! I had been touched by evil, and from now on it would always be a part of me. Wanting three men dead was evil in itself, but, nonetheless, I wanted them dead.

Finally, I fell asleep. When I woke up, I saw the suitcases and the keys to the car, but Cheryl wasn't there. She must have gone to get something to eat. I got dressed and went to the restaurant. She wasn't there, but I had something to eat anyway. It was almost eleven p.m. when I got back to my room. Cheryl still wasn't there. Maybe she had gone for a drink. I looked in the mirror and hoped that most of the bruises would disappear within the week.

Cheryl came back about fifteen minutes later. "You're awake. How long have you been up?"

"Almost an hour. How did it go?" I asked, purposely not asking where she had just been.

"Mark wasn't even there. He moved out, I guess. I was just down in the lounge. Are you hungry?"

"No. I just had something to eat down in the restaurant. I had a good sleep, and I feel much better. I bought a newspaper, and I was going to look through it, but I wanted to talk to you first."

"About what?" Cheryl asked, in a guarded tone, as if she had read my thoughts.

"Well, I'm supposed to get some money from Bob once the divorce goes through. We could buy ourselves a house. What do you think?"

"You mean you'll get enough money from Bob to buy a whole house?" she asked, incredulous.

"Well, beats buying a room at a time, doesn't it?"

Cheryl laughed, and I explained further, "I'm not exactly sure how much it's going to be, but I'm sure there'll be enough for a down payment." I retreated to half-truths. I didn't know yet exactly how much I would be receiving but I was sure I'd be able to afford two average-sized homes, maybe three. I really didn't know.

"Why not? Beats renting," Cheryl shrugged.

"Good. We can start looking tomorrow." I started looking through the ad section of the newspaper while Cheryl turned the television on.

"Do I get a say on where we'll live?" she asked, turning back to me.

"Of course. I don't have any strong preferences. I only know where I don't want to live." I was glad she was interested.

Two weeks later, I was en route to Toronto, a day before my divorce hearing. I went to my place on Woodbine and settled up with the landlord, telling him that after the twenty-seventh, I would no longer be needing the place.

On Wednesday morning, plastered with makeup to cover my bruises, I met with my lawyer Mr. Feldman, and we went to the courthouse together. Bob, Heather, and Barbara Radcliff were all waiting outside the courtroom, so I made a special effort to be busy talking to Mr. Feldman to justify my ignoring them. Inside the courtroom, everything went smoothly, although I was nervous when I was on the stand. I also experienced feelings of hurt and regret when an acquaintance testified about the extramarital relationship between Bob and Heather. But when it was over, I felt almost smug, since I was now financially independent, more than I had ever been before in my life.

I wasn't quite as smug as Heather, though. She had a possessive hold on Bob's arm as we left. Remembering the rage I had felt on that day of revelation, I was tempted to go up to them and say something terribly sarcastic, but since I couldn't think of anything, I left quietly with Mr. Feldman. He told me that his fee could come out of the settlement as we had agreed, and then I would receive the balance of the money through my bank within three weeks, at the latest. Later that evening, I was on a flight back to Winnipeg.

Cheryl had continued looking for a house while I was gone for the few days. When I got back, she had found a house she liked on Poplar Avenue. It was close to Henderson Highway, Watt Street, and the Red River. Come summer, we would be able to take walks and watch the boats. Ever since I had spent those long hours by the river when I was at the DeRosiers, I had found that water had a soothing effect. Sometimes, if I watched the water long enough, I got the feeling that it was I who was moving. I also loved to watch the birds circle overhead, diving now and then for morsels of food. I thought Cheryl's choice was a very good one, and I asked the saleslady what the earliest possession date would be. Unfortunately, she said it wouldn't be until the first of March. That meant another month of living in a hotel.

That same evening, Cheryl and I settled in our room to watch television. I happily thought that things were shaping up.

"I can't wait for March 1st, eh? We'll have to go shopping for furniture. Are you sure you want to take an upstairs bedroom?" I asked. "You could have the one on the main floor."

"For the fifth time, April, yes, I'm sure. That way, you'll be close to the kitchen, and when I come down in the morning, you'll have coffee and breakfast all ready for me. Right?"

"What? No morning paper beside your plate?" I asked.

"Oh yes, and the morning paper beside my plate," she answered.

I threw a pillow at her.

Then she looked at her watch and said, "Hey, April, you want to go down to the lounge with me and have a few drinks? To celebrate finding ourselves a new home?"

I had noticed that she had grown fidgety, and only then did I suspect why. An instant decision was required.

"Sure, sounds like a good idea."

Later that night when we were both in bed, I was unable to go to sleep. I had no idea on how to deal with Cheryl. It appeared she really needed those drinks. Maybe she was an alcoholic. And what would have happened if I had refused to go along with her? She'd been like a child asking me for a favour. Would she have reacted like a child and thrown a tantrum if I had not gone along? I thought that from now on, I would have to be careful with my words and reactions. That was the only way I knew how to deal with Cheryl.

I was also caught up in my own problem and spent hours thinking over the rape and its consequences. What would I and other "squaws" get out of my going to court? Maybe two years of safety from those particular rapists. Probably less, because hardly any criminal ever served a full sentence anymore. Rehabilitation, today, meant coddling the prisoners to the point of giving them every down-home comfort. Cheryl had told me of Native men who did something illegal so they would land in jail for the winter months. So what was the big deal about going to prison? I sighed at the hopelessness of so-called justice. Mostly because there was nothing for the victim. Nothing – especially for victims of sexual assaults – except humiliation in and out of the courtrooms. Nothing but more taxes to put more luxuries into the penal institutions. To keep a single prisoner for a year cost more than what a security guard earned in that year. I had read that somewhere, once. So, where was the justice of it? The only consolation I could derive was from killing them over and over again in my mind.

I had an appointment on February 8th to see Mr. Lord, who was handling the real-estate transaction for me. He was very happy to see me and, despite my fears that I would be embarrassed because of my divorce, everything went smoothly. When I came out of his office, it was almost noon. Roger Maddison came out of his office just then, and he seemed not at all surprised to see me. I was wondering if he remembered me, his old verbal fencing partner, when he said in a pleasant voice, "Hello, April, how are you?"

"Hello, Mr. Maddison. I'm fine, thank you. And what about you?" I half expected that he would say something sarcastic.

"Fine. Alex told me you were coming in today."

"Oh?"

"I was looking forward to seeing you again." He smiled, and then asked, "How about lunch?"

"Okay, I'd like that."

I did most of the talking over lunch. He listened and drew more out of me with appropriate questions. He asked me if I would go out with him sometime. This gentle, concerned side of Roger I hadn't seen before. I wondered why he had never gotten married. Then I wondered if he *had* gotten married.

"Have you ever been married?" I asked.

"No. I never found the lady I wanted to spend the rest of my life with." He was about to say more but I interrupted him.

"That's funny. When I first saw you, I thought almost the same thing, except in a positive way..." I stopped, suddenly embarrassed that I would tell him that. "Sometimes, not often, though, my mouth doesn't quit."

Roger was smiling.

"Well, I guess I'd better let you get back to the office. Thank you for the lunch." I told him where I could be reached.

Before I headed back to the hotel, I bought several books for Cheryl and me. There wasn't much that one could do in a hotel room. I picked up a book called *Bury My Heart at Wounded Knee* by Dee Brown. Cheryl would like that. Maybe it would keep her from going down to the lounge. Like, that morning, she said she was going over to visit Nancy. But Nancy was supposed to have a steady job, so why was Cheryl visiting her during the day? Maybe Nancy worked nights. Or maybe Cheryl was out drinking somewhere. No. Although Cheryl had a drink almost every day, she'd never been drunk or even appeared to be drinking. Maybe drinks to her were what coffee was to me. I couldn't get a day started without at least two cups of coffee.

On Thursday morning, Roger phoned to ask if Cheryl and I would like to have dinner at his place Friday evening. I told Cheryl about it, excited that he really had called. "I really didn't think he'd call me."

"Isn't this the same guy whose guts you used to hate when you worked at the law firm?"

"The same one. He's such a terrific person. Oh, you're not going to tell him about that tomorrow night, are you?"

"Don't worry. I'm not even going to be there tomorrow night," Cheryl said, winking at me.

"Oh, but you have to."

"Oh, but I don't. He really wants you there. I've got things to do. Besides, you don't need me to hold your hand." I tried to change her mind, but she wouldn't budge.

Friday evening started out with both Roger and I trying to make polite conversation. It wasn't like the lunch, where I only had a little time to say a lot. We had the whole evening ahead of us, and this was more formal. I guess he was as uncomfortable as I was. After the meal, over coffee, I asked him, "Roger, how come you were so nasty to me when I worked there?"

"I liked you," he smiled. That made me feel good. He added, "But I thought you were kind of snobbish, overly self-confident and..."

"All right, stop already. I get the idea. If you're going to give me a compliment, don't take it back. Anyway, that was no way to treat someone you liked."

"I had to cut you down to my humble size. Teach you some respect. Then, we could have fallen madly in love."

"There you go again. A replay of the past."

"Well, the important thing is that I liked you then, and I like you now." I just knew he was chuckling inside.

"As I accidently said before, I liked you, too. But I also detested you. I detested liking you. Of course, if I had known you liked me, then maybe things would have been different." I thought I was sounding nervous, so I stopped.

"Yeah, a few more years, and I could have taught you all the respect you needed to know. But then that man, Robert Radcliff, was it – came along and swept you off your supercilious feet."

"You can't use that adjective with feet. What kind of a lawyer, are you, anyway?"

"A humble one, one unacquainted with high and mighty words. So tell me, why didn't Cheryl come tonight? Have you been telling her tales about me?"

"No, she just figured we ought to be alone, I guess. It was a very good meal. Where did you learn to cook?" I asked.

"I've been a bachelor for a long time. You were telling me about your marriage. Care to tell me why the divorce," he added. "while you do the dishes?"

"I don't do dishes," I said in a haughty tone.

"There you go again, snobbish as ever, huh?" We both got up to do the dishes while I talked. I returned to being serious.

"Well, I divorced Bob on grounds of adultery. But that's not what bothered me the most. It was my mother-in-law, actually.

She didn't want to be grandmother to a 'bunch of snivelling little half-breeds,' as she put it." By now, my mood had turned completely serious.

"Why would she say a thing like that? You're not Indian, are you?"

"No. I'm...Métis." I had to force those words out.

"And from the way you said that, I gather you're not real proud of.it." Roger had a hint of an understanding smile on his face, but his eyes were serious.

"I'm not. It would be better to be full-blooded Indian or full-blooded Caucasian. But being a half-breed, well, there's just nothing there. You can admire Indian people for what they once were. They had a distinct heritage, or is it a culture? Anyway, you can see how much was taken from them. And white people, well, they've convinced each other they are the superior race, and you can see they are responsible for the progress we have today. Cheryl once said, 'The meek shall inherit the Earth.' Big deal, because who's going to want it once the whites are through with it?

"So, according to her, the progress is questionable. Even so, what was a luxury yesterday is a necessity today, and I enjoy all the necessities. But what have the Métis people got? Nothing. Being a half-breed, you feel only the shortcomings of both sides. You feel you're a part of the drunken Indians you see on Main Street. And if you inherit brown skin like Cheryl did, you identify with the Indian people more. In today's society, there isn't anything positive about them that I've seen. And when people say, offhandedly, 'Oh, you shouldn't be ashamed of being Métis,' well, generally they haven't a clue as to what it's like being a Native person. And those are the people who usually show discrimination.

"Oh, I'm sorry. I didn't mean it. I meant the words, I just didn't mean for them to come out all at once."

I was really embarrassed. I had held those words in for such a long time and now, I lay them on Roger, of all people.

"Well, believe it or not, I understand. And there will always be some form of discrimination, whether it is someone discriminating against an Indian on Main Street or your church telling you that you have to teach your children its beliefs because its the only right one. I've got a brother, an adopted brother, who's Ojibway. Joe thinks it's not important what others think of him. It's what he thinks of himself that counts."

"Well, Cheryl lives pretty much by that philosophy, and even so, she's come down with a drinking problem, I think. I'm not really sure. Anyway, only she has the right to tell me I ought to be proud of what I am, because she's worked so hard to do something about the Native image."

"Your sister sounds remarkable. If you think she's drinking, maybe she's just impatient to see the changes."

"I think my being back in Winnipeg will help a lot. It's funny; you're the last person I thought I'd be able to talk to about these things. Thanks for listening."

"I found it interesting. I find you interesting. I'm not going to tell you to be proud of what you are. Just don't be ashamed."

13

ON THE POSSESSION DATE, Cheryl and I moved into our very own home. By the second day of March, most of our furniture and appliances had been delivered. The following Saturday, we gave a housewarming party, but only Roger came. Cheryl had not invited Nancy or any of her other friends.

Next, Cheryl and I went looking for a car. It was wonderful to have money to be able to pay cash for a car. The salesman really catered to us, even offered us a two-car deal. But Cheryl absolutely refused my offer to buy her a car of her own. I really wanted a big, expensive luxury car but because of Cheryl, I bought a little Datsun, which I never did like very much, not after the Radcliff automobiles. Cheryl asked me again in that accusing manner, just how much money did I have. I countered by saying, enough to send her back to finish her university courses if she liked, adding that was about it. Of course, I had no idea how much that would have cost. But it was convincing and made Cheryl change the subject. She insisted she had no intention of becoming a social worker.

It was the middle of March, and I was half watching the evening news when a news story came on about an armed bank robbery or something. I'd been reading the newspaper at the same time, so I wasn't sure. If I hadn't glanced up at that moment, I wouldn't have seen the picture of one of the men who had raped me. Apparently, he had been shot to death by the police earlier that afternoon. It wasn't the leader, and it wasn't Stephen Gurnan. It was the one who had helped grab me and sat beside the driver. I paced back and forth in the living room, wondering if I should wait for the late news to come on again or call the police immediately. Since I was positive, I called the police right away.

I was told someone would be sent down to see me. While I waited, I thought things over. If only it had been the leader. Maybe the leader had been with him. Maybe they've got the leader. If they had arrested the other man, I would probably have to go to police headquarters to identify him. I was sure that those two would hang around together.

Then I hoped Cheryl wouldn't return while the police were here. I had never talked about the rape to her in detail, because she had initially blamed herself. So far, I hadn't even told her about Stephen Gurnan. For that matter, she had never told me what questions the police had asked her. I had wished those men dead, and now that one was dead, I was glad. But it should have been the other one.

Almost two hours passed before two officers showed up. They had brought some pictures for me to look at, and I picked out the dead rapist immediately. They asked if the other rapist was among any of the other pictures, but he wasn't. None even looked like the third man.

At the end of March, while Cheryl was out job-hunting in the afternoon, I got a call from the police asking if I could come down to the Public Safety Building immediately. They must have arrested the third man. After I got there, I had a wait of about forty-five minutes. Then, there in the lineup was the leader. He looked arrogant. He looked evil. It gave me great pleasure to be able to pick him out so easily, without any fear of being mistaken. At the same time, that cold chill came over me again. I began to tremble, just as I had that night. Not being able to control myself scared me. I really feared the possibility of losing my mind, going crazy. Rapists abused their victims spiritually, emotionally, physically, and mentally. Some victims' minds really did snap after brutal sexual assaults. So far, I'd been lucky. I was driven home in a police car, and I was grateful for that. The thought of being out alone, especially in the dark, was now terrifying for me.

Cheryl hadn't yet returned, so again I went through the ritual of trying to exorcise the evil within me by bathing. I poured half a bottle of perfumed oil into the hot water and then spent the next hour scrubbing vigorously. When the water got cold, I just added more hot water. All the while, I thought of the rapists, laughing crazily, pawing at me, coming down on me, putting their smell on me, putting their dirt on me. And no matter how hard I scrubbed, I couldn't get rid of the smell of their awful, slimy bodies, the awful memories. I wanted to scream aloud, that long silent scream I had kept in my head that night. I wanted them to feel my anguish. I wanted to gouge their eyes out. I wanted to whip the life out of them. Mutilate them. Kill them. Because bathing never worked.

I always got worked up like that whenever I took a bath, although it had never been with such intensity before. Back in the bedroom, I paced the floor back and forth, cursing Fate for having placed them on Elgin Street that night, cursing the judicial system because those two, if they went to jail, would get out again to rape again. When I had cooled down somewhat, I began wondering for the hundredth time why they had kept on calling me squaw. Was it obvious? That really puzzled me. Except for my long black hair, I really didn't think I could be mistaken for a Native person. Mistaken? There's that shame again. Okay, identified.

When Cheryl got home, we decided to order pizza and have it delivered. Cheryl had news that she was quite sure she was going to be hired at a downtown factory where she had put in an application that afternoon. She would have to phone back the following Monday. I asked her what she would be doing, because I couldn't see her working on an assembly line. She said she'd be doing a lot of different things but wouldn't specify. What a waste, I thought to myself.

That started me thinking of opening our own business, maybe a fashion boutique like the ones I used to visit on Yonge Street and in the Yorkville area of Toronto. From my shopping experiences with Mrs. Radcliff, I'd learned a lot and could have learned more had I paid more attention. Or, perhaps we could open an employment service agency. Having worked through them, I had an idea how they operated. There were other businesses that I could have invested my money in. But the main reason I didn't pursue those ideas any further was that Cheryl would insist on involving Native clientele.

For the time being, I decided to return to temporary secretarial work because I didn't want to be tied to a job until the whole rape ordeal was over, nor did I want to stay around the house brooding over it.

The snow had all gone, and I hoped that Cheryl and I would soon be able to take walks down to the river. I thought about buying a boat, but I wouldn't know how to handle the whole process of "going boating," so I dropped the idea. I would have to live on the memories of having gone sailing on Lake Ontario, with Bob and the others. Those were fun memories.

Roger, Cheryl, and I went out to celebrate my birthday. It wasn't often that we did anything together. Cheryl still hadn't brought a single friend over to our place. She went out a great deal. She would come home from work, have supper, change, and go out again. I spent more and more time with Roger.

In May, I was cleaning the house on a Friday because I didn't have a job for that day. It was when I was collecting the garbage from Cheryl's room that I came across an empty whiskey bottle in her garbage container. I was shocked to see it, the implication of it rushing into my head. Cheryl wouldn't do that – sneak drinks. So why the bottle? I had never seen her even slightly drunk. Of course, we hadn't seen much of each other over the past few months. I decided I was making too much of it. We were getting along all right, and I didn't want to change that. Cheryl never said anything to me, although she must have realized I would find the empty bottle when I cleaned.

A few weeks after this, I spotted a promotional piece in the newspaper about an Indian powwow coming up. I thought it would be good if Cheryl and I attended the festival, especially good for Cheryl. Perhaps it would renew her interest in Native issues.

That evening, as soon as Cheryl came home from work, I asked, "Hey, Cheryl, what's an Indian powwow?"

"Oh, it's mostly a dancing competition among different tribes who come from all over the place."

"Are they interesting?"

"Oh sure, I've been to several of them. I like going to them."

"Well, there's going to be one in Roseau on the July 1st weekend. I'd like to go to it and see what it's like. How about it? We could buy some camping stuff and make like we were teenagers again. Remember?"

"You really want to go?"

"Yeah, I really, really want to go."

"Okay, I'm glad you really, really want to go. You'll finally rub shoulders with real Indians." From the way she said that, I wasn't sure if she was happy or just being sarcastic.

I was anxious to go, and then I thought of Roger's brother, Joe. Funny that so many Indian boys were called Joe. Probably Catholic mothers naming their sons after Joseph, the foster father of Jesus. I wondered if Joe was married. Roger hadn't said. I thought maybe I should invite Roger to bring his brother and join us for the powwow. I'd have to ask him.

I never did ask him, though. I had supper at his place not long after, wondering how to broach the subject, but Roger had picked that night to decide it was time we showed our affection for each other. During the past weeks of seeing each other, I had subtly dissuaded him from giving me even a simple goodnight kiss. As far as I knew, Roger was most likely seeing other women, which was fine with me. Men, to my knowledge, did not tend to be celibate for long periods. And Roger and I were just good friends. But on this particular night, he kept getting uncomfortably close. At one point I went over to look out the window to avoid his touch, but he followed me. He made me turn to face him and was about to kiss me.

"Don't touch me," I heard myself say in a cold, icy voice that stopped him dead. He looked at me for a long time before he released me.

"I'm sorry. I wanted for us to be just friends, that's all. Just good friends," I said in a whispery voice.

"April, I can't figure you out. I thought we had more than just a friendship going for us." His voice was neutral and I couldn't tell whether he was angry or hurt. After that, he served me coffee, but our conversation was stifled. He saw me out to my car, but this time he didn't say he would call me. He just said goodnight.

I had an appointment on June 1st to see the Crown attorney, Mr. Scott. I had already received a subpoena from an RCMP officer for the Preliminary Hearing. Mr. Scott's office was in the basement of the Law Courts Building. The police had explained some of the general court procedures, but Mr. Scott went into further detail. For instance, as we went over my statement, he told me I was allowed to say things like "I smelled liquor on his breath," but not, "He was drunk." It had to do with hearsay evidence. One could testify to what was directly known. Anyway, it was complicated to me, and I worried about messing up my testimony. I also worried about the defense counsel misconstruing whatever I said.

On the day of the hearing, I went to Stonewall. I reread my statement. Mr. Scott reminded me of a few things, and before I knew it, we were at the community hall in Stonewall where the judicial process was to be carried out. Mr. Scott showed me to a small room where I was to wait for my turn to testify. By lunchtime, I still hadn't been called, and I was both bored and apprehensive.

After lunch, I went over my statement again, although I loathed going over the words that told the story of that night. I was finally called to give my testimony, and I started shaking as soon as I heard my name. My stomach had been tied up in knots all day, but it tightened up even more by the time I was in the witness stand.

Mr. Scott asked me to recount the events of January 11, 1972. I did, but minimized as much as I could. On occasion, he'd have me go into some details of the rape itself. I couldn't just say I had been raped; I had to describe the act itself. I tried at all times to look only at his eyes or his lips as they moved, pretending I was talking only to him and that no one else was there.

Of course, I could feel everyone's eyes boring into me. I knew darn well there were others in that room, listening to what I was saying. When that thought overwhelmed me, my voice would fade out, and the court stenographer would ask me to repeat myself. I wondered what those other people were thinking. It wasn't just simply a matter that a horrible degradation had happened to me. The thing was, I had been part of it. I'm sure that's what they all thought; that even if unwillingly. I had been part of that depraved sexual activity. I had known in advance that I would have to use explicit words when referring to private parts of the anatomy. And I had come across those words, as well as the slang words in the past. But to me, to say them out loud, in front of all those people, well, I faltered every time I had to say them. In the future, I would better understand why some women chose not to seek justice in the courtrooms.

Then I was questioned by the defense counsel, Mr. Schneider. He sounded skeptical, at times, even sarcastic. He made different insinuations, which made me feel defensive. By the time he was through with me, I felt like it was I who was on trial. He persisted in making me go into depth on some of the incidents, and I believed it was just to make me say those words I had stuttered on. I understood full well that it was his job to defend his client in any way he could, but I also felt what he did to me was morally wrong.

After I was allowed off the stand, a recess was called. I headed straight for the washroom. Once there, I threw up. One woman had been in there already. As she helped me, she expressed sympathy. I wished for the moment that I could stay in the washroom until everyone was gone. I fixed my makeup, braced myself, and returned to the courtroom, grateful that at least one person sympathized with me.

The court ruled that there was sufficient evidence to proceed with a trial. That's what the preliminary hearing was for. The court also ordered a ban on the publication of evidence, which meant I would still have my privacy. On our way back to Winnipeg, Mr. Scott was in good spirits because he had been successful. I was just relieved that this portion was over and done with. But there was still the trial ahead.

Cheryl and I left early Saturday morning for Roseau River. There was a parking area set aside for campers. As we made our way to the main area, we noticed license plates from Montana, the Dakotas, Minnesota, and even Arizona. Men, women, and children were in traditional tribal costumes. Somewhere in the background, drums could be heard, sounding the heartbeat of the people. Tepees had been set up, and

Indian women in buckskin dresses now tended to fires, making bannock for curious onlookers.

The main event, as Cheryl had said, was the dance competition. During the intervals, everyone was invited to participate in the dancing. Cheryl joined in, but I stayed on the sidelines. That night, we sat, Indian-style, around a bonfire, listening to the songs and tales of Indian singers. Cheryl told me that was probably how it had felt on those long-ago buffalo hunts. I was impressed by all the sights and sounds. I felt stirrings of pride, regret, and even an inner peace. For the first time in my life, I felt as if all of that was part of me, as if I was a part of it. It was curious to feel that way. I had gone expecting to feel embarrassment, maybe even contempt. I looked over at Cheryl. She, too, seemed finally relaxed.

She was deep in conversation with some people on the other side of her. I didn't attempt to join their conversation. I was happy enough just to see the old animation on Cheryl's face as she gestured and talked with her companions. Earlier that evening, an Indian family had set up their tent next to ours and had come over to offer help. At the end of the ceremonies, Cheryl and I returned to our tent.

"Well, did you enjoy yourself?" Cheryl asked.

"Yes, but, in this atmosphere, everything is staged. It's romanticized. On Monday we'll go home, and to what? I'll go back to see the drunken Indians on Main Street, and I'll feel the same shame. It's like having two worlds in my life that can't be mixed. And I've made my choice on how I want to live my everyday life."

After pausing to think this over, Cheryl said, "Yeah, but Indian blood runs through your veins, April. To deny that, you deny a basic part of yourself. You'll never be satisfied until you can accept that fact."

"How do you do it, Cheryl? How is it that you're so proud when there's so much against being a Native person?"

"For one thing, I don't see it that way. Maybe I have put too much faith in my dreams. But if alcohol didn't have such a destructive force on us, we'd be a fabulous people. And that's what I see. I see all the possibilities that we have. Nancy, for instance, you never did think much of her when I was attending university, did you? Well, she does drink and does other things that you would never dream of doing. But she also holds a steady job, and she's been at minimum wage for a long time. They use her, and she knows it. And she gets depressed about it. But with her education and the way things are, she knows she doesn't have many choices. She helps support her mother and her sister and a brother. The reason she left home in the first place was her father. He was an alcoholic who beat her mother up and raped Nancy. Okay, she doesn't have much. Maybe she never will have much, but what she's got she shares with her family. And she's not an exception."

"I didn't know that," I said. We sat for a time in silence before I spoke again.

"When we lived with our parents, I used to take you to the park. The white kids would call the Native kids all sorts of names. If they had let us, I would have played with the white kids. Never the Native kids. To me, the white kids were the winners all the way. I guess what I feel today started back then. It would take an awful lot for me to be able to change what I've felt for a lifetime. Shame doesn't dissolve overnight."

"I can understand that. I've been identifying with the Indian people ever since I was a kid. The Métis people share more of the same problems with the Indian people. But one of the things that Indian people had, which was theirs from the beginning, was spirituality. That's why it's easier to identify with them.

"I wrote this one piece in university, but they wouldn't publish it, because they said it was too controversial. I still know it by heart. Want to hear it?"

"Sure," I said. There was little in our conversation we hadn't discussed before, but sitting there in our tent, surrounded by proud Indians, everything seemed different.

White Man, to you my voice is like the unheard call in the wilderness. It is there, though you do not hear. But, this once, take the time to listen to what I have to say.

Your history is highlighted by your wars. Why is it all right for your nations to conquer each other in your attempts at dominion? When you sailed to our lands, you came with your advanced weapons. You claimed you were a progressive, civilized people. And today, White Man, you have the ultimate weapons. Warfare that could destroy all men, all creation. And you allow such power to be in the hands of those few who have such little value in true wisdom.

White Man, when you first came, most of our tribes began with peace and trust in dealing with you. We showed you how to survive in our homelands. We were willing to share with you our vast wealth. Instead of repaying us with gratitude, you, White Man, turned on us. You turned on us with your advanced weapons and your cunning trickery.

When we, the Indian people, realized your intentions, we rose to do battle, to defend our nations, our homes, our food, our lives. And for our efforts, we are labelled savages, and our battles are called massacres.

And when our primitive weapons could not match those that you had years and experience to perfect, we realized that peace could not be won, unless our mass destruction took place. And so we looked to treaties. And this time, we ran into your cunning trickery. And so, we lost our lands, our freedom, and we were confined to reservations. And we are held in contempt.

'As long as the Sun shall rise....' For you, White Man, these are words without meaning.

White Man, there is much in the deep, simple wisdom of our forefathers. We were here for centuries. We kept the land, the waters, the air, clean and pure, for our children and for our children's children.

Now that you are here, White Man, the rivers bleed with contamination. The winds moan with the heavy weight of pollution in the air. The land vomits up the poisons that have been fed into it. Our Mother Earth is no longer clean and healthy. She is dying.

White Man, in your greedy rush for money and power, you are destroying. Why must you have power over everything? Why can't you live in peace and harmony? Why can't you share the beauty and the wealth that Mother Earth has given us?

You do not stop at confining us to small pieces of rock and muskeg. Where are the animals of the wilderness to go, when there is no more wilderness?

Why are the birds of the skies falling to their extinction? Is there joy for you, when you bring down the mighty trees of our forests? No living thing seems sacred to you. In the name of progress, everything is cut down. And progress means only profits.

White Man, you say that we are a people without dignity. But when we are sick, weak, hungry, poor, when there is nothing for us, but death, what are we to do? We cannot accept a life that you have imposed on us.

You say that we are drunkards, that we live for drinking. But drinking is a way of dying. Dying without enjoying life. You have given us many diseases. It is true that you have found immunizations for many of these diseases. But this was done more for your own benefit. The worst disease, for which there is no immunity, is the disease of alcoholism. And you condemn us for being its easy victims. And those who do not condemn us, weep for us and pity us.

So we the Indian people, we are still dying. The land we lost is dying, too.

White Man, you have our land now.

Respect it. As we once did.

Take care of it. As we once did.

Love it. As we once did.

White Man, our wisdom is dying. As we are. But take heed: if Indian wisdom dies, you, White Man, will not be far behind.

So weep not for us.

Weep for yourselves.

And for your children.

And for their children.

Because you are taking everything today.

And tomorrow, there will be nothing left for them.

To me, Cheryl's message was emotional and powerful. When she finished, we sat in silence. The only sounds were those of the crickets. Somewhere in the distance, a child began to cry.

14

AFTER THAT LONG WEEKEND, I tried to keep the feeling I had alive, even though I was back in the city. I noticed Cheryl had gotten some good out of it, too, because she made more appearances around the house. She also seemed more relaxed, more willing to discuss events concerning Native people that appeared in the newspaper and on television. No matter what the issues were, she always found some way to defend the Native side of the question. Now when she began telling me that she was going to the Friendship Centre, I knew without doubt that she was indeed going there. The old fire had been rekindled. Cheryl began tearing clippings out of the paper, presumably to act on them, if possible. For Cheryl, I knew it was probable.

I returned to working as a temp, but the scenes I saw, on my way to and from work on Main Street gradually made that weekend's emotions disappear. I remembered my original evaluation of these people. Everyone always referred to them as "those Indians on Main Street," but there were Métis people there, as well. No, I felt no affection, sympathy, empathy, or anything else for those Native people. But for Cheryl, I faked an interest. So when she asked me to go to the Friendship Centre with her one evening, I agreed.

We decided to walk or, rather, Cheryl decided to walk. Walking was Cheryl's chief mode of transportation, even in winter. I suspected she was also snubbing my little car. However, it was a beautiful evening to be out, the kind where you could breathe deeply and smell the delicious night air. So, I enjoyed the long walk going there. Cheryl and I talked about the Steindalls longingly. We hadn't talked about our foster families very much, just in passing remarks. We admitted that we both felt too embarrassed to go back and see them, having been out of touch with them for so long. And perhaps our main desire would have been just to see and ride the horses. Cheryl and I decided we would go horseback riding a lot more often than we had been doing. It would be one way for me to get her into my car. Our car.

When we got to the Friendship Centre, we entered a large recreation room, filled with elderly Native people. Cheryl mixed among them immediately, with me tagging along behind her. While she conversed with them, I could only smile patronizing smiles and nod when it was expected. I knew that Cheryl saw their quiet beauty, their simple wisdom. All I could see were watery eyes; leathery, brown skin; aged, uneducated Natives who had probably not done much in their lives.

Cheryl explained that some of the people were in the city for medical reasons, or they were visiting relatives. When they returned north to their homes, they would resume fishing, trapping, and committing themselves to crafts.

"One thing you wouldn't like is the way they live in winter," Cheryl said to me. "Some of them have to walk miles and miles just for their water. They roll up newspapers inside their jackets for extra warmth. Cardboard and plastic replace broken windowpanes. Their furniture is wooden crates and blankets on the floor. Well, you've seen the pictures in some of the books I've given you."

"Sure, but I thought that was in the olden days. I thought they had new houses now."

"New houses, yeah, but cheaply made, no plumbing, no sewer system. Besides, those housing programs were thought up by Indian Affairs, which means only Treaty Indians get any of the supposed benefit out of them. Non-status Indians and Métis get welfare, and that's it."

I didn't know what to say. I felt it was good that they didn't have the federal government to rely on, that it would help them be independent, to a certain point. But I also knew what Cheryl said was true about non-status Indians and Métis having hard times finding employment.

Just then, an older woman came up to Cheryl. Thinking that she wanted a private word with Cheryl, I moved away and occupied myself by studying some Indian art hanging on the wall. Then Cheryl and the old woman approached me. The old woman suddenly reached towards me and put her hand on mine. I glanced down at her hand. It looked rusted and old. Her fingers were swollen at the joints, disfigured. The veins stood out, and it took everything I had not to withdraw my hand from hers.

Her hand felt so warm, so dry, so ancient. I'm sure my smile froze and then faded. I waited for her to take her hand away. I looked at her questioningly, but she didn't say anything. Her gaze held mine, for I saw in her eyes that deep simple wisdom of which Cheryl had spoken. And I no longer found her touch distasteful. Without speaking a word to me, the woman imparted her message with her eyes. She had seen something in me that was special, something that was deserving of her respect. I wondered what she could possibly have found in me that could have warranted her respect. I just stood there, humbled. At the same time, I had this overwhelming feeling that a mystical spiritual occurrence had just taken place.

Sheepishly, I told Cheryl how I had felt as we walked home. Cheryl smiled and said, "Well, you should be honoured. White Thunderbird Woman is an Elder. I told her that you were my sister but in blood only. I told her your vision was clouded but that when your vision cleared, you would be a good person for the Métis people."

"You do have a unique way of putting things." I said. "Comes from reading so many Indian books. Actually, most Indians today don't talk like that at all."

"It's a pity. It sounds so poetic."

When my vision cleared...Would it ever? And would it mean that someday I would come to accept those Main Street people?

I gave that incident a lot of thought over the following weeks. If I'd had such a grandmother when I was growing up, maybe I wouldn't have been so mixed up. My emotions were getting the better of me. Finally, I put it all down to the fact that it was a very emotional time of my life, with the divorce and the rape and all. Still, I continued to waver back and forth as to just how I felt about being a Métis. It was part of me. I was part-Indian. But, so what?

In September, Roger came over to my place on a Saturday morning. It had been two months since I had last seen him. I had missed him, of course, and I found it lonely without his company. But then I had Cheryl's company, and that made up for it, a little. I had consoled myself by thinking that with me, no deep relationship would ever be possible and therefore, it was better for Roger to stay away. When the doorbell sounded, I wondered who it could be, because Cheryl and I had virtually no one to call on us. Even though she had returned to her former self, Cheryl still had invited no one to our house. It was probably an Avon lady.

"Hello, April."

"Roger! What are you doing here? I thought you were the Avon lady." I was surprised and pleased to see him, and a smile came to my face instantly.

"Oh, I was in the neighbourhood, thought I'd drop by for a cup of coffee and see how you were," he smiled. "And no, I didn't bring my Avon products with me. Sorry."

"In the neighbourhood, huh?" I led him into the kitchen. When I had poured the coffee, we sat at the table, but didn't say anything.

Finally, he said, "Look before..."

At the same time, I said, "I missed you."

"Well, I missed you, too. I was hoping and waiting for you to call me. But then, knowing how obstinate you can be, I figured I'd better come here." Roger became more serious and continued, "Of course, if you don't want to see me, then I want you to tell me now, and I want you to tell me why. Is it because of your marriage? Did you get hurt by it? Is that why you've always held me at arm's length?"

"No. No, it has nothing to do with my marriage. I do like you, Roger. I just don't want you wasting your time with me, especially if you want more than just being friends. I can't give you more than that. And I can't tell you why. I won't tell you why." I sighed and put my cup down, emphasizing how hopeless the situation was.

Roger looked at me. I didn't look at him, but I knew he was looking at me. I could feel it. After a while he said, "Well, I'd rather for us to be friends than nothing at all. So we'll continue seeing each other, all right? And if you ever feel like telling me exactly what is bothering you, then don't hold back, okay?" He reached out and put his hand under my chin and made me look at him.

"Okay. But just don't count on it. And, it's not that I'm obstinate. I just can't tell you."

Roger smiled and sighed. "April, April, April. What am I going to do with you?"

Roger had some things to do, but we made plans to go out later that evening. When Cheryl came down later, I told her Roger had been there. Then I wondered if my going out with him again would have an adverse effect on her.

"You don't mind me going out with him, do you, Cheryl?" I asked, after much hesitation.

"Of course not. I think he's a heck of a lot better than Bob. I'm glad. You need a strong man to take care of you. You know what I mean? I'm the kind of woman who might feel smothered by a man after a while. But you, well, it's not that I think you're weak or anything. Just that I see you with a husband and kids and still doing what you have to."

I liked Cheryl telling me that. It wasn't quite the way things were between Roger and me, but if I hadn't been deranged by those rapists, that's probably how things would have been.

In the middle of September, a police officer came to my place to serve me with a subpoena to appear in court in the trial of *The Queen v. Donnelly* on October 10, 1972.

On October 3rd, I had to return to the basement office in the Law Courts Building to see Mr. Scott, the Crown attorney. He explained that Oliver Donnelly was going on trial only for the charges of unlawful confinement and rape. If a verdict of Not Guilty was reached, then he would proceed with the other charges of indecent assault, gross indecency, and assault causing bodily harm. If the verdict was Guilty, then the lesser charges would be stayed. When I left, I was well aware that the trial was less than a week away.

I told Cheryl about the trial, and she said she was going to attend. I told her I'd rather she didn't, but she insisted.

"Look, April, you've changed a lot, and I want to know why. You've never told me exactly what happened. You smile, you laugh, but I can see in your eyes there's no joy. I want to help you in any way I can."

"Cheryl, you blamed yourself in the first place, and it's not your fault. What happened to me was fate. But I know you; you're going to start blaming yourself, when you had absolutely nothing to do with it. Some terrible things did happen to me, and I don't want you to know about them. So please stay away, okay?"

"I won't make any promises," Cheryl said. "If I can take time off work, I still might come."

On Tuesday morning, I was at Mr. Scott's office by 9:00 a.m., in case I had to go over any last-minute details. Then I was secluded in a witness room while the jury selection took place. The professionals, like the doctors, had their turns to testify first, presumably so they could get back to their jobs. Lunch came and went. It was two thirty before I was called.

I could feel everybody's eyes on me as I walked to the witness stand. My insides were twisted into a knot. Nervously, I listened to the clerk ask me if I would swear to tell the truth, the whole truth, nothing but the truth, so help me God.

I said, "I do."

I was already trembling, and I hadn't said but those two words. While the Crown attorney shuffled through some papers on his table, I looked around, not moving my head. On my left were the jurors. On my right and higher up was the Honourable Mr. Justice Saul. There in front of me, enclosed in the prison dock, was Oliver Donnelly, intently staring up at me. I quickly averted my eyes.

Mr. Scott was quite different in his role before the jury. He was very sympathetic and seemed thoroughly offended by what he knew had happened to me. Again, I had to tell of the night of the rape. I answered in as much detail as I thought he wanted. I faltered at times, in a voice unlike my own. I turned red and looked at the floor. It was horrible to have to say in front of all those people what had actually happened to me. I had to fight to control my quivering voice. I had to pretend it wasn't as bad as all that. I was asked to describe the man who had raped me. I did so.

"Is that person whom you are describing present in the courtroom today?"

"Yes, he is."

"Could you point that person out?"

"He's over there," I said, pointing at Donnelly, as I had been previously instructed to do.

Mr. Scott said, "Let the record show that the accused, Oliver Donnelly, has been identified by April Raintree, the complainant."

When Mr. Scott finished with me, it was Mr. Schneider's turn. He was the defendant's lawyer. I expected him to be aggressive as he had been at the preliminary hearing, but he wasn't. He was taking a cool, calculated approach.

After going over my identification of Oliver Donnelly, he asked, "All right, you were in the car. What did you do while you were still in the city limits?"

"I sat in the corner of the back seat."

"Did you fight or plead with them to let you go?"

"No, I was..."

"So, you didn't do anything at all?"

"No."

"Now, would you say the defendant was intoxicated?"

"I don't know.""

"Didn't you state that you smelled liquor on his breath?"

"Yes, I did."

"You did what, Miss Raintree?"

"I did smell liquor on his breath."

"You stated that you were going to your sister's place to pick up her effects. Is that correct, Miss Raintree?"

"Yes."

"Do you know how your sister earned her living at that time?"

I answered, "No," and at the same moment Mr. Scott raised his voice, objecting that the question wasn't relevant to the case. The judge intervened to say he didn't have to make a ruling, because I had already answered.

After I had completed my testimony, the Crown Attorney called Stephen Gurnan to the stand. He was sworn in, but the judge called a recess until the following day.

That night, I wondered why the defense counsel had asked me what Cheryl did for a living. She seemed distracted, but I didn't think it was important enough to ask her. She said she was going out for a while. I took the opportunity to take my ritual bath. Maybe tonight I would be able to get rid of the nightmare visions, forever. But instead, everything was more intensified. The smell became stronger, as if the perfumed oil had somehow turned into their bodily scents. I could see and hear them again, their lunatic faces, laughing, sneering. I hadn't been able to say that in court! Frantically, I scrubbed and lathered and scrubbed some more. Finally, I quit trying. I dried myself off, roughly. Then I put my nightgown on and methodically began to brush my hair.

Suddenly, I could stand it no longer. I threw the brush down, and it hit the bathtub with a resounding clang. Then I snatched the bar of soap and the bath brush and threw them on the floor. With my arm, I swept all the perfume jars and other containers off the vanity. All I felt was a frenzied frustration. I began to cry, letting my sobbing grow louder and louder. I finally screamed out the weeks and weeks of pent-up frustration and anger. "You scumbags! You lousy dirty scumbags! I wish you were all dead! Do you hear me? I wish you filthy animals were dead!"

I slumped to the floor and pounded the ceramic tiling as hard as I could. I wanted to transfer the pain from inside to my fists. I cried until I had no more tears.

I stayed there for a while, allowing my mind to drain itself of thoughts. Gradually, some of my humour returned, and I chided myself for making such a mess, because it was me who had to clean it up in the end.

The second day of the trial started with the Crown Attorney having Stephen Gurnan tell everything that had occurred that night, reminding the jury that identity of Oliver Donnelly as the rapist was now made by two witnesses. I was now confident that the defendant didn't have a leg to stand on in the way of defense.

The defense counsel then got up to question Gurnan. As expected, he asked him what he had originally been charged with. He noted to the jury that Gurnan had gotten the charge reduced to forcible confinement. Mr. Schneider's tone when he questioned Stephen Gurnan showed his open contempt. The defense counsel brought out the fact that Stephen Gurnan had told Donnelly that the intended victim was a known prostitute. "How did you know that this certain girl you were supposed to scare was a prostitute?"

"Objection! That's hearsay evidence. Mr. Gurnan could not know that for a fact, since he didn't know the complainant."

"It is hearsay evidence, My Lord, but we believe this evidence is important not to prove that the girl was a prostitute, but that the witness believed her to be a prostitute."

Mr. Justice Saul said to Mr. Scott, "He does appear to have a point. Overruled."

The defense lawyer repeated his question, to which Stephen Gurnan answered, "My sister told me."

"And what is your sister's name?"

"Sylvia. Sylvia Gurnan."

I was indignant that I could be mistaken as a prostitute. If Mr. Schneider intended to prove that I was or had ever been a prostitute, he'd better forget it. I could prove beyond a doubt that I was a decent citizen.

It was after the lunch recess when Cheryl showed up.

"I lied at work and told them I was sick. I would have come a lot earlier, but I was stuck at something I had to finish. Anyways, how's it going? And how do you feel?"

"Well, I'd like to say I'm happy to see you, but I really wish you hadn't come."

"Well! That's gratitude. So, how's it going?"

"I think it's almost over, but I'm not sure. I think, too, that the defense counsel is trying to prove I behaved like a prostitute or something. They'll try anything."

Cheryl and I entered the courtroom together and sat near the front. A little later in the afternoon, Sylvia Gurnan was called to the stand. She testified that she had asked her brother, Stephen, to scare a certain prostitute. I figured that her testimony was to corroborate what Stephen Gurnan had said, thus making him a credible witness in the eyes of the jury. "You specifically told your brother, Stephen Gurnan, that this certain girl was a prostitute?" Mr. Schneider asked.

"Yes. We all knew she was a prostitute. It wasn't a secret," Sylvia replied.

"Did you know this girl's name?"

"Yes. Her name is Cheryl Raintree."

Shock waves went through me. There was whispering by people, sitting behind us. I looked sideways at Cheryl. She didn't move at all. It was as if she had been expecting it. I sat there shivering. My own sister? Champion of Native causes, a whore?

"Cheryl, say this isn't so," I said to her in a hoarse whisper, begging her to deny it. But she didn't. She just sat there looking at the floor.

What happened after that I'm not really sure. My mind was in a whirl. I know the jury left the room, but it didn't have anything to do with this recent disclosure. A police officer testified as to how Oliver Donnelly's statement had been obtained. I recalled Mr. Scott telling me about this *voir dire*. When the judge was satisfied that the statement had been given voluntarily, he ruled that the evidence could be submitted, and the jury was called back. Then Oliver Donnelly's statement was read to the court.

He said he had been first approached by Jason Steeps to help Stephen Gurnan put a scare into some hooker.

Under his lawyer's questioning, Oliver Donnelly politely and humbly told the story of the night, from his perspective. "Jason and I had been drinking heavily most of the afternoon before that evening. We sat in Stephen Gurnan's car, which was parked where the hooker was supposed to be living. When she came along, Stephen Gurnan told us she was the one, so we grabbed her and got her into the car. We drove around for a while, and the girl never said anything, so I figured it would be all right to have sex with her. I honestly believed she was a prostitute. When she did object, I thought it was because I hadn't paid her. I had never paid before, and I wasn't going to start then. The liquor made me lose control, and I hit her a few times. If I hadn't been drunk, I wouldn't have hit her. I believed at the time when I had sex with her, it was with her consent."

There were no further witnesses. Court was adjourned until the next day for the summations by the lawyers. Because it seemed Cheryl wasn't going to budge from her chair, even though the courtroom was almost empty, I said, "We'd better go now." My voice sounded cold, even harsh.

Cheryl stood up then and looked right at me with a questioning look in her eyes. I saw her face in that split second, before I turned away from her. I just couldn't look her straight in the eye, not at that moment. I didn't even know how I felt towards her. She followed me to the car, and all the way home we were silent. I then understood that she really had been to blame. I blamed her. At the same time, I didn't blame her – or was it that I didn't want to hold her responsible? I waited for her explanations, her excuses, but she didn't make any. When we had eaten supper, she went out.

I again checked the newspaper and was relieved to find they hadn't printed my name. I was simply referred to as the complainant. What a way to get into the papers, as a victim. A victim of my own sister's folly. A victim of Sylvia's revenge. Another victim of being Native. No matter how hard I tried, I would always be forced into the silly, petty things that concerned Native life. All because Cheryl insisted on going out of her way to screw up her own life. And, thus, screwing up mine.

For some reason, I didn't feel the urgent need for the ritual bath that night. I turned on the television to get my mind off Cheryl. It didn't help much. I kept thinking of the look she had given me that afternoon. The look I had so coldly turned away from, as if I had judged her guilty. Still, she was my sister, my flesh and blood, and when she returned I would tell her everything was okay. It really wouldn't be okay, but I decided I would try my best to forgive and forget. The late show came on, and Cheryl still hadn't come home. I fell asleep and woke up about three-thirty. The movie was over, and there was still no sign that Cheryl had returned. I went up to her room to make sure. Afterwards, I went to bed disappointed and worried.

The next morning I went to the trial alone. The Crown attorney made his summation to the jury. He went over all the testimony of the witnesses, emphasizing that the element of corroboration and legal principle had been met by both my testimony and that of Stephen Gurnan. Then he pointed me out and said, "Ladies and gentlemen of the jury, look at the poor victim, the victim of this deplorable crime. How she has suffered, not only from the physical and mental anguish, but also the emotional pain of the whole onslaught. Whether she was a prostitute or not, and I stress to you that she is not and never has been, is not the question at hand. The fact is, ladies and gentlemen of the jury, she suffered at the hands of Oliver Donnelly. She will never forget the torment of that winter night. Remember how she gave her account of what happened that night of January 11, 1972. Frightened, but honest. Not once did she change any of her testimony. Not once did she waver between truth and fiction. Ladies and gentlemen of the jury, there is one thing we can do on behalf of that girl, April Raintree. That is to find this man – the defendant, Oliver Donnelly – guilty of rape. We must give her justice."

I squirmed under their scrutiny. I objected to being pointed out like that, and being called that "poor girl." It sounded overly dramatic. It sounded like he wanted them to say the defendant was guilty on the grounds that I was such a pitiful creature. I wanted him found guilty because of what he had done. I was glad when he concluded his summation. I took the opportunity to look behind me to see if Cheryl had come. All I saw were strange faces staring at me.

Next, Mr. Schneider, the defense counsel, tried to convince the jury that his client was innocent. He emphasized that Donnelly had been drinking heavily, that Donnelly honestly believed that the girl was a prostitute, but more importantly, had consented by her own silence to have sexual intercourse. The accused further believed that objections by the complainant were made only because she had not received compensation for her services. I sat there thinking of only one thing. That man, the accused, that scumbag, Donnelly, had raped me.

He had done more than rape me. He deserved to be found guilty and nothing else. By the end of the defense counsel's speech, I began to worry that the jury would find him innocent. The judge called a lunch recess.

I walked down the corridor, then the stairs, wondering why Cheryl hadn't come, and feeling lonely and remorseful. I also wondered if Donnelly was going to get off. But then how could he get off when Gurnan had already pleaded guilty to one charge? Wouldn't that be ironic?

I was at the front doors when I heard Roger's voice. "April, what are you doing here?"

I looked at him, dismayed. I thought of lying but I couldn't think of any good lies. "I'm attending a trial."

"Oh? What trial? You didn't tell me about it."

"It's the Queen vs. Donnelly. It's a rape trial. I'm a witness. Or is *complainant* the proper word?" I looked directly at him.

Roger looked at me for a minute, a long minute. "You should have told me about it. I'm sorry. It must be rough on you. How is it going?"

"It's almost over, I think. I don't know how it's going to end. What are you doing here?"

"Oh, I had a few things to do, and I was going to do some searches at Land Titles for Alex. But it can wait. How about lunch right now? Is Cheryl here?" he asked, looking around.

"No. She didn't come today. She was here yesterday," I answered, not mentioning her involvement.

We had lunch, and afterwards he said that he'd come back to the courtroom later in the afternoon when he had finished his work. I talked with Mr. Scott in the hall, and he took time to explain what was to happen next. He assured me that things looked good.

I felt slightly better when I took my seat back in the courtroom. The Honourable Mr. Justice Saul gave his charge to the jury, summarizing once again the evidence given, explaining the law pertaining to the charges. It strained my patience to have to listen to him. I began thinking of what I should tell Roger. No doubt, if he hadn't read last evening's paper, he would read about the trial now. People had different reactions to rape, and I would like to have known what he was thinking this very moment. It was almost three thirty when the jury filed out of the courtroom to consider its verdict.

The courtroom emptied, and I walked out into the corridor, hoping to find Roger. He soon appeared, and we waited together, not saying anything about the trial. He asked me again about Cheryl.

"I'd rather not talk about Cheryl right now, Roger. I just hope she's fine, but I'm worried, because she didn't come home last night. But I'll tell you about it later. Right now, I'm just waiting to see what the jury decides."

It was a little over an hour later when we were summoned back to the courtroom. I was impatient, because it took everyone such a long time to get back in their places, especially the judge. I sat there, scarcely breathing, waiting for that one word: *guilty*. The jury filed back into the courtroom, and there was more of the legal footwork as I waited for the word. I looked ahead, not daring to look at the faces of the members of the jury. I heard the foreman of the jury respond affirmatively to the question of whether they had reached a verdict. Finally, I heard what I had wanted to hear: "We find the defendant guilty as charged."

I sighed with relief. Justice, to a certain point, had been done.

15

BEFORE ROGER AND I RETURNED TO MY PLACE, we went out for supper. When we did get home, I looked for signs of Cheryl, but it appeared she hadn't bothered eating or anything, if she had been home. Cheryl usually piled her coffee cups and dishes in the sink, and there were none. I made coffee, knowing Roger was waiting for me to talk.

When we were both at the table, I began. "Well, you found out what my big secret was. Do you understand why I felt the way I did?"

"Of course. But you should have told me."

"Rape isn't something you talk about, Roger. I never even discussed it with Cheryl. Cheryl...she blamed herself, you know. She blamed herself, because she was in the hospital, and I came to Winnipeg to be with her. It was when I was going to her place that I was raped. And then in court, we both found out that those men were after *her*. It wasn't just my bad luck. She caused them to be there at that time. She apparently had angered some woman, and that woman wanted her to pay for it. And instead, I paid for it."

"How do you feel about Cheryl?"

"I don't know. They said she was a prostitute. I can't resolve how I feel about her. I just don't know. One minute, I want to hug her and tell her it doesn't matter. And the next, I just want to give her hell. I feel like her babysitter. As soon as I leave her alone, she goes out and does all these incredibly stupid things. And I always thought she had it all together, more so than me. What is the matter with her?"

"Well, what you went through is traumatic. There's no denying that. It will take time."

"You're right. It's not as if she made me lose all my money. That doesn't even seem so important anymore. Once, all I wanted was money, lots of it. And now, what I did lose was more precious than money. I'll never be the same as I once was. You know, when I was married, I didn't want children because I thought they might turn out looking Native. Lately, now that I can't have children, I would really like to be able to. Settle down and raise a dozen kids."

"Why can't you have any children?" he asked, with concern.

I looked at him. Couldn't he figure that out? "Because, I was raped. I'd be scared to ever let a man get close to me."

"And how long are you going to feel that way, April?"

"I don't know. I suppose I'll always feel that way."

"Do you like feeling sorry for yourself?"

"I don't feel sorry for myself," I said indignantly. "I just know how I feel inside. I feel dirty and rotten and used. I'll never be what I was before. I'll never be the same. Can't you understand that?"

"From what I understand, you're keeping what you feel inside of you alive. You're not even trying to let go. Now that the trial is over, April, let it go. Let time do its healing. The big tragedy now is not that you've been raped. It's that you might refuse to let yourself heal."

"You men! You haven't a clue as to what a rape does to a woman. To men, rape is just a word! Well, it kills something inside. That's what it does."

I was angry with Roger. Perhaps what he was saying had some truth to it, but I felt he was being very insensitive to my feelings on that day. In my anger, perhaps because of the emotional roller coaster I'd been on, I ordered him to get out of my house. I wanted someone to comfort me, not make me feel that I was wrong in my reaction.

"I'm sorry, April. Maybe I shouldn't have said what I did, but I really believe you're going to have to let go of your hatred and resentment sooner or later. I'll call you tomorrow," he said, in a kind, understanding tone.

"Don't bother!" I said obstinately.

My anger continued to burn after he left. Who was he to tell me my reactions were wrong? What did he know about rape? I stormed into the bathroom and began to run the water for my ritual bath. Then I realized Roger would think I was just wallowing in self-pity, so I turned the water off, stormed back into the kitchen, and poured myself another cup of coffee. It was cold, and I slammed the cup back down on the table and sat there staring at nothing in particular. What could any man ever understand about rape? They just had no comprehension!

But as I sat there, I began to think about what he had said. It was true that I had come to look forward to those ritual baths. I enjoyed killing them over and over again in my mind. But who was I hurting by it? I had wanted Roger to comfort me, but maybe what I really wanted was his sympathy, maybe even pity. It was something he hadn't given me, and I resented it. How was I supposed to just "let go," as he said? It simply wasn't possible. When I finally tired of waiting for Cheryl, I went to bed, my mind still in a muddle about my feelings. I was still full of hatred, but I was also beginning to admit that perhaps, Roger was right, and I should try and let go. The thoughts were with me when I awoke the next morning. I spent the day wandering aimlessly around the house trying to read a book or watch television. I was making supper, when Cheryl walked in. "Cheryl, where have you been?"

"None of your business."

I was taken aback by the bluntness of her answer. "Sorry. I was just worried. There's no need to snap at me."

"Oh? You think things should return to normal, do you? Well, good luck! I've got to go up and change." With that she quickly went upstairs, not giving me a chance to say more.

I walked back to the kitchen. Then I went back to the foot of the stairs and called up, "Hey, Cheryl, supper's almost ready. Are you going to come down soon?"

"I'm not hungry," she called back.

While I was washing the dishes, I heard Cheryl coming down the stairs. I was glad. Maybe we could talk. But she called, "I'm going out. See you later."

"Cheryl, wait – "

But the front door slammed. I could just see myself, scurrying down the street, pleading for her to come back so we could talk.

Roger called a little later and asked if I wanted to go out to a movie or something.

"A movie would be fine." I said, thinking it would take my mind off Cheryl. "Roger, I also wanted to apologize for the way I acted. I was wrong."

"No, I was the one who was wrong. I should have been more understanding. I'm sorry."

"Okay. Your apology is accepted," I said, allowing him to take full blame. Without saying it, we both knew we were equally at fault. Well, maybe I was more at fault.

I didn't go to court the day Donnelly was sentenced, but I learned on the news that he had been sentenced to five years at Stony Mountain. I wondered if those five years – he'd prob-ably be out on parole after three – would leave as deep a mark on his life as he had left on mine.

In the following weeks, Cheryl absolutely refused to talk to me, unless it was in little, biting sentences. At first, I was patient, but then I became impatient and unsympathetic towards her. Sometimes I'd come home from a date with Roger and she'd go upstairs, leaving me in mid-sentence. Sometimes she'd come home, drunk. That really upset me. Then she'd say all kinds of nasty things about me that weren't true or were only half true. Those things would hurt me the most, and once she saw the hurt in my eyes, she'd seem satisfied and would leave me alone.

One Saturday afternoon, she came in the front door. She looked in pretty rough shape, her hair dishevelled and her eyes reddish and dopey-looking. She immediately went upstairs, as I expected. But a few minutes later, she came down, carrying one of her whiskey bottles.

"Thought I'd keep you company today. I haven't seen my big sister in such a long time. I'll watch you clean up the place. It's like an Indian having a white maid. Well, go ahead, don't let me stop you. I'll just go and get me a glass. I can drink this stuff straight, you know. Want to see?" She took a swig from the bottle, then smacked her lips.

"Well, I'm sorry to disappoint you, Cheryl, but I've already done the cleaning. And while you're getting a glass, get me one, too, will you? There's Coke in the fridge. I'm not up to drinking it straight."

Cheryl looked at me suspiciously. "Oh, I get it, if you can't beat 'em, join 'em, eh? And what is poor, sweet Roger going to think?"

"Doesn't matter. Once I told you that we were going to make it. Well, if you're not going to try, then why should I?"

"Oh, no. Don't lay that crap on me, big sister. You turned your back on me a long time ago. You think I don't know why you married Bob? It was to get away from me, that's why. I'll bet you wished you were an only child. I bet you wished I was dead."

"You know that's not true!"

"And now you're back here, right in there, with another white man. Half-breeds aren't good enough for you. You're a bigot against your own people. You want to know something else, April? I'm ashamed of you. Yeah, ashamed. You're not my sister. You're my keeper, buying this house, paying for my keep. That's all you are, just my keeper. You're disgusting. And you have the nerve to look down on me?"

"I've never looked down on you, Cheryl. Never. Just on what you do. What you're doing to yourself. I don't understand why."

"Don't give me that bull. You heard what they said in court, and I saw what you felt. You think you're better than me. You've always thought you were better than me. And you'll never understand me. You'll never understand me." Cheryl repeated the last line more to herself than to me. Then in a louder, more aggressive tone, she said, "You know, April, you sure have lied to me a lot. You tell me one thing when you know it's an outright lie. It's pretty bad in this stinking world when you can't even trust your own sister."

Cheryl never did pour me a drink. She went back upstairs, I assumed to sleep it off. I felt as if I had been in a physical fight with her. I was breathing hard. It was unreasonable of Cheryl to accuse me of all those things. She wasn't faultless. So why, why, why did she tear into me all the time? I thought of Alcoholics Anonymous. Cheryl would never go there. That would be like admitting that she was a down-and-out drunkard. In the previous several months, I hadn't seen her sober, because when she was sober, she avoided me like I was the plague.

In December, Roger invited me to go to Killarney with him to meet his parents. They lived on a farm, and Roger went out to visit them as often as he could. I felt I couldn't leave Cheryl alone, and Roger said I was to invite her, too. I knew Cheryl wouldn't go, and in the end, Roger decided he would remain in the city for Christmas and spend it with me. I protested, of course, but he remained firm in his decision.

We waited most of Christmas Day for Cheryl to return so we could open our presents together. Cheryl didn't come. I was embarrassed. Roger had forsaken Christmas with his family to be with Cheryl and me. I had forsaken a Christmas with his family for Cheryl. And Cheryl didn't even do us the courtesy of staying home.

We spent New Year's with his parents. I also met his brother, Joe, who wasn't Indian at all. When we were by ourselves, I said, "You lied to me, Roger Maddison. You said your brother Joe was Ojibway."

"Well, I figured that would help you open up a little," Roger grinned. "You know, give us common ground. Actually, the guy I was talking about was a good friend in school. "

"My, my, you don't have any scruples, do you? And here I was going to ask if Cheryl could meet Joe and, you know, maybe get together."

By this time, I was fully relaxed and comfortable with Roger in every way. It was almost a full year after the rape. Roger had succeeded in making me feel good about myself again. I'd have moments when I'd remember, but they weren't all-consuming. It would take a long time before I would heal completely. But Roger was right. Time was the best medicine.

Still, I couldn't get through to Cheryl. There was virtually no communication between us. I had resumed my temp work. One day at the end of February, I didn't have any assignments for the day. I sat around for most of the day, bored. Late in the afternoon, I decided to do some baking. It was already dark when I removed muffins from the oven. That's when Cheryl came home. I heard her as she came down the hall and into the kitchen. She took off her jacket and placed it over the back of a chair.

"Aren't we domestic today?" she said in sneering voice. "Practising up, are you?"

"No, I just thought it would be nice to have some home baking. It's a little early, but do you want supper?"

"If I wanted something to eat, I'd fix it myself. After all, I do live here, don't I?" Cheryl said.

"Well, excuse me. I was just offering."

Cheryl got up and went upstairs. I figured tonight if she wanted to grind away at me, I was going to give her some of her own medicine. Sure enough, a few minutes later, she came downstairs again with a full bottle of whiskey. She set it on the counter, got herself a glass, and poured some Coke in after the whiskey. It was about half and half.

I watched her do all this, and then I said, "Is this private property, or can I have some, too?"

"Go ahead, help yourself. Don't expect me to serve you." She returned to sit at the table.

I decided to join her with my drink.

"So, are the three of us going to have a nice cozy little chat?" Cheryl asked, looking at me. Her eyes were glassy, and she had to focus to look straight at me.

"What do you mean, 'the three of us'?" I said, looking at her stomach area, avoiding her eyes.

Cheryl laughed and said, "You, me, and my good friend there," she said pointing back at the bottle of whiskey. "He's going to keep us company. Yes, sir, the family that drinks together, stays together," Cheryl laughed again.

"Well, do take off your boots and stay awhile," I said sarcastically. I had washed and waxed the floor the day before, and I noticed then that Cheryl had tracked watery marks on it. Cheryl ignored me and took a long sip of her drink.

"Cheryl, I wish you'd tell me what's been bugging you these past months. Ever since that day in court, you've been treating me as if I'd done something wrong."

Cheryl looked at me but didn't say anything.

"I wish we could get everything out in the open. I wish there were no secrets between us. I want to help you, Cheryl. That's all I want to do. Put that away for tonight. Go to bed, and tomorrow we can have a real honest discussion, okay?"

"Quit it, April. All you ever do is nag at me. Nag, nag, nag. Is that how you drove Bob away? And how long is this new one going to last, eh? How long is Roger going to last before you try to run his life? Ex-Mrs. Radcliff. Socialite of the East. Big shot. You're such a phony. Couldn't manage her own life, but she wants to manage mine." Cheryl finished her drink and got up to pour herself another one. She brought the bottle with her and set it down beside her glass.

I sighed and said, "Cheryl, don't."

Cheryl cut me off and mimicked my plea, "'Cheryl, don't, Cheryl, don't. Don't do this, don't do that. You're only hurting yourself, poor, dear Cheryl.' Well, I know darn well what I'm hurting. Because of me, you don't bring any of your white friends here, do you? And with Roger, you had to explain all about your poor, drunken sister, didn't you? So he would understand about me. And pity me? Same way you pity me. Well, I don't need your factitious pity."

I studied Cheryl. This was far worse than it had ever been before. I didn't know what to do. Should I try to appease her or provoke her into talking to me about what was making her say these things?

"You're ashamed of me," she continued. "You're ashamed of what I do. If you were ever proud of me, you'd be proud to be a half-breed. Proud, I tell you." Cheryl glared at me, daring me to say differently. She was swaying from side to side, as she again refilled her glass.

I said in a quiet voice, "Go look in the mirror and tell me what I've got to be proud of."

"Oh, so the truth comes out. As long as I act like a proper whitey, I'm something, eh? But a few drinks and I'm a stinking, drunken Indian."

"You're doing all this to hurt me, right? Why? Do you hate me, Cheryl?"

"Hate you? No, I don't hate you. I hate a lot of things about you. You're a snob. You have double standards. You were so shocked when they said I was a hooker. Well, look at you. How did you buy this house, April? How did you buy that car out there? How, April? You prostituted yourself when you took Bob's money, that's how. You never loved that man. You loved his money. You figured you were going to be Miss High Society. But you figured wrong. But you still came out of it with your pay. A nice, big, fat roll for a high-class call girl. Yeah, your kind makes me sick. Big white snobs who think they're the superior race. Your white governments, your white churches, sitting back in idle, rich comfort, preaching what ought to be, but making sure it isn't. Well, Miss Know-It-All, I know something you don't. And you won't feel so high and mighty once I tell you what I know."

Cheryl put her finger across her lips as if to warn herself to keep silent. "Shh, I'm not supposed to tell her," she said to herself. She smiled a silly, secretive smile, then frowned to herself. It looked as if she were debating on whether to keep her secret.

I was waiting, hoping she would continue. I felt that what she was on the verge of saying would help solve the mystery of what had made her give up on everything. I felt it wasn't just that she blamed herself for the rape. Something had happened before that. She had started drinking before that. Maybe it was something I had done. Whatever it was, I wanted to know. To goad her into more angry outbursts, I said in a cold voice, "Cheryl, you've had enough. Come on, I'll help you to bed."

I got up and put my hands on her arm to help her.

Cheryl shook them off, viciously. "You take your hands off me. I'm gonna have another drink, and no one's gonna stop me. Especially not a superior white madam. I can take care of myself. I don't need anyone. Not anyone."

I recoiled at her loud outburst and sat down again. I watched the liquid in Cheryl's glass go down once again. The bottle was half-empty.

"I don't need anyone," Cheryl repeated to herself. Then she looked at me and said maliciously, "Especially not you. I couldn't care less about your fancy ways. You're just a social climber who didn't make it."

Cheryl was slurring her words badly, and when she saw that I winced every time she used a vulgar word, I could see that she was delighted.

"So, April Raintree, you think you got all the answers, eh? But you can't tell me anything, can you? Because in reality, you know zilch. I'm the one who knows what life is really all about. Me. That's who. I got the answers. I found the answers all by myself. You lied to me, and I lied to you. I did find our precious dear ol' Dad. He's a gutter-creature, April. A gutter-creature! All the tricks I turned, well, that helped him, you know? That kept him in booze. Not only that, I joined him, too. Ah, but that's not all. The best part is still to come." She smiled a lopsided smile, as if she had lost control of her facial muscles.

"Mother, you know what happened to our poor, dear Mother? She jumped off the Louise Bridge, is what she did. Committed suicide. You know why she stopped seeing us? Because she couldn't bear the pain. Yup, she committed suicide. They were bums, you know. Both of them. Bums. Boozers. Gutter-creatures. Dad took all that money from me. He didn't know where it came from. He didn't care where it came from.

"Mark DeSoto. Jack-of-all-trades. Drug pusher, bootlegger, stealing, breaking and entering, pimping – if it was illegal, he was into it. And guess who was right there in it with him?

Your little sister, Cheryl Raintree. Your baby sister. Pardon me. There was another one after me. Baby Anna. Did you know about her? Well, she died when she was still a baby. She was the luckiest one of us."

Cheryl leaned her head on her arms which were crossed in front of her on the table. She was weeping to herself, repeating the last sentence, "She was the luckiest one."

I was shocked by her revelations. I didn't believe them. Cheryl was only trying to shock me. Except she wasn't watching me for the desired effect. She wasn't lying.

I was going to make coffee for us. Then I was going to see Cheryl to her bed. Tomorrow, we were going to have a long talk. Now that I knew the reason behind her actions, I knew I could do something about it. I was also relieved that it wasn't because of me that Cheryl had given up. I took the bottle over to the sink and began pouring the liquid down the drain.

"What the hell do you think you're doing?" Cheryl screamed, at the top of her lungs. She frightened me, and I dropped the bottle into the sink as I jumped. For all of Cheryl's drunkenness, she moved as swiftly as a mother cat coming to rescue her endangered kittens. "Give me that, that's mine!"

I had a hold of the bottle again, and Cheryl lunged for it. We both struggled for control of it. I guess all Cheryl could see was that her precious liquid was seeping away. All I wanted was for her to quit drinking for the night. When the last drop was gone, I let go of the bottle. I started turning towards Cheryl. She was enraged. She glared at me with hatred, and before I could speak to her, she brought her hand up and struck me as hard as she could across the face. I was already off balance, and the blow sent me reeling backward across the kitchen. I hit the refrigerator hard with my back and shoulders.

I put my hand to my face where Cheryl had struck me and looked at her in disbelief.

Cheryl, momentarily horrified by what she had just done to me, seemed to come out of her drunken stupor.

"Well, you shouldn't have done that." She grabbed her jacket and I heard her go down the hall. Then the front door slammed.

16

I SHOOK MY HEAD TO CLEAR IT. This was all too much. I went back to the sink and put the empty bottle into the garbage container. My mind started activating again, and I realized I should have gone after Cheryl. I went to get my jacket and boots, and then I had to look for the house keys. They weren't in my purse, and I couldn't remember where I had put them. When I found them, I went out the front way.

The closest bus stop was at Watt Street, so I walked in that direction. At the bus stop, there was no sign of Cheryl. I went back towards Henderson. I was sure that if Cheryl had intended to take a bus, she would have gotten on one by now. I waited at the bus stop for the next bus heading downtown and got on. I tried looking out both sides of the window, but with it being dark outside and lit up inside, plus the condensation on the windows, I couldn't see the sidewalks very well.

I got off in front of City Hall and decided to walk back home, by way of the Disraeli Bridge. That meant walking down Main Street to Higgins Avenue. I walked on the north side, because there were more people on that side. If Cheryl were among these people, I could spot her. But I walked all the way home, without running into her.

I couldn't sleep at all that night. The wind had picked up outside, and I was sure there was a blizzard going on out there. Mixed in were the noises of the house – all those creaks one doesn't notice during the day. I listened to them, deciphering what may have made them. Several times, I thought Cheryl had returned. I got up and went upstairs to check her room.

The next morning, I got up, tired. I thought perhaps I had made too big a deal the night before when I worried about never seeing Cheryl again. Nonetheless, I called where she worked and found out that she had quit a few months earlier. Later, I called the Friendship Centre, but the person who answered didn't know Cheryl. I made coffee. I spent most of the day waiting and worrying. When my employer from the agency called, asking if I wanted to start a job Monday, I said no, that I'd be taking some time off again.

At four-thirty, Roger phoned to say he was going to pick me up in an hour. We were supposed to go out for supper, but I had forgotten.

"Oh, Roger, I can't go. Cheryl left last night. I don't know where she is. She's not going to come back."

"Well, April, Cheryl has been away overnight before. Why are you so worried?"

"We quarrelled. A lot. She was drinking heavily. She told me everything, Roger, all the things that have been bothering her. I have to find her."

"Okay. We'll have supper, and then we'll go and look for her, all right?"

"You don't have to come with me. I don't even know where to begin."

"I'll come with you. Don't worry, April, we'll find her."
While I waited for Roger, I decided we could go down to the
Friendship Centre and talk to anyone who might know where
Cheryl would be. I tried to remember places Cheryl had men-
tioned in the past. Was it Carlo's or was that the name of
a beer? I got my coat and boots on and waited for Roger. I
returned to the kitchen and looked in the phone book. There
was a place called DeCarlo's. That was it. I noted the address.
Since it was a Friday night, I thought we might even find Nancy.
I cursed myself for not taking more interest in Cheryl's friends.
I didn't even know Nancy's last name.

After we had a quick supper, we went to the Centre. A few
people said they knew Cheryl, but they hadn't seen her for the
past couple of months. From there, we drove over to DeCarlo's,
which was on Carlton. There was a lineup of people waiting
to get in, different types of people, and it reminded me of the
Hungry Eye. My crowd once. When Roger and I got in, we
looked the crowd over. A smoky haze hung over everyone's
heads. Music was blasting from the amplifiers. From the way
we were dressed, Roger and I were obviously out of place. We
ordered drinks but were barely able to talk because of the
noise. I watched for Cheryl or Nancy. I even felt I'd be able to
tell who Mark was if I saw him. I wondered if this was where
they all still hung out.

On the other side of the room, there was a girl who
reminded me of Sylvia Gurnan. I couldn't see clearly because of
the dimly lit, smoky atmosphere. People kept passing between
us, and sometimes I was sure it was Sylvia, and then I wasn't
sure. She wouldn't have been any help, even if it had been her,
but I would have known there was a possibility of Cheryl being
here, too. I studied the other people at the table. They were

all white. Mark, as far as I knew, was Métis. When the band took a break, Roger asked me if I recognized any of Cheryl's friends. I said I didn't, so we left.

We drove around for a while, up and down the downtown streets, as we searched the faces for Cheryl's. We were not successful. We returned, but she hadn't. We took our coffee into the living room, and I turned the television set on.

"You know, Roger, I'm to blame. No, I'm not going into a 'this-is-all-my-fault' routine. It's just that I wanted her to have all these good memories of our parents. I always told her only the good things that happened when we lived with them. I knew that they had drinking problems. That's why we were taken away. I should have told her that when I gave her those addresses so she could look for them. But I didn't. I just gave her the stuff and hoped that her search would come to an end. And she went out and found our father and found that he was an old drunk. I'm sure she never told me all of the things she discovered, because she felt she had to protect me from the truth. She carried that around with her all alone, not wanting to share her problems. And I knew about it! Well, not the part about our mother committing suicide. So many lies to protect. And in the end, they destroy anyway. I just can't understand why all that would have such an adverse effect on her."

"I wish I could say something that would help," Roger said.

"Maybe, maybe she just used these things as an excuse to start drinking. Maybe she was an alcoholic all along, and she just needed some real good reason to start into it. Do you think that's possible?" I asked.

"I guess anything is possible. The reasons for drinking can be complicated."

"Sometimes I think if we really were white, we wouldn't have all these complications in our lives. I'd just be a wife, maybe a working mother, just an ordinary person. You know what I mean? There probably wouldn't be any problem with alcoholism. Our lives would be so different. But as it is, I lie to protect her, and she lies to protect me, and we both lose out. I don't know. If I was more like her or she was more like me, maybe we wouldn't have pulled apart."

"Maybe you've both pulled too much in different directions. Cheryl has identified with the Indian people and all the wrongs that have been done to them. And you, having identified with the white people, well, she's taken everything she's felt out on you. Earlier, when you told me the things she used to say when she was drunk, well, she wouldn't believe them herself when she was sober. I think, from what you've told me, Cheryl saw you in a typical white role. You supplied her with all her needs. You stayed in Winnipeg to help her, to be by her side. You've made her take handouts. You've stressed that she can depend on you, right?"

"Well, I am her big sister. I had to watch out for her."

"Maybe you could have told her that you needed help from her, in return. Or, at least, not have made it so clear that you were in charge. People need to feel that they are needed and worthwhile. On top of all that, she blames herself for your rape, and she knows you blame her, as well. I'd say Cheryl has a very low self-image right now. Drinking helps wipe out that image. And she can't let herself become sober, because it hurts when she's sober. So she drinks again."

"What kind of help could she have given me? I have everything I need."

"April, I'm sure Cheryl could have given you something that is very important. Right now, I don't know what, exactly. But something to do with your attitudes about yourselves."

"That night, I just wanted her to go to bed and sleep off the alcohol. I wanted for us to really talk when she was completely sober."

The weeks passed, and Roger and I continued to look for Cheryl. She had never come back to the house. Every day when I'd get home, I'd look in her room, and everything was always just as it had been that first night. We returned to DeCarlo's regularly, but always without any luck. Sometimes, we'd drive around and I'd spot someone who I was sure was Cheryl. I'd get Roger to park the car, and I would jump out and go after that person. But when the woman would turn around, my excitement would turn to disappointment, because it was never Cheryl.

The month of April brought erratic temperatures. Some days were warm enough to tempt people to dress lightly. The nights brought back the cold temperatures, though, sometimes even below freezing. April 18, 1973, my birthday, was a cold rainy day. I stayed home, hoping Cheryl would remember and come home. But she didn't. Roger and I celebrated alone.

Ten days later, it was the same kind of dismal day. The winds started early in the afternoon, first in short bursts, as if gathering momentum for the gales that would follow. It had drizzled off and on for the previous several days. Since it was a Saturday, Roger and I had been out combing the city – more specifically, the hotels. We'd even gone to all the hotels along Main Street. The rain began to fall more and more heavily as the day wore on, and the wind had also picked up. Early in the evening, we decided to call it quits after I had rushed out into the rain thinking a stranger had been Cheryl.

When we got to my place, I was soaked to the bone. I felt so discouraged. While I changed, Roger made us coffee. Then we sat silently in the living room, just listening to the steady pelting of the rain against the windows. I wondered what Roger was thinking. Maybe he thought I wasn't worth all the trouble and aggravation. Maybe he wanted to call it quits with me but not at this time because of Cheryl. I sighed.

"What's the matter?" he asked.

"Oh, nothing. Just wondering about all the trouble I've put you to, and how much time and gas you've wasted, when you could be out enjoying yourself."

"Well, the gas and time is nothing. And even though we're not out living it up, I do enjoy being with you. So stop thinking that way. Everything will be worthwhile once we find Cheryl."

"You really and truly don't mind?"

"In spite of her current problems, I think Cheryl is quite a person...and she is your sister."

I stretched out on the sofa and rested my head on his lap, reassured. It felt so good to be near Roger. It seemed hard to believe I had held him away for so long. I would have been completely content, except for Cheryl. Suddenly, the phone rang, exploding into the stillness of the house. I jumped. By the second ring, I got there and picked up the receiver. "Hello?"

"Is this April?"

"Yes."

"I don't know if you remember me. It's Nancy. Cheryl has been staying with me." Nancy's voice sounded shaky.

"I remember you. What about Cheryl? Is she okay?" I said anxiously, shooting out the questions.

"She just left here. I didn't want her to go. She seems okay but in a funny way. I wanted her to stay here. But she said she had to go. She said goodbye to me as if she wasn't going to see me again." Nancy sniffled.

"Do you know where she was going?"

"No. And I couldn't go after her, because I've been sick the past couple of days, and I'm not dressed. My mom thinks she's going to do something terrible. My mom's the one who told me to call you. Maybe you can do something. I'm so worried."

"Oh no." I leaned against the wall. My voice was barely a whisper.

Roger was at my side, and then he took the receiver from me. "What's going on?" he asked Nancy. He listened to her for a few minutes and then asked for her address. Then he asked some questions about what Cheryl was wearing. When he hung up, he immediately called the police. He explained the situation, gave them Nancy's address, and told them we'd meet them there.

It was still raining but not as heavily as we drove to the address on Henry Avenue. There were a number of look-alike, rundown shacks, and we found Nancy's house among them. Nancy opened the door before we could knock.

"Anything new?" Roger asked immediately.

"No. I didn't know how to stop her. I just didn't know how to stop her," Nancy sobbed.

"It's all right, Nancy, don't worry. We called the police, and I'm sure everything is going to be okay. Thank you for calling me." What I really wanted to say to her was that she should have called me a lot earlier. But she looked so sorrowful.

"Let's drive around and see if we can spot her," Roger suggested.

We had pulled away when Roger noticed a police car arrive and stop in front of Nancy's house. He braked and put the car in reverse. We both got out and walked back to the car. I was hoping they had found her. I looked in the back of the car for Cheryl, but there was no Cheryl. Roger exchanged some words with the officer, who then turned and asked me if I had even the vaguest idea where she might have gone.

"No, I don't. We've been looking for her and looking for her, and all this time she was here. If only Nancy had called us before this. Now I just don't know where she could be."

Cheryl's words flashed across my mind: *...and you know what our poor, dear mother did? She jumped off the Louise Bridge, is what she did. Committed suicide.*

"She jumped off the Louise Bridge..." I said out loud.

"What's that?" Roger asked.

"Our mother. Our mother killed herself by jumping off the Louise Bridge. Didn't I tell you that?"

"No, you just said that she did it, you didn't say...Never mind; let's go over there."

Roger briefly explained this to the officer, and he agreed to drive over to the bridge to check it out. Roger and I jumped in the car and followed the police cruiser. It was only a few minutes ride, but it seemed to take a lifetime.

"Why doesn't he put his flashers and siren on, for crying out loud?" I said impatiently as we stopped at a red light on Main Street. My eyes were still combing the sidewalks. Maybe she had stopped for a drink someplace. Maybe she had gone back home. Maybe her goodbye to Nancy meant she was going to move back home. Oh, I'd give her such a big hug if that's what she had done.

Finally, we reached the Louise Bridge. I could see some figures on the bridge waving towards the police car. Roger parked behind the cruiser, its lights now flashing. I jumped out into the rain, which was coming down in torrents, and ran to where the police officer was talking to two strangers on the bridge.

"...not five minutes ago," one of them was saying. "She just stood up on the railing, I tell you, and jumped off. Ask Stan here. He was with me. We both saw it. We tried to stop it, Officer. We slammed on the brakes but we couldn't get there in time. Christ, one minute she was standing there, balancing, and the next, nothing. Why would she want to do a thing like that? Those Indians are always killing themselves. If they aren't shooting each other on the reservations, it's this. Holy jumpin' Jupiter! What a night this has been. And now this. I tell you, it's unbelievable."

I was looking down at the waters, looking for Cheryl. It was too dark to see anything, too murky. The man's words rang in my ears. What did he know? Someday, maybe, I could explain to people like him why they did it.

Roger had placed his arm around me. I was crying. My tears were mixed with the rain, and they dropped down to where Cheryl was, in that murky water I had once loved to watch. Now I watched, hoping that Cheryl was somewhere down there, alive. But I knew there was no hope. Not for Cheryl. Not anymore. I ached inside. I wanted to let loose with my tears. I felt like sobbing, screaming, wailing. But I just stood there, using the railing for support. Hiding the agony I felt. The agony of being too late, always too late.

After answering some questions for the police officer, Roger and I drove back to Nancy's house. When she opened the door, she saw right away from my expression that the worst had happened. She burst into tears. Her mother saw Nancy cry and walked over and put her arms around her and hugged her. Then she came over to me, a complete stranger, and also gave me a comforting hug. Roger quickly and briefly explained what had happened.

While Nancy's mother busied herself making tea, she said, "Cheryl was like a daughter, you know? She was such a good person. She helped Nancy, you know."

"Yeah, whenever I needed help, she was there." Nancy started sobbing again, but between sobs she continued, "Sometimes, when we needed money, Cheryl would give it to us. She never made us feel like we owed her, you know? When I would get depressed, Cheryl would cheer me up, make me laugh."

"Cheryl would buy groceries," Nancy's mother said, "and she would always joke that they ate them all up anyways."

Nancy and her mother exchanged looks.

Then Nancy said, "I'm not the only one Cheryl helped. She did a lot for other girls, too. Especially at the Centre. She had these big plans, you know. And she used to organize lots of things at the Centre for young people. Then she quit. She changed real sudden, but I never knew why. Oh, she'd still help people, but she wouldn't go out of her way anymore. And then she met that creep, and he moved in with us, so I moved back home 'cause Dad left."

I appreciated them comforting me. I sat in silence, because I could think of nothing to say to comfort them in return. We stayed until Nancy's mother said, "Well, enough for tonight. You're probably tired. You go home, and get yourself some sleep."

"Thanks for coming back to tell us about Cheryl," Nancy came over to where I was standing and hugged me. Then she said, "Cheryl left some things for us to take care of. Like the typewriter you sent for a gift. She didn't want Mark selling it on her. And the other is – well, you come back when you're feeling better. Tonight is not the right time. You will come back?"

It seemed very important to Nancy that I return, so I promised I would.

When we were back in the car, I said to Roger, "Imagine that. They're so poor, and yet they kept that typewriter for Cheryl all that time, when they could have sold it. And the way they talked about her, like they really did love her. They give out such a family feeling. Cheryl must have liked that a lot. No wonder she felt more at home with them than she did with me."

"I think you should come over to my place tonight, all right?"

"All right; thanks. Cheryl hasn't been home for a long time, but somehow the house would feel much emptier tonight."

When I finally got to sleep, it was long past midnight. I dreamt of Cheryl. I could hear her laughter, but I couldn't find her. I looked and looked, but all I could hear was Cheryl laughing. When I did find her, she was in some kind of muddy quicksand. I put my arm out to reach her, to help her, but she wouldn't take my hand. She just kept laughing and sinking down, deeper and deeper. I begged her and begged her to take my hand, and I began crying uncontrollably. When I woke up, I was still crying, and Roger was hugging me. When I had quieted down, I lay my head on his chest and listened to his heartbeat. A couple of times, the leftover sobs would shake my whole body, and Roger would hold me a little tighter. Gradually, I went back to sleep.

The next morning, the police called and asked if we could identify the body they had pulled out of the river. When we returned a few hours later, I was in more of a daze than I had been before. It was final. It had been Cheryl.

Roger did almost everything for me, and helped me with the funeral arrangements. I was mostly silent, but occasionally, I would reminisce about Cheryl. That reminded me there was one thing I had to do.

After some hesitation, I phoned the Steindalls. I had a long talk with Mrs. Steindall, telling her of Cheryl's death and explaining the absence of our visits. She was very understanding and very sympathetic. That same evening, the night before the funeral, they came to Roger's place to see me.

The funeral service was small and simple. Most of the people who came were Indian and Métis. They had heard about Cheryl's death through Nancy and her mother. They gave me an insight into Cheryl's past by the glowing remarks they made about her. Again, I wanted to cry for the waste of such a beautiful life. But I didn't. I remained outwardly emotionless.

Nancy asked me again to come over to their place in the near future, and I promised I would.

When it was all over, and Cheryl was buried, I knew it was time to return to the house, alone. Roger seemed to understand my need and drove me back. He didn't come in with me. Before he left, he said, "Take as much time as you need, April. Then call me. I'll be waiting for you."

"Roger, thank you for everything. I love you."

Roger smiled, "I love you too, April."

17

I ENTERED THE HOUSE, which now seemed so empty, so cold. I decided I would pack all of Cheryl's things away in a big trunk, even her clothes. That way I'd always have part of her. And being able to touch her belongings would strengthen that feeling.

I opened the door to Cheryl's room, and the first thing I noticed was an empty whiskey bottle. I hadn't really noticed it before when I had gone into her room to look for addresses or names. But there it stood on Cheryl's dresser, mocking me. Suddenly, I was filled with a deep hatred of what it had once contained. I grabbed it by the neck, raised it high, and smashed it against the edge of the dresser. Again and again. I was screaming, "I hate you! I hate you! I hate you!" My tears came flooding out, and I continued screaming, "I hate you for what you've done to my sister! I hate you for what you've done to my parents! I hate you for what you've done to my people! Our people!"

I threw myself on Cheryl's bed, letting all my pent-up tears pour out. I pounded my fists into the bed, allowing my emotions to tumble out. I felt a frenzied rage at how alcohol had torn our lives apart, had torn apart the lives of our people. I felt angry for having done so many wrong things at so many wrong times. And I felt self-pity because I would no longer have Cheryl with me.

"Oh, Cheryl, why did you have to go and kill yourself? All those people at the funeral, they loved you so much. *I* loved you so much. Didn't that count? Didn't it matter to you? You had so much going for you. You didn't have to kill yourself, Cheryl! Why? Why?"

I writhed on the bed as if I were in physical pain. At times I would become still, but not for long. Stronger emotions would come crashing down on me, and I would toss and turn again, trying to exorcise the painful anguish from within. I pounded my fists into the bed, again and again, in frustration. "If only..." Those words repeated themselves over and over in my head. But it was too late. Cheryl's death was final.

When I had spent the last of my tears, I sat on the edge of the bed and surveyed the mess I had made in the room. The floor had scattered fragments of the whiskey bottle all over it. Cheryl's pillow was soaked with my tears. I looked again at the floor. If only I could smash the problem of alcoholism as easily as I had that bottle.

Temporarily void of all emotion, I systematically began to clean the room. I put the Kleenex tissues into the garbage container. I began picking up the larger pieces of glass. I grabbed one piece a little too savagely, and it cut my hand. I looked at the blood oozing out in a thin red line.

"Still after more blood, are you? Well, you cut down my sister, my parents, my people. But no more. I'll see to it. Somehow. Some way."

When I had finished cleaning Cheryl's room, I sat down again on Cheryl's bed. I wondered where to start, yet not wanting to start. Then I remembered all of Cheryl's papers, the journals she had kept. There were two boxes under her bed, and I began going through them. The first was full of newspaper clippings, but I wanted her journals. They were in the other box.

I began looking through them. The last entry she had made was in January 1972. That was the month I had been raped. I looked for a 1970 journal. It was this one that I was most interested in, because that was when I had first lost touch with Cheryl.

The entries for January indicated she had started the search for our parents. February had occasional references to her continued search. There was more in March.

I see more and more of what April sees, broken people with broken houses and broken furniture. The ones I see on Main Street, the ones who give us our public image, the ones I see puking all over public sidewalks, battling it out with each other, their blood smearing up city-owned property, women selling what's left of themselves for a cheap bottle of wine. No wonder April ran. She was horrified that this was her legacy. She disowned it, and now she's trapped in that life of glitter and tinsel, still going nowhere. Charitable organizations! What a load of crap. Surrounded by a lot of people, business-wise but empty. Just like the Main Street bums.

The more I see of these streets, the more I wonder if April isn't right. Just maybe. Better to live that empty life than live out on the streets. What if I do find our parents? Sometimes I can't help it; I feel like April does. I despise these people, these gutter-creatures. They are losers. But there is a reason why they are like this. Everything they once had has been taken from them. And the white bureaucracy has helped create the image of parasitic natives. But sometimes I do wonder if these people don't accept defeat too easily, like a dog with his tail between his legs, on his back, his throat forever exposed.

Happy Birthday, April. What do you give the person who has everything? I can give peace of mind with a few lies.

May 1970 – Struck pay dirt with a new address on Austin. The place is rented by a woman named Josie Pohequitas. I knock on the door, and it is opened by this little, bent, old woman who is stoned out of her mind. But happy as hell. I have figured out by now it's better to see these people at certain times of the day. You have to be late enough so they can start getting over last night's drunk and early enough so they're not whacked out of it yet. I ask if she knows Henry or Alice Raintree.

"Henri, Henri Raintree?" she says in a French-type accent.

"Yes, I'm his daughter, and I've been looking for him," I say in a pleasant voice.

"Ah, yes, mais oui, we're good friends, you know. Come in. Here, sit down, here. He comes to our place when the snows are gone. He goes north for winters. He is welcome here. He stays. Sometimes, we have big party. Sometimes, we have big fight. Then he goes. But he always come back, Henri does. He will come back. You come back in a couple of weeks. You will see. He will be here then."

I'm tickled a deeper shade of brown, you might say. I tell the toothless woman with her toothless smile that I will be back.

June 1970 – I knock at this door again, having been here a few times with no luck and expecting none this time.

"Ah, Cheryl, it's you again. Come in, come in," her face lights up into a big grin, still toothless.

"Henri, Henri, come out here and see the surprise that is here for you. Hurry up, Henri," her voice is high-pitched and squeaky. She never pronounces the *h*'s.

An old, grey-haired man comes walking out of the kitchen. He is trying to keep his balance; curiosity is piercing through his drunken haze. I assume that Josie has told him about me, but still it's a few minutes before he realizes it's me.

My smile disappears, but a smile slowly appears on that leathery, unshaven face.

"No, no, it can't be. Not my little daughter, Cheryl. My little baby. You're all grown up now."

He chuckles and staggers a little closer to me. He makes a visible effort to draw himself up, but he has drunk too much already, and the feat is beyond him. His clothes are worn, dirty. and dishevelled. Tears of happiness and perhaps awakened guilt pour from his watery eyes.

The woman, Josie, is beaming with pride as if this "joyful" reunion were all her doing.

"It is like a miracle. It's like a miracle," she cackles over and over again, watching father and daughter facing each other. I am rooted to the very spot, absorbing the true picture of my father. I make no effort to move towards him. This goes unnoticed, and the old man approaches me.

"I cannot believe that we are standing here, face to face, at long last. At long, long last," the decrepit old man says.

I stand quietly, hiding the horror that is boiling inside of me. I hadn't known what to expect. But it wasn't this, this bent, wasted human form in front of me. My father! I am horrified and repulsed: by him; by the cackling, prune-faced woman;

by the others who have crawled out of the kitchen to watch all this "happiness," all of them with stupid grins on their faces; by the surrounding decay; by the hopelessness. The cancer from the houses I've been to has spread into this house, too. To destroy.

All my dreams to rebuild the spirit of a once-proud nation are destroyed in this instant. I study the pitiful creature in front of me. My father! A gutter-creature!

The imagination of my childhood has played a horrible, rotten trick on me. All these years, until this very moment, I envisioned him as a tall, straight, handsome man. In the olden days, he would have been a warrior if he had been all Indian. I had made something out of him that he wasn't, never was. Now I just want to turn and run away, pretend this wasn't happening, that I had never laid eyes on him. Pretend I was an orphan. I should have listened to April.

Awkwardly, he hugs me. I smell the foul stink of liquor on him. Hell, he probably sweats liquor out of his pores. I close my eyes so no one will see what's in them. I hold my breath against the gutter smell. Seems like ages before he releases me. When he does, he turns to the others and says, "Don't just stand there, bring her a drink. Now we have something to celebrate. I found my little girl after all these years. Tell me, Cheryl, where is your sister? Where is April? I missed you both so much. Ah, here we are."

He hands me a beer and wipes his tears and runny nose on the sleeve of his shirt. I don't answer. I just think, "April is far away from you, and she'll never know what you are, you gutter-creature!"

Gratefully, I swallow some beer. Disgust, hatred, shame... yes, for the first time in my life, I feel shame. How do I describe the feeling? I swallow more beer.

I stay for the rest of the day in spite of my desire to flee. I stay, because I want to know about Mom. But I want Dad sober when I ask him about Mom. Funny, I can still refer to him as Dad. I drink away the hours and feel the dizzy, nauseous sensations, as I laugh stupidly with them. Josie puts me to bed, just in time, on a battered couch in the living room.

Next morning. I wait patiently for Dad to get up. It is almost noon. He comes into the kitchen. He looked in rough shape last night, but now he looks worse, with his weak, flabby arms showing, because he's in a torn, greyish undershirt. His dark-coloured baggy pants are held up by suspenders that are frayed to the breaking point and all twisted. I get coffee for Dad. Josie is busy puttering around the kitchen. No one talks, the only noises come from Dad slurping his coffee.

Finally, I ask him, "Dad, could we talk?" Sounds like I'm shouting. I lower my voice. "I want to know about Mom. How is she? Do you see her?"

Dad makes a gesture as if he doesn't want to talk about her right now but I persist. "Please, Dad. Tell me about Mom. Where is she?"

Tears come to his eyes again. He says simply, "She died last July."

"Died? Mom died?" I ask, not believing. I then figure out that Mom was in poor health when we were kids, and that's why she died. I wish I could have seen her. Poor, dear mother. Maybe that's why Dad turned to booze. He misses her so much he can't live without her. I can forgive that, retract all the bad thoughts about him.

But Dad speaks again. "I may as well tell you everything." He sighs and lapses into another long silence.

I try to make it shorter by urging him to continue. "Tell me what, Dad?"

"Your mother took her own life. She killed herself," he says at last. "She left a letter for me, but I had gone up north early that year. I have a nephew in Dauphin. I stop in there sometimes. They sent the letter there. She jumped off the Louise Bridge last July. I took the letter to the RCMP and they checked with the Winnipeg police. They had found a body, and everything matched your mama. She was not happy with her life. Once she lost you girls and Anna died, she knew she would never get you girls back again. Those visits were too hard on her. So she stopped going. She tried to kill herself before, once a long time ago."

I digest what he says...too hard on her? What about April and me? In those foster homes? Okay, only one was real bad, and April suffered most in that one. But I suffered for April. And the other ones? Those people weren't our flesh and blood. They weren't even our race. I remember now, those promises you made us, promises we believed, all the waiting for you to take us back home, all the loyalty we gave you...all for nothing.

"Who's Anna?" I'm angry but I don't want to fight. I want information.

Dad looks at me, surprised. "You don't know about Anna? Oh, of course not. You were just a baby yourself when she died. April must remember her. Maybe not. She was just little, too, and Anna wasn't with us very long. She was your baby sister. But she was a sick baby. They should have kept her in the hospital longer, but, no, they sent her home too early, and she died. They blamed your mama and me. That was their excuse for taking you girls away from us. No, my girl, your mama was not a happy woman."

"Why didn't you come to see us when we were kids?" I ask in a soft voice, afraid of an honest answer.

There is another long pause. "I went up north for a long time. I was never here to visit you again," he says, as if that was a good enough reason. "No, your mama did not want you girls to see the way she was. She was too ashamed. She couldn't face you again. They shouldn't have taken you away from us. The baby was just sick, that's all." Dad drifts off into silence again. Dad asks me to come back and see him tomorrow. I say I will.

I do. Josie says Dad left that morning to see some friends of his for a few days. Here I thought he would be impatiently waiting for me. Ha! What a joke!

I sat on the bed with the journal clutched to me. This was the second mention of Anna. I'd been thinking of Anna after Cheryl had told me about her. Baby Anna. I remembered that's what I had called her. Recollections of my mother rocking a baby had come back, much clearer. I'd always had vague pictures in mind, but I'd never realized the baby was our own sister. Baby Anna. She'd been with us for just a fraction of our lives. But she was sick and had to go to the hospital. And now, here, in Cheryl's journal, were Dad's words saying the same thing. Baby Anna. Such a small part of our lives. Yet she had changed our lives the most.

This was exactly how Cheryl felt when she found Dad. After all that he told her, she still went back to see him the next day. She was still loyal to him. How was it she had the natural family instinct? I had instincts only for self-preservation, pushing anyone away from me who might hurt me. I was a loner. Only recently had I let Roger in, then Nancy and her mother, hugging me that night, giving me all that they had felt for Cheryl. Before Roger, who else besides Cheryl had hugged me and meant it?

Well, maybe Mrs. Dion. I remembered wishing many times that I could be as affectionate as Cheryl. That meeting with Dad, maybe it destroyed her self-image. Strange though, since she had seen that side of Native life before. I wondered what sort of image she had built up about our parents. Was it that image of long ago that had sustained her, given her hope?

> *February 18, 1971* – So…a son is born to me. It should have been a very special day for him. A day when his aunt and his grand-parents and all his relatives rejoiced. Instead, it's just him and me. What's that joke I read? If he had known what was going to be in store for him, he would have cried a whole lot louder?

> *February 22, 1971* – Having pondered over what to call you, my dear son, I've decided on Henry Liberty Raintree. May you grow up to be all that your grandfather is not.

A son? Cheryl had a son? I felt anger and bewilderment. Not at Cheryl or anyone else; the anger was for me, for being the way I was. Because it had caused Cheryl to feel so alien-ated from me that she couldn't share the most important event in her life with me. Henry Liberty Raintree. Then I smiled. A part of Cheryl still lived. After a while, I continued reading.

> *March 10, 1971* – Nancy is babysitting, and I'm free for a while. Feels great to be let out. Henry Lee's been so cranky lately. On top of that, we've got to move out 'cause kids aren't allowed. Landlord's just a bigot, always looking down his nose at me when I pay the rent. I thought Henry Lee would change my life for the better, but I can see I thought wrong. Must say I do feel good about this watering hole. Don't think Nancy will mind my coming home late. She'll understand.

April 8, 1971 – Sure am glad Nancy's mom is letting Henry Lee stay at her place. I'm not so tied down anymore. She sure gives him some good mothering. I don't think motherhood was meant for me. I'd rather be out partying than sitting at home changing dirty diapers.

June 1971 – Nancy's mom is keeping Henry Lee for me for good now. Do I feel guilty? Only when I'm sober. And I try very hard to see that doesn't happen. I give her money all the time, so I'm sure she doesn't mind. Wish I had a mother like that.

October 1971 – Today Dad says he doesn't know where he is going to stay, because he can't pay his rent. I know what he wants, so I give him forty bucks. His eyes bulge. Usually I only give him ten or twenty.

At DeCarlos with Nancy. The gang is all here, too. Already we got suckers to pay for our drinks. It's cheap coming here. I give my money to Dad so he can go get tanked, and I come here and get mine free. I have to laugh at dumb jokes, let these guys run their hands up my legs. They think they're going to get more later, but I can avoid that.

Mark DeSoto. Now if all these guys were like Mark...but they're not. Nance says Mark's ol' lady, Sylvia, is going to have it in for me if I hang around with Mark. He's over there at another table. He comes to say hello. I ignore him. He was supposed to call during the week and didn't. The suckers at my table are really playing up to me tonight. Got to go say hi to Marie.

Walking back to my table, I hear this shrill voice. "Hey, squaw, I don't share my man with no one. You hear me? Especially no squaw." Sylvia comes into my path and stops. I stop. I look her in the eye.

"What's your problem, sweetheart? Can't hang on to your guy? And I ain't no squaw, I'm a half-breed." I feel ridiculous and powerful at the same time. I know what I'm capable of. I give her my coldest stare. I know I've won this round. She can't match my gaze. The blonde bombshell jabs a finger into my shoulder, telling me what she's going to do to me. I twist around slightly and bring my fist into the side of her face, not real hard but hard enough to back her off. The dumb broad trips over a chair and sprawls on the floor. Everyone laughs, hoping for a fight. I step over her and continue on my way.

"You're going to pay for this, Cheryl."

"Yeah? Well you'd better give it your best shot, Sylvia."

Mark struts over to my table. My precious companions scatter. He sits down and grins.

"So, you're my prize," I say to him sarcastically. But the evening ends with Mark in my bed.

Mark moves in. Nance moves out. Landlord requests that we remove ourselves after the first party. I find a cheap place on Elgin.

November 1971 – I'm working. Mark is working the streets. We're always broke. I sell all the furniture, except the typewriter. I wonder why April gave it to me. She's the one with the writing talent. I give it to Nance for safekeeping, so Mark won't sell it.

We're stone broke. Mark owes everyone, so we can't hit anyone up for a loan. Mark says to me, "You know that guy who comes to Neptune's, and he always looks the chicks over? Well, he's loaded, and sometimes I sit and talk to him."

"I know who you mean. What about him? You're going to borrow some money from him?"

"He never lends money. But sometimes he sees a chick he likes and asks me if I can arrange a meeting. So, I go to her, and if she's interested we share the money he pays, see?"

"You mean you're some kind of pimp?"

"Not a pimp, Cheryl. I just do two people a favour, and I get some money out of it. We need money now, bad, and I know he's got the hots for you. I just thought you might consider it, just this once."

"You're asking me to go to bed with another man?"

"Well, it's not like there's any feelings between you. Just think of it as a business transaction. I told him you were a very special girl, and he's willing to pay more for you. Come on, Cheryl, one hour's work, and you could make fifty bucks. I'll try to get more."

"Forget it." I'm bloody mad. "I ain't no prostitute." I storm out of the house. A week later, we're still broke. I'm drinking at Neptune's. I'm almost drunk. Mark comes over. This sucker who's been buying me drinks leaves quickly. Funny the power Mark has. "Cheryl, please, we gotta get some money: The land-lord today said he'd give us another 24 hours and no more."

"Is he kinky?" I'm just dirt. Who cares if he's kinky?

Later, I'm back at Neptune's. We have our rent money now, plus some. I have a drink. Another one. Another one. My parents deserted me, April has left me, Mark...is a good-for-nothing woman user. Make that last word *abuser*. I have another drink. And another one. Let Mark use me. I don't care. Let April sit in her fancy white palace. I just don't care anymore.

January 1972 – I'm an old pro now. I'm working the streets full time. I avoid the pigs by picking johns who are obviously not pigs. Well, they're pigs, too, but in another way. Mark arranges a lot of meetings, too. I've gotten into other things I bet

Mrs. Semple never heard of in her old "syndrome" speech. I'm still broke. First thing Dad says when I see him is, "Cheryl, I need twenty for groceries."

"I don't have any."

He goes into a rage. "What do ya mean, you don't have any? You got enough to go drinking, but you can't spare your poor Pa any? Did that bum you're shacked up with tell you not to give me anymore? You're just as bad as your ol' lady was, you know that? A lazy no good for nothing. Running around all the time, living with bums. I need some money. I need groceries, and I got to pay the rent. Now I got nothing, just 'cause you couldn't hang onto a simple job."

I tell him he's worse. I swear at him. I tell him what I think of him, that he's a parasite, a gutter-creature. I tell him it's his fault Mom killed herself. The tears spring to his eyes. I leave him. Let him stew in his guilt. I sure as hell stew in mine.

At home. Mark comes in. I'm angry and still brooding. Mark is angry. I'm supposed to be at Neptune's. We need money real bad. He yells. I yell. He beats me. I'm used to it. He avoids hitting my face. He has learned it's not good for business. He leaves.

I walk along Main Street. This is where I belong. With the other gutter-creatures. I enter a hotel. I don't know which one. The word BEVERAGES is all I see. I need a drink. A couple of drinks. The depression is bitterly deep. The booze doesn't help this time.

I'm back on the street. I'm drunk. I want to run in front of a car. The guy who was buying my drinks comes with me. What a creep. We head to my place on Elgin. We take a shortcut down a back lane. The creep wants to fondle me and kiss me. He can't wait. "Back off, you ugly old man. I'm no whore, you know?" I don't know why I say that, but I repeat it. I can scarcely keep my balance. It's like there's two of me, one watching, one doing.

"I wanna kiss you. I know what you are. So don't pretend with me, I paid for you."

"You stink. Leave me alone, you filthy pig!" I slur the words. He gives me a push. I slam into the wall and fall into a sitting position. My legs have given out. They're sprawled out in front of me, like they don't want to go on, anymore. I close my eyes. I like the sensation of everything spinning around at full speed. I half open my eyes. I watch the man. He's looking real scared. He turns and runs, clumsily, boozily. I smile and shut my eyes again.

I come to. I'm still just lying around with my legs out there in front of me, still going nowhere. I notice the garbage cans and garbage bags on either side of me. "Hello there!" I says to them. "I've come home. At long, long last."

I chuckle to myself. I hiccup. I chuckle some more. I think in the morning the garbage men will take us all away, me and my friends. I giggle. I try to get up. I can't. So I stay put. Every once in a while I chuckle to myself. And hum a tuneless song.

I wake up. April's holding my hand. I can't see her, but it's April. I squeeze her hand.

For a long time, I sat very still, thinking. Then I looked at my watch. And sighed. It was 3:00 a.m. I knew what I had to do. I knew now why it had been so important for me to return to Nancy's place. I'd have to wait until morning. I paced around the room and finally returned to the journals. I put them back in the box and set them on the floor. Then I lay on Cheryl's bed, on top of the covers, still clothed. With my hands under my head, I stared up at the ceiling. The clock downstairs was abnormally loud and so, so slow. A few hours more and I could be on my way to Nancy's place, to Henry Lee.

For the moment, I thought of Cheryl. Memories came back, memories of her voice, the memory of her reciting her powerful message at the powwow. Why, oh, why didn't she talk to me? Why couldn't we have talked to each other? And would it have helped? At times I was overwhelmed with memories of her, and tears would trickle down the sides of my face.

The next morning I woke up, dismayed that I had fallen asleep. Then I was dismayed to find it was still too early to go to Nancy's place. The sun was just beginning to rise, spreading orange yellowish hues across the skies. I went downstairs to make coffee and freshen up. My eyes felt swollen. Again the house seemed so empty, cold, lifeless. With my cup of coffee in hand, I opened the front door and stood looking out at the still, empty street. The birds were just beginning to sing their morning praises to their Creator. It had rained during the night. Everything was wet. The smell of wet earth was invigorating, so clean.

I stood there breathing deeply when I noticed there was a letter in the mailbox. I thought of leaving it for the moment, but didn't. The moment I saw it was Cheryl's handwriting, my heart started to pound. I tore it open and sat down, heedless of the damp step.

Dear April,

By the time you get this, I will have done what I had to do. I have said my goodbye to my son, Henry Liberty. I couldn't bring myself to tell you about him before. Now I know you will do what is right where he is concerned. I also know that Mary and Nancy will do as you wish. They're taking care of Henry Lee. All my life, I wanted for us to be a real family, together, normal. I couldn't even mother my own baby!

Do not feel sorrow or guilt over my death. Man thinks he can control Nature. Man is wrong. The Great Spirit has made Nature stronger than Man by putting into each of us a part of Nature. We all have the instinct to survive. If that instinct is gone, then we die.

April, there should be at least a little joy in living, and when there is no joy, then we become the living dead. And I can't live this living death any longer. To drink myself to sleep, day in and day out.

April, you have strength. Dream my dreams for me. Make them come true for me. Be proud of what you are, of what you and Henry Lee are. I belong with our mother.

Love to you and Henry Lee,
Cheryl

An hour later, I was at Nancy's place once again. She opened the door for me, as if she had been expecting me at that precise moment. I followed her down the hall to the kitchen. Sitting at the table was a small boy eating some cereal. He looked up at me as I walked into the room. He smiled, the same kind of smile I had seen a long time ago on his mother's face when she was that age, the age of innocence.

Nancy began explaining but I stopped her. I told her I understood everything. As I stared at Henry Liberty, I remembered that during the night, I had used the words, "my people, our people," and meant them. The denial had been lifted from my spirit. It was tragic that it had taken Cheryl's death to bring me to accept my identity. But no. Cheryl had once said, "All life dies to give new life." Cheryl had died. But for Henry Liberty and me, there would be a tomorrow. And it would be better. I would strive for it. For my sister and her son. For my parents. For my people.

About the Author

Born in St. Boniface, Manitoba, in 1949, Beatrice Mosionier was the youngest of four children and was taken from her family by Children's Aid Society at age three. Following the suicides of her two sisters, Vivian in 1964 and Kathy in 1980, Beatrice was compelled to write a book. Her first novel, *In Search of April Raintree*, was published in 1983. The school edition, *April Raintree*, was published in 1984.

Beatrice spent a total of twenty years living in Toronto, and, in 2004, returned to Winnipeg permanently. She is the author of several children's books, including *Spirit of the White Bison* and *Unusual Friendships: A Little Black Cat and a Little White Rat*. Her second novel, *In the Shadow of Evil*, was published in 2000, and *Come Walk with Me: A Memoir*, was published in 2009.

From the First Edition

One cannot read this moving account of two Métis sisters without feeling their terrible anguish, bewilderment, and anger as they try in their different ways to live in a society that frequently rejects and abuses them, as it has rejected and abused their parents and ancestors. The story is a tragic one, yet its final outcome is one of affirmation and bitterly won resolve. – MARGARET LAURENCE, AUTHOR

In the past few years, there has been much controversy regarding Native children and the question of foster homes and adoption. Reams of papers and reports have been written. How many of those papers were written by people who have lived through that experience?

This is a powerful story because, with gentleness, it deals with the sickness in our society and our people. It is the kind of writing that will begin the healing of our people and help a dominant society understand and feel the lives of a people it almost destroyed. – MARIA CAMPBELL, AUTHOR

From Readers

I have just finished your novel *April Raintree*, and I am both deeply moved and full of excitement. Delighted to have found such a fine piece of writing. – J.P., ENGLISH PROFESSOR

Within a month the novel has established such a reputation, that every day, students ask to borrow copies to read on their own. Few of our kids normally read much on their own, so this is quite pleasing to me as an English teacher – J.T., TEACHER

The students in [my] class come from many different countries.... I believe that your novel has been successful in bringing about a greater understanding of people from all cultures. – J.P., TEACHER

I read your book for the first time when I was twelve years old, and I liked it so much I read it again..... It's hard to put the book down; it's exciting and addicting. – K.B., STUDENT

Th[is] book ... shows many events that people have been through and how they have overcome them. I'm not normally much of a reader. However, I was unable to stop reading your book because it seemed so real. I also know and have grown up with many people in similar situations to what you have written about. – T.B., STUDENT

Your novel was so good that once I started to read it I couldn't put it down until I completed it. For me... to read a book and finish it, it has to be good. – L.M., STUDENT

Your book speaks the truth about us Aboriginals. After reading this book, I wanted to help Aboriginals across Canada. I'm not exactly sure how yet, maybe as a politician. But whatever I do for my people... *April Raintree* has inspired me! – J.G., STUDENT